UNFINISHED
FLIGHT

ALSO BY KEN FILING

Awash in Mystery

UNFINISHED
FLIGHT

BY

KEN FILING

Order this book online at www.trafford.com
or email orders@trafford.com

Most Trafford titles are also available at major online book retailers.

Printed in the United States of America.

ISBN: 978-1-4269-3656-2 (soft)
ISBN: 978-1-4269-3657-9 (hard)
ISBN: 978-1-4269-3658-6 (ebook)

Library of Congress Control Number: 2010909926

*Our mission is to efficiently provide the world's finest, most comprehensive book publishing
service, enabling every author to experience success. To find out how to publish your book,
your way, and have it available worldwide, visit us online at www.trafford.com*

Trafford rev. 7/20/2010

Trafford
PUBLISHING®   www.trafford.com

North America & international
toll-free: 1 888 232 4444 (USA & Canada)
phone: 250 383 6864 ♦ fax: 812 355 4082

To my granddaughter, Rosie, whose spirit and sweetness inspired me to give real life to the daredevil lady pilot in *UNFINISHED FLIGHT.*

PREFACE

UNFINISHED FLIGHT is pure fiction. Writing it as a prequel, that prefigures *AWASH IN MYSTERY,* seemed a perfect way to bring the story to fruition. Using my granddaughter, Rosie, as a guide to the personality of the main character also just seemed to fit. I've interspersed names of famous characters such as Amelia Earhart, Jimmy Doolittle and others to add a touch of realism to the story. Most historical facts on World War II are true. Dates may not be entirely accurate, although I've tried to be as close as possible without disturbing the flow of the story. The U.S. Navy ships named were real. I was aboard the U.S.S. Dixie for my first cruise at sea, at age 17. I served aboard the U.S.S. General J. C. Breckinridge for two years as a Seaman in the early 50's. The U.S.S. Cod is a submarine now docked in Cleveland, Ohio and is a tourist attraction. Its war record is true and documented. My research was by internet and historical facts were found at The History Place. World War Two in the Pacific, Timeline of Events. Also History of the Coconut Crab from Wikipedia, Amelia Earhart from Wkipedia and The History of Air Racing and Record Breaking. Other World War II facts were brought back to my memory from a scrapbook of news articles that I kept as a boy during World War II. The events taking place on the island of Tongolo are as fictional as the island itself.

PROLOGUE

Early in the fall of 1940, a small dual engine aircraft was winging its way east from its flight origin in New Guinea. All had gone well and the flight was according to schedule during the first leg...maybe too well.

Rosie apprehensively gazed ahead into the increasingly darkening skies. She could feel some slight turbulence now tugging at the controls of her Lockheed Electra L-10E twin engine prop plane. She glanced over at her napping husband, Chris, sitting in the co-pilot's seat and then nudged him with her elbow.

"Better wake up honey. Looks like some bad weather ahead."

He opened his eyes and sat up straight "Holy mackerel where did that come from?" he said with anxiety in his voice.

"I don't know. It just seemed to come from nowhere and it looks like its still growing. Those black clouds look fierce." She answered.

Suddenly the bottom seemed to drop out from under them and the plane hit heavy turbulence with a teeth rattling collision. They plunged downward in a sickening side slipping free fall. Rosie was fighting the controls.

"Help me Chris. I can't get control. We're going to go into a spin."

Chris grabbed the controls in front of him and the two of them struggled against going into a dreaded spin. But they were overcome by the force of the storm and started into that sickening spiral. They whirled downward and only after some very anxious moments, they finally pulled out of it and regained some control. The plane leveled off at about 500 feet below their cruising altitude and they settled on a course fraught with massive turbulence. They were bouncing like a bucking bronco but at least they were in an uncomfortable control.

"Decrease power Chris or we'll shake the rivets right out of the wings. They're almost flapping now."

With decreased power, the Electra took the storm a little better but they still surged violently up, down and sideways with sickening lurches.

"I swear honey I would have taken us around this if I would have had some warning that it was ahead of us." said Chris.

"Not your fault. It seemed to form out of no where. Nothing we can do now except try to get through it. We'll be okay if it doesn't get any worse. Whoa…whoa…whoa… it's a bad one" yelled Rosie, as the plane hit another air pocket that felt like they hit a brick wall and she struggled to right the plane's attitude. She fought off the increasing vertigo brought on by the twisting and turning of the gyrating Electra.

"I'll help you all I can Rosie." yelled Chris above the shrieking wind.

The clouds seemed to close in on them and it got even darker. It was a virtual monsoon and made visibility non existent. They strained to see beyond the nose cone.

"I'm going to climb higher. I don't think we can get high enough to get out of this but just maybe the air won't be quite as rough in the upper part of the storm." she called out in a quavering voice.

She pulled back on the wheel and said "give me a little more power Chris. I need both hands on the wheel in this mess."

The Electra nosed up and bounced along like a rubber ball but slowly climbed up through the turmoil. Suddenly they seemed to hang up and almost stop. Rosie yelled "POWER – POWER -- MORE POWER OR WE'LL STALL."

Chris gave it all the acceleration he had in both engines. The plane surged ahead and quickly regained headway.

"Wow that was close, okay ease off a bit, we're using too much fuel and we still have 300 miles or so before we get to Howland Island. We have no fuel to spare and that gauge seems to be going down awfully fast. I'll level off at this altitude. It seems to be a little less rough."

They bumped along for 30 minutes or so and Rosie maintained a good course. She heaved a sigh of relief and smiled at her spouse, relaxing a little.

"Speaking of fuel, Rosie, I swear that I'm getting an odor that smells like gas. I hope we didn't spring a leak in all that turbulence. We put some pretty good stress and strain on this baby."

"What's the gauge say?" she asked.

"Oh boy. Not Good." he answered.

"Of all the damn luck! At least the storm seems to be diminishing. I see some breaks in the clouds up ahead and not near as much lightening now. I'm going to go back down and see if we can get a visual on where we are. With any kind of luck we might spot an island. We should be pretty close to the Phoenix Islands."

"I don't know Rosie. That wind pushed us all over the place. I'm not even sure I can find Howland now....seems like we should be west of the Phoenix Islands. The way that fuel gauge is dropping I don't think we'll have enough to make it much further."

"Okay. I think you're right. We better look for a place to set her down. See if you can raise anyone on the radio and let them know our situation. Send a mayday, maybe someone is close enough to help if we have to ditch."

Chris grabbed the radio microphone and started transmitting a mayday. He gave the coordinates as closely as he knew them. They suddenly broke through the cloud layer. It was still raining but there was some visibility and they both scanned the horizon for a likely spot to set her down.

The starboard engine suddenly coughed, sputtered and stopped running. Then it started back up for an instant before it quit running altogether. The port engine kept running but they knew it wouldn't be long before it too would give up the ghost.

Finally it did and the Electra went into a glide. The relative quiet was eerie and the two passengers also were very quiet, both staring off into the, now clearing skies, looking hopefully for something other than that vast expanse of ocean.

They entered a dense cloud bank...so thick that it seemed like cotton rushing passed the windows. When they broke out, the sunshine was brilliant. Chris shaded his eyes and looked off to his right. "Rosie, look to starboard, I see something."

Rosie banked the quickly descending airplane and homed in on what appeared to be a small atoll. She was attempting to keep as much altitude as possible and felt if she could keep in the air a little longer she could reach the small island.

As with many, many islands of this type, a coral reef surrounded the perimeter and formed a lagoon. There was a spot on this one where the lagoon was wide enough to give them a good chance of belly flopping in. Rosie aimed for the best shot that she had. She glided in over the reef with little room to spare and then used the flaps to slow as much as she was able, without dropping suddenly like a rock. When she reached the wide spot she gave it full flaps and pulled the wheel back as far as she could. The plane hit the water, tail first, and then the nose dropped. They submerged about half way, plowing through the surf, and suddenly stopped. They popped back up for an instant and then settled in a shallow spot. The upper part of the plane was above the water line for now but it slowly took on water and was slipping under. It would soon come to rest just under the surface.

"Rosie, I don't know how you did that, but honey you saved us. Hey, are you okay? Your forehead is bleeding. Let me look at that."

"I'm okay honey, just a little woozy from a bump on the head."

"It doesn't look too bad. We better get out of here, we're starting to sink. Can you swim to shore?"

"Sure I can, but let's grab what we can, especially the survival pouch. Maybe we have time to inflate the life raft and carry some food into shore. Let's go."

CHAPTER ONE

EARLY IN THE YEAR 2006

The small, tropical island of Tongolo is located in the South Pacific just west of and a little north of the Phoenix Islands. It is sometimes thought to be a part of those islands but is, in fact, its own entity and owned by no country. It is far removed from the shipping lanes in that part of the Pacific Ocean and is seldom visited by anyone other than the occasional cruising sail boat and a supply ship that visits it every two or three months. It's located close to the intersection of the equator and the International dateline which gives it a year around tropical climate and because of the unique currents and upper atmosphere winds, typhoons very rarely happen. The severest weather for over one hundred years on this island has been an occasional tropical storm.

It is in this idyllic setting that we find Kent and Teddi Allison sitting in the shade of a palm tree enjoying their breakfast. Their two children, Eva Rose and Ross have just left to walk to the village school, which is taught by their good friend Marte, the wife of Adam, an old crew member of Kent's and a very close friend.

As they were finishing their breakfast, the village chieftain Ben Fletcher Adams approached and said "Good morning you two. Are you ready for our trek into the hills?"

"We sure are" said Kent "we've got our hiking and camping gear inside and all packed for a three day trip. The kids will stay with Adam and Marte while we're gone and I'm sure they will have a great time with their kids. It will be one long sleep over and I'm sure Adam will be pulling his hair out by the time day three rolls around."

Ben chuckled "Yes when those five youngsters get together its non stop fun and games. Okay let's make preparations. The boys will be along in a few minutes with their machetes. We've got some pretty thick jungle to go through before we start the up grade to the caves where the old villagers stayed during the Japanese occupation. It will take most of the day to get there and set up camp. We may have some time left to locate some of the caves today but tomorrow is when we'll really get to explore them. It's been several years since I've been there and I really never got deep into the caves where they lived. Some of our villagers have explored them and found many artifacts of their ancestors. The only one still alive that survived the war and remembers the horrors they went through is Kellea. She's old and frail but still pretty sharp and will talk about the war if asked."

"I'm so anxious to see the caves" said Teddi "it just intrigues me how a group of villagers could fight back and survive the horrors of the occupation by a modern Japanese army. After we get back I'm going to sit down with her and record everything she remembers before it's lost forever."

"Grab your gear" announced Ben "I hear the boys approaching and we don't want to lose any daylight."

The group of five loaded their backpacks and trudged through the village to the edge of the jungle. The first part of the journey was easy going. There were well worn paths leading away from the village but it wasn't long before the growth got thicker and the two strong, young men started hacking away with their machetes to clear a path so they could make some headway.

Even with the growth cut back, Ben, Kent and Teddy found the hike a struggle. There were the ever present insects buzzing around their heads and biting their bare arms and legs and the stray uncut branch, with leaves as sharp as a knife that would snap back. At one point, one did so and put a neat little gash on Kent's forearm. Ben called the procession to a halt and insisted that Kent tend to the wound with an ointment that Ben carried in his pack.

"What is this stuff Ben?" said Kent "it sure has a strong odor. In fact it smells awful."

"You don't want to know" said Ben with a slight grin "but it will keep it from getting infected."

The two machete wielders mumbled something in Polynesian, glanced at Kent with a sly grin and then both rose to their feet while chuckling in that deep guttural way of these island people.

Kent wrinkled up his nose, picked up his pack and started off walking next to Teddi.

"She gave him a strange look and wrinkling up her nose sweetly said "why don't you just trail behind us for a while honey?"

They soon were back on their way and after another hour or so the terrain became less dense and the going was much easier. The machetes were only used occasionally and soon not at all. Most pleasant of all, the temperature seemed lower and the humidity lessened. Kent's aroma also lessened as the day wore on.

Ben said "The thick jungle is behind us but soon we'll have some steep elevation to contend with. Let's break for lunch."

While they were resting and enjoying a bite of lunch, Ben asked "You've told me the story of your trawler, Kent and how you and Teddi met and married in Honolulu, did you always live there?"

"No Ben" said Kent "I was born on a farm in Ohio which had been in the family for well over one hundred years. I was told that the land was some kind of grant from Connecticut and was known as the Western Reserve in the early days. My early life was one of helping out in the orchard in which we grew mostly apples but also some peaches, plums and cherries. Apples were the cash crop and the Ohio climate was very good for them. My dad took us boys to Lake Erie one summer and when I saw that huge expanse of water, I was dumbstruck. I knew that some day I would end up going to sea. Every chance I got I'd make my way to the lake and one way or another, hitch a ride on a boat or volunteer to crew on racing sailboats at a yacht club in Cleveland. I'd do anything to be near the water. I loved it, especially the sailboats. I graduated from high school at seventeen and left for the U.S. Navy within weeks of graduation. My mom and dad died in a house fire while I was away and after the funeral I agreed that my brother should get the farm. I knew that I would remain at sea after my tour was done and that's when I settled in Honolulu and became a fisherman. The rest of the story you know. How I met Teddi, bought the trawler, got hijacked, sailed the Caribbean and ended up here on Tongolo."

"Well I'm glad you found your way here. You and Teddi are like family" said Ben. "Okay let's hit the trail."

The next several hours were a steady rise to the top of a foot hill that led to the two twin peaks at the center of the island. When they crested the top of the hill a beautiful, lush valley came into view.

"Isn't it beautiful?" said Ben "We'll go through the valley and about one third of the way up the south peak we'll find the caves. There's a pasture area near to them where we can pitch the tents. That was the common area for gardening and a pig sty for the war time villagers. It was pretty well hidden until you rounded the outcropping"

They reached the small pasture just before sunset and Ben said "Let's pitch the tents and set up camp. We can locate some caves later but we better wait until tomorrow to explore them. Some of them might be populated with wild boar or some other varmints."

Later, as they sat around the camp fire after the evening meal, they reminisced about how the island must have been an entirely different kind of place back in the early 40's. Suddenly there was a rush of wings and high pitched squealing.

Teddi bolted upright and moved closer to Kent. In a quavering voice she said "What was that?"

"Don't worry Teddi" said Ben "they are only bats and they'll eat the mosquitoes. By the way, we've heard about Kent's upbringing, now tell us about your life and where your ancestors came from."

"Well I guess I'm pretty much of an island girl. I was born and raised in Honolulu. I didn't get to see much of the world until I met Kent. Unfortunately I didn't have much of a family either, my mother Eva died at 33 shortly after I was born. My father was so distraught that he grieved himself to death. I was only two, too young to remember them at all. After my dad died I went to live with my grandmother, Rosemarie, also in Honolulu. She was 65 at that time and the sweetest lady you'd ever want to meet. She raised me but in her later years became afflicted with Alzheimer disease and finally passed away at 76."

"Before she became afflicted, when I was very young, she told me stories about her life. I didn't write anything down so I'm only talking from memory and what I was told after she died. I was only 13 when she passed away. As I remember she was born in Kansas. Her family farmed and raised some cattle and had been there since the pioneer days. When she was 18 she somehow became interested in flying. A lady at her funeral told me that my grandma knew Amelia Earhart. I don't know if this is a fact or not. It's pretty hazy, but I know she married my grandfather in the late 30's and he worked for Lockheed. Somehow, and I don't know the details, while flying a test plane in the Pacific, they had an accident. From what I can determine it must have been just before World War II because they were captured by the Japanese somewhere right in this part of the world. Of course it is now known that the Japanese were planning the attack for years and did a lot of scouting of these islands to build airstrips and establishing bases of operation."

"At grandma's funeral, a very kind retired navy officer talked to me briefly. He said that he knew both of my grandparents during the war and both were brave and resourceful. They were instrumental in helping our forces capture an island here in the Pacific. He was sure that they somehow became separated and then reunited. I know that my mother was born in 1942, but I'm not sure where, or if it was while they were prisoners, or maybe after. She had no birth certificate only a certificate of birth issued in Hawaii. No place of birth had been noted. Sometime after the war they were united and came to live in Hawaii. The story becomes confusing of how and when all three ended up together. Grandfather died at an early age due to the wounds he had suffered. Grandmother raised me alone. My mother met and married my father in Honolulu where he was born and raised. That's about it in a nutshell, Ben. I lived in foster homes until I went on my own and then met this handsome brute who has given me a wonderful life and two perfect children."

"Well that's quite a story, Teddi. It's really too bad your grandmother didn't document some of what happened. I've heard many other stories about World War II hereabouts and they all are very interesting." said Ben. "Well, let's turn in and get an early start in the morning."

CHAPTER TWO

The next morning at first light, Ben roused the two young village boys and instructed them to get the fire going and to prepare breakfast. He then grabbed a big soup spoon and the frying pan and banged on it loudly outside of Kent and Teddi's tent. He called "Okay you sleepy heads, it's time to get started. We've got a lot of exploring to do.'

The married couple sleepily crawled through the tent flap and suddenly became wide awake when they smelled the coffee brewing.

"Wow" said Teddi "I slept like a rock. I didn't realize how tired I was until I crawled into my sleeping bag. I conked right out and didn't stir until I heard you banging on that frying pan, Ben. By the way let me show you what else that pan is good for." as she grabbed the pan and headed to the fire to help with breakfast.

They all were famished and wolfed down their breakfast so they could start the exploration of the caves. The three of them started off, leaving the two boys to police the area and put the campsite in order. The boys agreed to have lunch ready for them at about noon so they wouldn't lose any exploration time.

They climbed to the first cave and found that it was pretty bare. There was evidence of some animal life so they went on higher to a group of 3 caves. These also were empty of much except one that was quite large and opened up on the inside after you entered through a smaller opening. It had some nooks hollowed out for what was probably sleeping areas. It looked like it may have been a home for a couple of families. It went deeper than the rest and Ben lit a torch to see better. There was a stirring on the ceiling and a multitude of bats came into view. The explorers became very quiet and the bats seemed to settle down.

Teddi said in a shaky voice "I think I've seen enough of this cave." And she slowly and silently backed away towards the entrance. Ben and Kent grinned at each other and went on in a little deeper until they came to a solid wall and could go no further. The wall was smooth and flat and had many hand drawn pictures of ancient warriors and animals.

Ben said "These drawings were made centuries before our villagers made these caves their homes. Legends have told of them but this is the only time I've seen them first hand."

Kent tried to duplicate a few of the drawings. They obviously told a story. Maybe one of the older men could translate some of the drawings. If so he would bring them here to see what they could determine.

After they exited the cave and met up with Teddi they decided to return to the camp for lunch and then explore the upper caves that probably hadn't had as many previous visitors.

The two village boys had the camp shipshape and had a great lunch ready for the explorers. Teddi was disappointed that the only significant find was after she left the cave and she was quiet all during lunch. Ben and Kent thought better of telling her that it was her own fault for being so squeamish about the bats. She stood up and firmly announced that she intended to see everything this afternoon and she sauntered off to her tent to freshen up.

They made their way back to the caves and immediately found artifacts from the World War II settlers. One cave in particular looked a cut above all the rest and you could see that someone made it very habitable. The three of them spent most of the afternoon there. Just as they were getting ready to call it a day and head back to the campsite, Teddi spied a nook deep inside the cave in the corner, of what appeared to be, a shelf used for a sleeping area.

She called "Kent could you come here and take a look at this?"

"Sure thing. What have you got?" answered Kent

"There's a nook here in the wall that is covered with a flat rock and I can just barely see something behind it, but I can't budge the rock."

"Here let me see what I can do" he said.

The flat stone was wedged in and it looked like it was purposely jammed in to hide something. Kent took his knife and chipped away at the edges of the stone. Soon he was able to insert the blade and he popped it loose.

"You were right Teddi. There's something wrapped in an oil skin. There...I've got it now. Let's take it out into the light and take a look."

The three anxiously went to the mouth of the cave where they could investigate their find. The sun was getting low but still plenty of light to see by. Kent laid the parcel on a rock and slowly undid the oilskin. It looked to be about the size of a hard back book. Kent said "It feels like a book or maybe a stack of papers"

Sure enough when he peeled away the waterproof covering it was a book. And when he turned back the cover he could see that it was some sort of a diary.

"This is a great find" said Ben "it could very well tell us many things about the villagers."

"Well here's another surprise guys" said Kent "the entries are written in English. From what I've heard of the original inhabitants that were on this island, as brave and resourceful as they were, I doubt if any of them had the education to keep a diary in English."

Teddi said "Oh Kent, lets hurry back to the campsite, I'm so anxious to read some of it and it's going to be dark pretty soon so let's hurry."

They loaded the artifacts into cloth bags and struck out for the camp. When they arrived they gathered around the campfire and Kent carefully took the oil skin wrap from around the book.

He folded back the cover, quietly read something under his breath and gasped. He gazed at Teddi and said "Honey, I'd like you to read the first line." And he handed the book to her.

She took it with a questioning look on her face and said "Why, Kent? What's the matter?"

"Go ahead honey. Read it out loud." He said somberly.

"Okay" she carefully opened the book to the first page and read:

"My name is Rosemarie Conner. My husband Chris Conner and I are living on this island with a group of escapees from a Japanese Army base where we were held prisoner. This date is sometime in February in 1942."

Teddi looked up. Her eyes were glistening with tears. "Oh my God, Kent, I think we have found my grandmothers diary. It probably was somewhere near here that her plane went down. I know it was in this general area. Oh Kent, could we have found my mother's birthplace?"

"Teddi, this is mind boggling" said Kent with wonderment. "What are the odds? What could have guided us to this island? It's pretty spooky but I think God has a lot to do with it. At least this confirms it with me. I think He wanted you to find this spot."

"I'm overwhelmed too, honey. Can we leave for the village early tomorrow? I want to read every word and I especially want to talk to Kellea. I just know she had to know of my grandmother."

"We'll leave at first light, Teddi" said Ben. "I, too, want to learn more about those brave souls that lived through the occupation of our island."

They all arose well before sunrise the next morning and wasted no time in packing up for the trek back to the village. It was barely light when they hit the trail and there was little conversation as they hiked on, with everyone deep in his own thoughts.

CHAPTER THREE

…how did we become Japanese prisoners? It's a long story and I guess it really started back on the farm where I met Chris flying his crop duster….

EARLY IN 1929

"Rosie! Rosie! You have chores up here! I don't know what pleasure that girl gets out of watching that crop duster airplane flying over our fields. You'd think she never saw one before."

"I'm coming Mom. That's Chris Conner's plane. He's coming over tonight. I'd like you and Dad to meet him."

"Well I hope he comes in something other than that airplane. He might have a pretty tough time finding a place to land."

"Oh Mom, don't be silly. He has a truck and of course he'll drive over. Hi Daddy! Chris is coming over tonight. He's the boy that I met at the air show."

Rosie's dad walked up the porch steps and said "Just who is this boy? Where's he from? And I suppose he's one of these vagabond crop dusters who travel's from town to town praying on sweet young girls who think every boy that flies a plane is some kind of super hero."

"No daddy, that's not so. He's from Wichita where he graduated from high school and his family still lives there. He became interested in flying when some barnstormers came through and he went on a flight with one of them. He took lessons while still in school and bought an old plane. He spent a whole year working on it to make it into a crop duster. Now he's saving the money he makes dusting crops so he can go to college. Oh daddy, I hope you like him."

"Humph! Well, we'll see." He said as he glanced at the smiling mother.

Later that evening after the dinner dishes were done, the three family members were sitting on the front porch of the farm house. Her father, sitting in his rocking chair enjoying a smoke on his pipe, her mother busy with her knitting and Rosie anxiously staring out at the road trying to catch a glimpse of a set of head lights coming their way.

Finally it happened. A Ford pick up truck pulled in off the road and slowly came up the winding driveway. After it stopped, a tall handsome young man unwound himself from the driver's seat and approached the porch. Rosie immediately ran down to meet him.

Her mother said, "Oh I wish that girl would use a little restraint."

The two young people climbed the porch steps and both parents rose to their feet.

"Mother and Father, I'd like you to meet Chris Conner. Chris this is my mom and dad Mr. and Mrs. Sterling."

"How do you do, young man." said the mother and father in unison.

Chris extended his hand to Mr. Sterling and said "It's a pleasure to meet both of you" as they shook hands.

"Please sit down Chris. May we offer some lemonade?" said Rosie's mother. "I have a pitcher cooling in the ice box."

"I'd like that very much, thank you." said Chris.

"Rosie, would you get that for Chris?"

As Rosie left for the kitchen the father asked "I understand you are from Wichita."

"Yes sir I am, but I'm living out at the airfield for now instead of trying to make that two hour trip each day. I can stay for free if I watch over the place at night. That way I can save for college quicker."

"Hmm. That seems like a pretty good way to do it." agreed the father.

"Just how safe is that airplane?" said Mrs. Sterling.

"Well ma'm it's probably as safe as the person doing the flying. I know some guys that are real hot shots and they are not safe at all. But I'm not of that type. I believe in following all the rules. Now I must admit that the low flying needed to dust crops carries some risks but I'm only doing that until I finish school."

"What are your plans after that?"

"Well I'm planning on studying Aeronautical Engineering at Purdue. It has the best program in the country and has a tie in with Lockheed so that may be what I'll pursue. My dad would like me to try for that.

The evening passed quickly and soon Chris stood and announced that he had an early day coming up and needed to hit the hay.

Rosie walked him to his truck and when they reached it he asked "Would you like me to pick you up on Sunday and take you for a short plane ride?"

"Oh I've been dying for you to ask me. It seems like so much fun just to be up in the air free of the ground. Yes, Yes I'd love to go."

"Okay I'll pick you up after church on Sunday. Maybe we could have a picnic." He said.

"I'll have a picnic basket all packed for us when you get here" she said.

He reached for her and hugged her tightly while he kissed her cheek and said "Good night, Rosie."

"Good night Chris. I can't wait for Sunday."

She dreamily watched as he drove off and then walked up to the house and into the parlor where her mom and dad were sitting.

"Did you like him, mom? How about you dad?"

Her dad chuckled "Now, now Rosie just relax. Yes he seems like a nice young man but a bit older than you. After all you are only 16 and still in high school."

"He's only a little older dad. He just turned 19. He asked me to go on a picnic Sunday and then out to the airfield. I told him I could go. I hope its okay."

"Well I guess it will be alright but I don't want you to get any ideas about riding around in one of those airplanes. I know what a dare devil you are."

"Oh dad" she said as she turned to go up the stairs to bed. Her face felt red and hot.

After she lay in bed she thought about Sunday. She would be with the two things that she wanted to be with the most, Chris and flying. How perfect it would be.

TWO YEARS LATER

"Hurry Rosie, we don't want to be late for your graduation. You worked four years for that high school diploma and you don't want to miss walking up on that stage."

"I'm coming mom. I'm having a problem keeping this cap on my head." called Rosie as she came running down the steps.

"Good gracious young lady, you're going to trip over that long gown. Let's go outside, your father's waiting in the car."

They loaded themselves into the Chevy and Mr. Sterling headed out to the road. He glanced over at Rosie and said, "Well honey I guess I'll not badger you anymore about going to college to get your teaching degree, like we kind of planned before you got this flying bug."

"Thank you daddy, I've interviewed at Cessna for an office job and I'm pretty sure they'll hire me. But I also have an appointment with Ken-Aire a new company and I think I'll be happier with them. They seem to be on the cutting edge with more streamlined designs, according to Chris "

"I suppose flying lessons are somewhere in your plans while you're in Wichita. Am I right?" piped up Mrs. Sterling.

"Well, yes. Oh mom, you know I'll be careful."

"Please do sweetheart and I know that young man of yours has influenced you on this, but he seems to have his head on straight, so listen to him. He has some experience with aircraft and I must say that I do trust the young man. By the way, will he be here today?"

"Yes daddy" said Rosie with a smile and a blush.

"Well here we are. Rosie, go join your classmates."

After they parked the car and were walking to the auditorium, they spied Chris up ahead. Mr. Sterling hailed him and Chris waited to join them.

"Well Chris, how did your first year at Purdue go?"

"Just fine Mr. Sterling. I really like it although it sure requires a lot of studying. A social life is out of the question."

Mrs. Sterling perked up and laughingly said "Well I'm sure that Rosie will be glad to hear that."

"She need not be concerned about any of that Mrs. Sterling" said Chris with about the same shade of a blush that Rosie had. "I can't wait to tell Rosie that Amelia Earhart will be coming to Purdue next year to be on staff. I sure would like to meet her. I guess you know Miss Earhart is Rosie's role model."

"Yes, we're very well aware of that, Chris. Rosie collects all the news stories she can about that famous lady and her travels."

They settled in their seats and enjoyed the festivities. When it was over, all the graduates and parents gathered for hugs, kisses and tears. A milestone in their lives had passed. It was now time for new accomplishments and adventure…..especially in Rosie's case.

Several weeks later, Rosie had moved to a small apartment in Wichita, which she shared with another girl also recently hired by Ken-Aire. They both worked in the office and were well liked by Ken-Aire management.

Time passed quickly but now she missed Chris and her only communication with him was by mail. She kept him up to date on her flying lessons and he kept her up to date on his aeronautical studies. She was a natural and her instructor marveled at her ability to learn so quickly.

Rosie was soon caught up in a group of other women flyers and was able to buy in on a joint ownership of a small plane.

She also was picking up some extra spending money doing some crop dusting for a few farmers. She loved skimming close to the ground and other daring stunts just for excitement.

She had been with Ken-Aire over two years now and was earning a good enough salary to start thinking about owning her own plane. When she approached her boss about looking at a used plane, that Cessna owned, he asked if she would be interested in obtaining a sponsor that would furnish a plane to fly in the air races for women. He knew of a group within this organization that wanted to enter a plane in the newly established Powder Puff Races which were becoming increasingly popular. They felt that it would be a very good promotion for the company.

"Oh that would be an answer to my dreams" said Rosie "but what about my job?"

"I'm not sure of all the details, but I'm certain that you would still be associated with Ken-Aire, since the airplane is a company experimental project. It's been thoroughly tested by our pilots but the company is looking for a woman pilot to enter it in the local races and see how well it would do. Of course the goal is to enter it into the big race from Santa Monica to Cleveland.

Rosie left his office in a daze. She contacted the management group for an appointment which was set up for the following day and went home to write a letter to Chris.

CHAPTER FOUR

....my love of flying started at an early age and Chris was a big part of nurturing this love as well as nurturing our love for each other. I became an avid lady racing pilot....

Her appointment went well. The race group explained that this was an experiment and that Rosie must follow instructions and accept the advice given by the test pilots. She agreed in a calm, confident manner but internally the butterflies were fluttering. She left the interview with determination to be the one they would choose to fly in *the big one* when they felt it was time.

The next several months were different than anything she had ever imagined. The experimental plane frightened her at first. But as always with Rosie, she quickly became proficient and soon the day came with they entered her in one of the shorter, preliminary races close to home.

She was quite nervous before take off, but once in the air and in the element where she excelled, she was calm and efficient. It was almost like she was part of the plane. Since this was her first attempt she was instructed just to get the feel of the environment and not push it to the extreme. She followed instructions to the letter and came in dead last. She held back and several times did not make a move up when she could have.

As she landed, she said to herself "I could have done better...I know I could have. I'll hold back for a while but they've got to let me turn her loose...they must let me...or I'll do it on my own."

The team was happy with the way she followed their plan and set out to schedule more races in anticipation to race in the big race from Santa Monica to Cleveland. She squirmed and fidgeted all the while.

The team leader called to Rosie as the meeting broke up "Stay here Rosie. Let's talk about the race."

She sat down and gave him a questioning look.

"Okay little missy, I'm a lot older than you so I'm going to talk to you like a father. I know that you are just dying to open that baby up and prove that both you and that plane have a lot more guts than we showed today and some day we will. But don't you do anything foolish. I've seen other hot shots in my time that aren't around today because they didn't respect better judgment. You are a fine pilot and you can go a long way with Ken-Aire and beyond. But don't let over confidence cloud your judgment. Be patient just a little longer."

She sat quietly for a short time and then said "Thank you sir. I want to be a good pilot and I know I get over exuberant at times. I guess it's just my nature."

"That's okay Rosie. That's why we chose you."

The team scheduled her in more races and in each one she did better and better until she finally came in first. She was ecstatic. She bounced out of the cockpit screaming "Yahoo" and pumping her fist in the air. "I'm ready. I'm ready." She yelled.

"Slow down, little lady. Slow down. One more race and then we'll talk about the big race." said her boss with a loud happy laugh.

She won the next race by a huge margin. At the meeting after the race they completed the application for the Santa Monica to Cleveland Race naming Rosie as the pilot.

In the last letter from Chris he said that Miss Earhart would not be competing or even attending this race since she was preparing for a trip around the world sponsored by Purdue University. The school had financed and had taken delivery of a Lockheed L-10 Electra for her use in July 1936.

Although others had circumnavigated the globe, hers would be the longest at 29,000 miles. To do this she would follow an equatorial route. Rosie marveled at the accomplishments of this wonderful woman and followed her feats with an obsession.

Also he had great news about landing a job with Lockheed as soon as he got his degree and was looking forward to being able to see Rosie a little more often.

LATER IN SANTA MONICA

Rosie had just arrived at the air field in Santa Monica where the race was to begin. She looked around in amazement. Never in her life had she seen so many airplanes of every shape and size. And the women pilots.... some not very friendly at all.....and some that seemed to just tolerate her. She did meet a lady who took her under her wing and was showing her around. "My name's Vera Jennsen. What's your name honey?"

"I'm Rosie Sterling. Thanks for talking to me."

"Oh don't take offense. The old timers always act that way to the young ones.....especially if they're as pretty as you. They're just jealous."

Rosie's plane had been shipped in by rail and a group of Ken-Aire technicians were just finishing reassembly of the wings and making fine adjustments. They had now given it the official name of XP-R. Rosie walked into the hanger where the XP-R was docked and was checking out the adjustments with a technician. She heard a door close in the back of the hanger and footsteps approaching. She glanced up and froze. She stood there with her eyes opened wide and her mouth agape and then suddenly bolted in a sprint, racing to meet this tall, handsome, well dressed young man.

He stopped and stood with his arms spread wide, a beaming smile on his face, waiting for this exciting dream of mass hysteria with tears streaming down, and her hair flying straight back, to reach him and to leap into his arms.

He smothered her with kisses and then blurted out "Marry me Rosie. Let's not wait. I planned on asking you at some romantic dinner or in a rose garden or something but I need to ask you now. Will you marry me?"

She didn't hesitate more than a second and loudly proclaimed "Yes, Chris. Yes! Yes! Yes!"

The Ken-Aire technicians all stood and stared at this emotional greeting. And when they heard Rosie's answer they all broke out in a big, very loud, boisterous cheer.

"Atta girl, Rosie." They yelled.

The happy couple walked out arm in arm, smiling among the din of her fellow workers. They had a lot of catching up to do. Rosie said "Let's go someplace where we can talk."

"There's a little coffee shop around the corner here on the field. Let's go there for now. I'm still kind of nervous." said Chris.

Chris continued "Wait a minute Rosie. Do you think I should talk to your dad first? What if he objects? Maybe we should wait."

"Hold on mister. Are you backing out already? I'm not letting you get off the hook that easy."

"No, no honey, I just mean that your dad and I should at least discuss it. I think he likes me but he's going to ask me, what are my plans, not only for the wedding, but for our future. Let's sit down for a minute and let me catch my breath."

She looked at him sheepishly "Okay. I guess I just got too excited. Let's sit down and make some plans."

They walked to Chris' car where they drove towards the Lockheed plant. Chris had moved into an apartment to be nearby the plant. They had to continue their discussion and now understood that many things must be considered before they rushed into anything.

By the end of the night they both agreed that a marriage was definitely in the plan. But first things come first. Chris must settle in on his job. Rosie had commitments to Ken-Aire, not the least of which is the up coming race.

Both were very happy and content with leaving things just as they were. They were in a position to see each other more often and still work on ambitious goals that each had set for themselves.

Preparation for the race was long and arduous. It was Ken-Aire's first attempt to design a racing aircraft exclusively built for a woman pilot.

Also it was Rosie's first attempt at this grueling race. Though it was tough to qualify, some team members still treated her like a naïve little girl.

As a result, the team and the lady pilot sometimes didn't agree on everything to the point where one day Rosie stormed out of the hanger, loudly exclaiming "I QUIT!"

Everyone got quiet and finally the boss said "Let's knock off for the day and come back tomorrow with a new attitude. I'll talk to Rosie."

He caught up to Rosie a little later in the coffee shop sitting in the corner booth with a cup of black coffee.

He slid in across from her and said "Looks like you like your coffee black now, huh?"

She eyeballed him and said "Well I don't really like it this way but if you don't do everything like a man does, they treat you like a little school girl."

"I know Rosie, but you've got to understand how women were treated before this. For some men it's a bust in the chops for a women to be able to do something better than they can and you can fly circles around any guy on that team. But you've also got to remember, some of those guys helped design that plane and they really do have more technical knowledge than you do. So that's why we're called a team. There is no way we could ever compete in this race without input from every person on the team both male and female."

"Well I know they know more than I do about aerodynamics but can't they just listen to me about how it handles up there?"

"Yes they can and yes they will. Tomorrow morning we'll all sit down over coffee and donuts and talk about this in a calm, sensible manner. Are you with us?"

"You know I am boss. I'll see you in the morning."

A few days later, the airfield was bustling with activity. Engines were revving up everywhere. The sound was deafening. Rosie felt great. This was finally the day she could give it her all.

She climbed into the cockpit, turned to the crew, gave a thumbs up and a radiant smile. When she got the signal to taxi onto the runway, she eased out and stopped in position for take off. The starter waved and she eased the throttle forward and felt the surging powerful engine move her forward. She gave it more power and was airborne quicker than she ever had been in her life. She was so exhilarated that she felt light headed. She knew it was that surge of adrenalin and tried to calm herself but this was a thrill that she would never forget.

The first leg of the race to San Bernardino went well.

The second day was two legs. The first to Yuma, refuel and then on to Phoenix. She lost minimal time at the refueling tank and the plane was running well. She felt that she moved up some what and poured the coals to her. It was getting dark when she spotted Phoenix and wanted to land before she lost daylight. As a result she came in too fast and hit hard. She bounced along the runway and when she came to an abrupt stop at the end of the runway she slowly nosed over and then dropped back on her tail wheel. She had heard an ominous crack when her nose hit the runway and swore at herself for being so stupid and impatient.

She clamored out of the cockpit, ran to the front of the aircraft and sure enough the prop was askew and a big wide crack was visible.

"Oh no." she lamented.

Two of the team had been sent ahead and they came running up to the damaged plane.

"It'll be okay Rosie. Let us take a look. If it's only the prop, don't worry, we've got a spare."

"Oh guys, I'm so sorry. I was making such good time."

"You made great time and don't worry. You did your job, now we'll do ours.

She did as they said and when she checked back she was very happy to hear that the plane would be in tip top shape, refueled and ready to go by takeoff time.

Day three went well and Rosie used a little more caution but she didn't lose any time either. Day four brought them into El Paso and dead reckoning was getting more difficult.

Day five was all Texas. El Paso to Fort Worth. Rosie was exhausted but the next leg was Wichita, really familiar territory.

After a good nights sleep she was anxious to start on the Wichita leg. The terrain was flat and they could all fly closer to the ground.

The sky was clear and she could fly low enough to have excellent visibility to pick out where she was. Soon she spotted the airfield and banked for a landing. She could now see people standing by cars and trucks and could swear she heard cheers for the local girl coming in for a landing. She made a perfect three point landing and taxied to her designated spot.

She gazed at the throng and sure enough, standing taller than anyone else was Chris just beaming with a proud smile. And was that mom and dad beside him? It sure was. She clamored out of the cockpit and ran to her loved ones not even hearing the cheers from the crowd.

Later at dinner with Chris and her family, her dad said "Rosie, Chris and I had a chance to talk while waiting for you and he told me how much he cared for you and he asked for your hand in marriage."

Rosie gulped and said "Oh…oh..I..ah…didn't think….ah..ah"

"Well honey, I want you to know that both mom and I couldn't be happier and we fully give you our blessing. We also respect the maturity of both of you to wait until you've both gotten a little more established."

"Oh thank you daddy, thank you. I love you both so much."

The next day was bright and sunny and all flyers took off without a mishap. The destination was East St. Louis which had a postage stamp size air field. Rosie landed her plane by reducing speed almost to the point of a stall. But she made it in and stopped short of the end of the runway. Others weren't so lucky.

Several came in too hard and bounced down the runway. One went clear off the end and mired itself in deep mud. The landing gear was beyond repair. And the other screeched off the side of the runway, careening along an access road. Workmen scattered as the wildly bouncing plane finally dug a wing in the mud and flipped around at right angles, continued on and finally came to rest wiping out a maintenance shed. The two workmen inside the shed heard the plane coming and escaped just before it hit and burst into flames.

The pilot didn't make it. She was badly burned and died that night in the hospital. Rosie was one of the throng who attempted to rescue her but got there too late. The two evacuated workmen were the ones who pulled her out and they both suffered burns on their hands and smoke inhalation. They survived and were released after hospital treatment.

Rosie had gone to the hospital to offer support and vigilantly stayed by Vera's side until she passed away. Vera was the kind lady that had shown her around that first day.

Vera's said these last words to Rosie before she closed her eyes and slipped away "You're a good pilot honey. Don't let any body tell you any different. But don't keep racing forever. Marry that young man before he gets away."

And she was gone.

Rosie told the other girls in the waiting room that Vera passed on while she was in there. They silently left the hospital and returned to the field where they gathered for a meeting to take a vote on continuing the race.

The vote was unanimous to continue.

CHAPTER FIVE

....racing was in my blood. I reveled in it and following the career of Amelia Earhart only made me want to do more.

The pilots manned their planes the next morning, on a somber note. The usual bantering, kidding and laughing is non existent. The next leg is to Columbus and then from there the final leg is to Cleveland. The weather was good and both Columbus and Cleveland have excellent air fields. The runway where one of the pilots had crashed into a bull dozer had been completed and was state of the art. The mood lightened somewhat when all planes landed safely in Columbus and excitement was high in anticipation of the final leg into Cleveland.

Rosie was notified at check in that she was in the top ten. She so wished that Vera could be here to congratulate her......but she must carry on. Vera would have wanted her to give it her all.

Dinner that night with a few of the girls was nervously jovial and everyone left the table immediately, when dinner was over.

The next morning was tense and each of the pilots manned their plane with grim determination. Rosie was even more nervous than she was at the initial takeoff in California. The final start went smoothly and all planes made it safely into the air. Now it was time to show the flying skills of each of them. The final, no holds barred, race to the finish. As soon as Rosie's wheels left the ground she got to top speed quickly. The plane just ahead of her seemed to slow down for a beat so she sling shot past her. That was a trick Vera had taught her. She lost sight of the others and hoped that

22

she hadn't strayed off course. Dead reckoning was still the only way to navigate. But instinct told her to stay the course.

The distance from Columbus to Cleveland was only about 125 miles so it was a short leg and wide open throttle all the way was her plan of action. The wind was coming from the southwest, directly on her tail so she was literally flying at the top of the chart. She would face the disadvantage of this great wind when she reached Hopkins Airfield which is south and west of the city. She must fly past the airfield and bank around to land into the wind. Landing with the wind on her tail would create too much of a risk of a cartwheel. But then they all faced this dilemma and only the most foolish would try such a risky landing. But she must admit, it did cross her mind.

Soon the approach to the airfield was in sight.

She banked around to the west and started her descent into this huge airfield. As her wheels touched and squealed when rubber met the surface she glanced ahead and could see that she was not the first one here. She couldn't grasp how many others were there but definitely there were several.

She slowed down, made her turn and taxied to the holding area where she was assigned. As she deplaned she looked up and saw several Ken-Aire people running towards her with happy grins.

"Congratulations Rosie. You did well. Mr. Kennard is here and wants to see you as soon as you check in." one of them yelled.

Mr. Kennard, President of Ken-Aire was waiting for her in the hall. "Rosie girl, come here and let me hug you." And the giant of a man enveloped her in his arms. "Little girl, you have put Ken-Aire on the map. We have proven that we can fly with the big boys. There's no stopping us now. With a few minor changes and with you at the stick, we'll mow 'em down."

"Oh thank you Mr. Kennard, but I had a lot of help. Without the team helping me, at just about every stop, I couldn't have done it. I just know I wouldn't have made it."

"You did just fine. I want you to take it easy for a while after the awards banquet and all the ceremonies and such. Take some time off….maybe you can fly back to L. A. on a commercial flight…and spend some quality time with that young man of yours."

"Well I'd really like to see Chris. We have some plans to discuss."

"Okay young lady but after we get back to the plant and have some meetings and make the design changes, I'd like to sit down with the entire team and make out a schedule for the next year.

She checked into her hotel and called Chris to tell him about the race and that she'd be coming to L.A. in a few days. He was excited about both. She then called home and both mom and dad where happily relieved that the race was over and that she was safe. She didn't tell them that this was only the first of several more cross country races that she'd be in during the next year.

When she got to Los Angeles, Chris was at the airport to pick her up. It was a happy time with both having had great success and to relax without the pressures. Chris took a one week vacation and they spent time just being two young people in love.

The week went by all too quickly and they both promised to try to see each other more often but both knew that the next year was going to be a busy one.

On the way to the airport Chris said "I guess you knew that Amelia Earhart's Electra L-10E was in Oakland and that she and Fred Noonan along with Harry Manning and Paul Mantz were going to leave for Hawaii in March."

"I knew that she was planning the circumnavigation but I didn't know all those people were going."

"Well Noonan is the navigator and the other two are technical advisors, I guess. I don't know but I think there are some problems with both equipment and possibly people."

"Gosh I hope nothing goes haywire. The Electra is a good plane isn't it?"

"Oh yes it's the best that Lockheed puts out and it's tried and true. I just heard a few rumblings about the variable pitch prop and how it was lubricated….or maybe the lack of it. But they are pros and I'm sure they'll be okay."

He continued "Well sweetheart, here we are saying our goodbyes again. I love you Rosie and whenever you want to tie the knot, I'm ready, and it can be under any conditions that you name."

"I love you too Chris. It won't be long, I promise. I have some obligations to Mr. Kennard and to Ken-Aire, for the next year, and also some goals of my own. But it's not all bad. Ken-Aire is paying me well to race the XP-R. With both of us earning good money, it will give us a good start. Just bear with me a little longer, honey, I'm anxious too."

They parted with a kiss

When she reached Wichita she checked into a hotel and called her mom. She explained that getting away to visit them on the farm on this trip was going to be next to impossible, because of all the planning meetings and evenings of review. Mom understood. When she reached the Ken-Aire plant, the whole team was already there and ready to set up an itinerary.

The biggest race was the Bendix Trophy. This prestigious race was inaugurated in 1931 and non other than Jimmy Doolittle was the winner.

It was a known fact that the Bendix brought unusual fame and distinction to the designer and builder of the racing aircraft as well as to the pilot who raced it. For this reason Mr. Kennard was extremely interested in placing well with the XP-R. "Can you imagine the prestige of winning with a woman pilot?" he said.

Rosie was giddy with the anticipation of the race. She was so exited about the added horsepower and the speed that it generated that she could hardly contain herself. She flew the new version of the XP-R with added confidence and it showed. The crew chief greeted her as she alit from the cockpit after a practice run and yelled "Rosie you made that plane do things I never thought it could do. It was like you were built right into it."

Mr. Kennard came walking up and said "That's right Mac, this plane was designed for someone exactly like Rosie and I feel very fortunate to have her as our pilot."

Mac said "Hey did you hear the bad news about Amelia Earhart?"

"Oh my God" said Rosie "she didn't crash, did she?"

"No, no" said Mac "they only got as far as Honolulu and had mechanical problems."

"Thank the Good Lord that she's okay. What happened? Was it an accident or a malfunction?"

"From what I heard, there was a galling problem in the propeller hubs' variable pitch mechanism. Sounds like a lubrication problem to me. They're going to try to correct it at Luke Field on Ford Island."

"Well I'll be darned" said Rosie "I guess that man of mine has some pretty good knowledge of aircraft."

"Okay gang, enough talk about that. Let's get busy. Rosie I want you to explain how you did some of those maneuvers up there. It might be very helpful when we enter the Catterton after we do the Bendix. Let's go into the conference room."

When she arrived at the apartment one afternoon days later, Chris met her with more bad news about Amelia.

"Tell me what happened Chris." She said.

"Three days after they serviced the prop hub variable pitch mechanism, Earhart, Noonan and Manning resumed the trip. Upon takeoff from Luke Field, Earhart ground looped. Witnesses say they thought they saw a tire blowout. What ever the cause may be, the aircraft is severely damaged and is being shipped by sea to the Lockheed plant here in Burbank. I may get the opportunity to help on the project."

"Oh I feel so sorry for her Chris. Do you think that she'll come to the plant?"

"That certainly is a very good possibility."

"Oh Chris, do you think I could meet her? She's such a great lady and has done so much for women flyers. I'd rather meet her than any one else."

"I can't promise honey, but if there is any way in the world that I can arrange it, I will."

Back to preparing for the race, tomorrow was the big day and there was nothing more they could do. They were as prepared as well as they possibly could be. Rosie left early so she could get to bed and get a good rest. There would be no overnight rest stops on this one. It would be any where from 8 to 12 hours depending on where she placed with two refueling stops. This was no race for sissies.

Early the next morning all were ready to start. Most of the technicians had spent the night tuning everything to perfection.

The airplanes were spectacular. Some of these planes she had only seen as pictures in magazines.

A little later the race started with a deafening roar. Hundreds of horse power all howled at once. Rosie's ears were ringing with the resounding thunder. She poured the coals to her refitted high horsepower engine and it responded with a jolt that pinned her to the seat back. She was flying again at break neck speed and that familiar adrenaline rush was again throughout her body. It was just a marvelous high that had reached its zenith. All the pressures of getting ready and all the meetings of business planning and promotional tours were now behind and this is what she really wanted to do. Let the others do all that. She would fly and Mr. Kennard must understand.

It was a grueling race and when it was finished and she landed in Cleveland again she was completely spent. But it was a good feeling of accomplishment. Rosie was again in the top ten but averaged 185 mph, much lower than the winning speed of 258 mph.

Mr. Kennard was a little disappointed that she didn't do better but considering that the best pilots in the world competed he certainly was not embarrassed, especially when Ben O. Howard, the winner of the 1935 race complimented him on the fine design and even made a suggestion on an upgrade.

He said "Don't you fret, little girl, next year we'll knock 'em dead. I've come up with some good ideas of how we can get more speed out of this baby."

"Thank you sir, I'm really tired. I think I'll get a bite to eat and hit the sack. Can we talk in the morning?"

"Sure thing, sure thing. We've got to plan for the Catterton next so get a good nights rest. We'll all be leaving for the plant right after the awards tomorrow."

Rosie quietly said "Wow" as she walked away.

CHAPTER SIX

…..it was becoming evident that being a woman racing pilot had its drawbacks. My time with Chris was limited and some races were grueling…..

There wasn't any break after the Bendix. Mr. Kennard wanted the whole team back at the plant to plan for the Catterton and also the promotional tour before the race.

When he gathered them together he said "Sales has reported that orders for the Avenger surged after the Powder Puff Race and they expect the same to happen after the Bendix. I've called a meeting of all departments in one week. It's a command performance. That is, I want 100% attendance. We are about to embark on the most aggressive campaign that this industry has ever seen.

He continued after a dramatic pause to let his message sink in "I hope everyone understands that each of us has a specific part in making this campaign a success and you…the race team….are the cutting edge. Rosie, it has been requested that you make the entire marketing tour trip with that group. You've only got a few days after the meeting before you leave so I want you to contact the head of the marketing department tomorrow to meet him and lay out a plan. I've booked you on a commercial flight leaving this afternoon so get packed."

Rosie stood and started to leave. She stopped and turned to ask "Will I be able to go home before I leave again?"

"I'm afraid you can't this time. Maybe not even before the Catterton. Let's play it by ear."

She went back to her room and packed for the trip to the plant.

While on the plane she thought she'd better write a letter to Chris to explain everything. He's going to be disappointed.

My Darling Chris,

I'm writing this on the flight back to Wichita from Cleveland. I'm sorry I didn't call but it's been a real whirlwind.

I won't be coming home for a while. Mr. Kennard wants me to prepare to go on some big promotion tour with the marketing people. There has been a surge in sales of the production design of the XP-R... You may have seen it...and they expect more. Anyway they want me, as the pilot, to be available to answer questions and give instruction on its uses. I don't like this kind of work. I'd rather be flying.

I also am not crazy about some of these marketing people. My dad has a term for them...fast and loose...at least that's how they act. Maybe it's just an act, but I think it's disgusting. There are two other women going so at least I'll have some company.

I miss you so much Chris. You are so different than these people. You are such a genuine person and these fictitious people could not hold a candle to you. Oh by the way that is another one of dad's sayings.

After the Catterton I'm going to talk to Mr. Kennard about not doing these tours. I hope he understands.

Well darling we are going to land soon. I want to get this posted as soon as we land. I promise I will be in touch as much as I can.

I love you,

Rosie

The next day Rosie went to the Marketing Dept. to meet Mr. Smither. He had a manual all prepared for her. A meeting was scheduled in two days. Read it and she could ask questions then.

He then stood and dismissed her. It was all very informal. She went to her desk and started reading the manual. The first three pages were a travel itinerary. It appeared that they'd be constantly on the move.

As she was reading, two well dressed young ladies approached her desk and one said "You must be Rosie, the pilot. Hi, we're Pam and Betty."

"Oh...Hi. Yes I'm Rosie. Do you work here in Marketing?"

"We sure do honey. In fact we'll be seeing a lot of each other in the next few weeks or more. We're also going on the tour."

"That's great. This will be my first real tour. I've worked at a few customer viewings with Mr. Kennard but I'm strictly a novice at this tour thing. I'll need some guidance from you gals."

"Well first of all honey do you have any decent clothes? You can't wear those farmer togs."

"Gosh I have some dresses and stuff at home but they're in California. I didn't bring dress up clothes since I flew in the race and didn't really need them."

"Tell you what. I'll go see Mr. Smither and see if we can break loose some expense money for some clothes for you. The old boy owes me a favor anyhow" Pam said as she winked at her friend.

Rosie went back to studying the manual and by lunch time her two friends were back.

Betty laughed as she said "Okay Rosie, Pam was pretty successful in getting some expense money. Old man Smither must have owed her a big favor."

"Let's get some lunch and then the three of us are going on a shopping spree for the afternoon." said Pam.

By the end of the day Rosie was loaded down with packages. She marveled at how those two girls could find the bargains of the cutest stuff and then haggle on the price. It was beyond her shopping capabilities. She unloaded her bags of new clothes and spent the evening trying everything on.

The two week tour went by very quickly and Rosie met many potential customers. All were very curious how such a little girl could fly such a powerful aircraft. And there were those who doubted her abilities until they questioned her and she gave all the right answers.

Mr. Smither complimented her on the way she handled the questioning.

"As long as they keep the questions on flying and on the XP-R I can hold my own but there were a few who asked other questions that were of a personal nature and I just turned away. I'm not that kind of girl."

Mr. Smither stood silently for a moment, started to say something, and then turned and walked away.

Finally the tour ended and the group headed back to the plant. Mr. Kennard wanted a report the following morning at the inevitable meeting.

Before Rosie went to bed in her room that night she called Chris and explained that she had been constantly on the go for two solid weeks. He understood and asked "Can you come home before the Catterton?"

"It doesn't look like it honey but as I told you in my letter I'm going to let Mr. Kennard know that I would like to forego any more long tours. An occasional customer meeting is okay but that's all. The Catterton is only two weeks off and they again have modified the plane so I'll have to check it out. Oh it will be so good to get back to flying."

The meeting went well and Rosie was excused after several hours. Mr. Kennard complimented her on customer contact and told her to check in with the Technician Crew Chief to go over the modifications on her airplane.

He said "We want you to get it in the air in a few more days to make sure everything is working up to snuff."

She was very proud that he called it 'her' airplane in front of the whole group.

The Ruth Catterton Air Sportsman Pilot Trophy Race was finally here and Rosie performed exceptionally well doing all the required maneuvers and adding a few of her own. Some of the exercises included, soaring to a stall, a barrel roll, both kinds of a loop, nose dive, tailspin, touchdown and go, instrument landing and finally a three point landing.

Rosie was not first in the overall but did win a first in maneuverability. Mr. Kennard was very pleased.

Again after the awards she was told to report back to the plant in Wichita. That was okay because she wanted to have a discussion with Mr. Kennard.

The morning after her return she went to Kennard's office and asked the secretary if she could have a moment with him. When the secretary called him on the intercom he affirmed that Rosie could enter.

"Good morning sir"

"Good morning Rosie. I'm glad you came up. I was going to ask to see you today anyhow. We are very proud of what you are doing here and I'm planning a little bonus for you right after this next marketing tour and then some time off to unwind."

"Thank you sir, I appreciate your confidence in me. And actually that's what I wanted to talk to you about."

"You mean the bonus?" he said with a chuckle.

"No, no I mean the tour. I don't really enjoy them, especially being away so long, and some of the people I have to deal with are kind of rude."

"From what I understand, you handle yourself quite well with those that are rude. Unfortunately, in sales, you must put up with a certain amount of rudeness from moneyed people. Pam and Betty can handle any extra customer requests. Just treat them nice, and don't be rude in return. Always use good judgment, as to the situation."

"I'd prefer not to go Mr. Kennard."

"Okay. I'll tell you what. The first stop on the tour is Chicago. There is a very important customer that has requested to meet you. Just go to that one exhibit, meet the customer and we'll discuss the next step. Okay?"

"Okay Mr. Kennard. I'll do this one time."

After she left Kennard picked up the phone.

"Smither, I just met with Rosie. You were right. Come on up. We'll figure out something. She must be made to understand how important this order can be. I hope she's smart enough to cooperate."

CHAPTER SEVEN

.......the time finally came when I realized that this kind of life was not for me. I wanted no more of living in the fast lane. I wanted a life with the man that I loved. I left Ken-Aire and the air races....

The tour made its way to Chicago and the first night of the exhibit was very busy. The special customer was a large corporation that was interested in a fleet of corporate planes.

The president of the company was a middle age, well dressed, handsome man and Pam and Betty were paying special attention to him. His champagne glass was never empty and soon it was evident that he was getting tipsy. He had been over to meet Rosie earlier, before he had been imbibing heavily, and asked many questions about the Avenger's performance. Smither was glowing and it appeared that he also was heavily into the champagne.

Rosie had been talking to one of the corporate engineers when she noticed Pam and the corporate VIP talking discretely and looking her way.

Soon Pam walked over and said "Okay honey, it looks like its show time for you tonight."

"I don't understand" said Rosie.

"The big wig president wants you to go to his room." she said.

"I'll do no such thing" Rosie said adamantly.

"Look here girly, I tried to get him to ask me and so did Betty. We knew you were skeptical about such things but he's insisting on you. Now here he comes. Shape up."

"Okay Rosie girl. I've got a magnum of champagne on ice in my room. What do you say we head up there?"

"Sir, you've got the wrong idea about me. I will not go to yours or anyone else's room."

Just then Smither walked up, "Are we having a problem here?" he said

"Smither you better straighten out your girl here. You know what's on the line and I'm sure you remember our earlier conversation on entertainment for me and my boys."

"Please go have a drink and let me get things on track here." said Smither haltingly.

After he left, Smither turned to Rosie and said "What's the matter with you? Don't you realize the size of the order he's giving us? We're asking that you cooperate just one time. Mr. Kennard said that once you realize the magnitude of this, you'd go along with it."

"No!" said Rosie.

"Look I know about you women pilots. You're all out for the big thrills and the good times. Don't think I don't know that. I've been around for a long time girly, now get up to his room."

Rosie hit the boiling point. Before she could contain herself, she let loose with a round house right hook with every bit of the 110 lbs. of her lithe body behind it and caught Smither right on the point of his chin. He went down like a stricken steer at the stock yard. He laid there with his eyes closed and his mouth slack.

The room got deathly quiet. Rosie turned on her heel and stomped towards the door. As she passed the corporate VIP he reached out for her arm. She pulled away before he could grab on and turned to face him. "If you want some of the same mister, just try grabbing again."

He stepped back and raised his hands, palms facing Rosie, and said "Whoa. Whoa little girl. I've seen what you can do and I want to congratulate you on a great right hook. Good night and good luck."

She turned and left. She went straight to her room, packed her clothes, left the hotel and caught a cab to the airport.

At the airport, she was able to book a flight to Wichita that was leaving in 30 minutes. She checked her bags and boarded the plane.

It was a short flight and she was deep in thought the whole way. She had some decisions to make and by the time she arrived in Wichita late at night, she had made up her mind. She took a cab to the temporary apartment the company had furnished for her while she was in town and packed all her personal belongings.

The next morning she made her way to the plant at the start of the work day and took the elevator to the floor of executive offices.

"Good morning Ann" she greeted Mr. Kennard's assistant "May I see Mr. Kennard?"

"Just a moment, Rosie, I'll see if he's available." she answered in a cool tone.

She rose from her desk and closed the door after entering his office.

Rosie thought to herself 'Obviously word has traveled fast.'

After a few tense moments Ann returned and said "Mr. Kennard will see you now."

Rosie entered and said "Good morning Mr. Kennard. Thank you for seeing me."

"Please sit down Rosie. I guess we have something to discuss." he said in a very business like tone.

"I'll come right to the point sir, and make things easier for all concerned. I'd like you to accept my letter of resignation" she said as she handed him an envelope.

"Well termination isn't necessarily mandatory in this case but some sort of chastisement is certainly in order. Smither was able to salvage the fleet order but concessions had to be made. Ken-Aire was embarrassed and has a red face. This is not acceptable"

"You don't understand sir. I QUIT! As of this moment I no longer work for Ken-Aire. I'm leaving with a clear conscience. I performed the duties that I was hired to do to the best of my ability. I was a good pilot for you and I was willing to help promote your new design but never did I agree to act as a prostitute or anything associated with that. I will agree to keep that reason within these walls and I hope that you are a gentleman enough to do the same. My resignation merely states that I prefer to explore other avenues in the industry, mostly in the teaching field, and no longer care to participate in racing."

Kennard read the resignation and sat silently for a minute, staring into space and then turned to her.

"Okay young lady. You've probably made a wise decision. Resigning will take the pressure off of all concerned. Rest assured there will be no repercussions here at Ken-Aire. All employees will be instructed that this is a closed matter and no further discussion or speculation is to be made. A simple memo of notification of your resignation will be made. I'll notify the C.F.O. to have your final check ready for you immediately."

He picked up his phone, called accounting and said "Cut a check immediately for Rosemarie Sterling for her salary to date. And also include the bonus that we talked about last week."

"Thank you Mr. Kennard. I'm sorry that it had to end this way but I guess I'm just not cut out for the corporate world."

"I too am sorry Rosie. I just wish the corporate world had more people like you in it. Maybe it wouldn't be such a rat race. Good luck and latch on to that engineer boy friend of yours. He sounds like a good man."

Rosie left the plant and felt as free as a bird. She stopped at the first phone booth and called the farm.

"Hi mom" she said as she heard her mom's voice "are you up for a house guest for a while?"

Her mom was baffled and Rosie just laughed and told her that she'd be there in a few hours and yes everything was okay and that she would explain everything when she got there.

The next call was to Chris at the Lockheed plant.

When she got him she said "Honey I'll explain everything in a letter but I'm now unemployed. No everything is fine. In fact it probably couldn't be better. And by the way....on that marriage thing that we talked about? Well...later has just become now."

There was a moment of silence on the other end and suddenly there was a loud "Whoopee."

Rosie laughed and said "I'm going to the farm for a while honey and talk to mom and dad. Do you think you could get a few days off and come here so we could make some plans?"

"I've got a few things to wrap up but it shouldn't take more than a few days and I'll be on my way honey. You don't know how happy you've just made me. But I'm really anxious to hear your story."

Rosie loaded her belongings into a cab and struck out for the farm. Everything felt so clean and fresh. She could hardly wait to see Chris again. She was just sure that mom and dad would go along with a small wedding there on the farm. She had enough of the fast life and just wanted to settle down with Chris and teach flying to others.

She caught a cab to the apartment and asked the driver for help loading her bags and other belongings and to drive her out to the farm.

On the ride to the farm, she smiled all the way. She was so happy and so relieved.

The time on the farm settled into a daily routine after the first few days. Mr. Sterling wanted to make a trip into Wichita and confront the whole Ken-Aire Marketing group and clean house.

Rosie laughed and said "Dad, I'm a big girl now and believe me they all know that this little girl can pack a wallop. Everything is finished now and that page in my life is closed. I want to thank you and mom for the fine Christian up bringing that you both have given me. It certainly brought me through some very tough times and helped me make some life changing decisions."

"We're proud of you Rosie, both dad and I, and we're so happy to have you home again even though we know it probably won't be for long."

"You're right mom. Chris should be here any time now and we'd like to discuss wedding plans if that's okay with you two."

"Oh honey, that would make us so happy. Yes! Yes! We've been looking forward to the day that you two tie the knot."

No sooner did they get those words out of their mouths when a cab pulled up the winding drive. As it stopped in front, Chris stepped out of the back seat with a glow on his face.

Rosie rushed down before he could even pay the driver and jumped into his arms. Mr. and Mrs. Sterling were not far behind and could hardly wait until Rosie unwound herself from Chris to get in their own hugs.

Chris laughingly paid the grinning driver who drove away with a tear in his eye.

And then the happy wedding planners all adjourned to the parlor.

Mr. Sterling composed himself, straightened his back to draw himself to every inch of his compact height and with a very formal tone of voice said "Chris… we gather that it's going to be wedding planning time for you two."

The silence was deafening.

And suddenly the room exploded with raucous laughter from the three Sterling family members as Chris stood there and turned a ghastly shade of white.

The color came back into his face as Rosie said "Don't worry honey, you'll get used to this crazy family."

"I hope so darlin' because I hope to be a part of it for a long, long time." Chris said.

"Would you like to call your folks, Chris?" said Mrs. Sterling. "Maybe they could come over for lunch tomorrow and get in on the planning."

"That would be great, Ma'm. They know I'm here and I feel that they would be pleased to be a part of it."

The wedding plans went well and a June wedding was planned. Chris was able to schedule time off from work for the wedding and a short honeymoon.

He and Rosie went back to Los Angeles to tie up loose ends on their housing plans. Both had small apartments, not really suitable for a newly married couple, and Chris had some projects at work to complete.

It was in May of 1937 and the wedding was planned for the first week of June so they had to move quickly.

They spent most evenings together and on one of them Chris came to Rosie's apartment all excited.

"Rosie, you're not going to believe this." Chris blurted out.

"What? Why are you so excited?" Rosie said.

After a short pause and with a big smile, he said "Amelia Earhart and Fred Noonan are in the plant inspecting the Electra L-10E that they plan to use to continue the circumnavigation."

"Oh Chris, did you see her?"

"Not only did I see her but since I was assigned to help with the modifications I'm working with her and Noonan for the next week or so until it's ready to fly."

"Honey I'm so happy for you. But I'm really jealous too. I wish I could just meet her and tell her how much I admire her."

"Let me tell you the best part." Chris said. "I told her about the crazy woman pilot that I'm going to marry and guess what? She would like to meet you."

Rosie let out a blood curdling scream and jumped on Chris, wrapping arms and legs around his frame.

"Easy, easy little girl. The neighbors will think I'm murdering you." As he set her down he said, "Can you be ready for me to pick you up tomorrow at noon? They said they will meet us for lunch. That's the best I can do. Security is getting tight at the plant with all this stuff going on in Europe and I can't get you inside anymore."

"Oh Chris, I'm so happy. Thank you, darling, thank you so much for thinking of me."

CHAPTER EIGHT

......the wedding was beautiful and my husband is so caring and thoughtful. I was finally able to meet Miss Earhart but a double tragedy was soon to happen.....

The next day was a whirlwind. Rosie was on cloud nine all morning and she could hardly contain herself when Chris arrived. She ran out to his car, not even waiting until he was fully stopped.

"Let's go!" she said.

There were many Lockheed people at the restaurant and she finally was able to meet the famous lady and engage in a very short conversation about women pilots and air racing. Amelia was very gracious and even said she had seen Rosie's name in some of the races. They spoke of mutual friends and before you know it, the lunch was over and Amelia and Fred excused themselves. Rosie and Chris sat for a moment. She basked in the pleasant warmth of this memorable meeting even though it was short and amidst a crowd.

She looked at Chris, took his hand and kissed it while whispering "Thank you. Thank you."

They arose and slowly left the restaurant.

Time passed quickly and soon the happy day was upon them. They had made all preparations for living quarters and they left for Kansas.

The wedding took place at the farm, in the flower garden, under the rose trellis, which was picture perfect. An old family friend, Reverend

Father McIntyre performed the ceremony and all the friends and relatives gathered under a tent, out of the blazing sun, to witness the betrothal.

The reception was held under the tent with plenty of food and drink. It was a joyous occasion for all and was quite evident as family and friends celebrated the union of this wonderful couple.

Rosie was a vision of loveliness as she moved gracefully among the guests receiving their good wishes for happiness. Chris was along side of her beaming with happiness and graciously accepting the congratulations of all.

The starry eyed bride and the nervous groom left the happy celebration late in the evening for their wedding night in the finest hotel in Wichita. The next morning they caught a plane to San Francisco for a somewhat abbreviated honeymoon.

Chris had to be back at the Lockheed plant and Rosie needed to set up housekeeping in their newly rented apartment.

After they got back, Chris told Rosie that Earhart and Noonan had secretly flown from Oakland to Miami sometime after they had lunch with them. It was rumored that they wanted to fly the modified plane on the first leg overland as a semi test with no publicity. In case of a failure or an aborted flight they didn't want all the hullabaloo they had in Hawaii.

"In fact," Chris said "It went so well that they continued on going east instead of west as before. A much better plan because they'll get more favorable winds going east. They left Miami on June 1. Their route will take them to South America, Africa, South East Asia, into the Pacific, New Guinea, Honolulu and back to Oakland."

"How long will it take them?" Rosie asked.

"Depending on the weather, of course, probably a little over a month."

"She's such a brave lady. I just love her."

The next several weeks were busy ones for the newlyweds but Rosie tried to keep track of the circumnavigation on the radio and newspaper. Sometimes Chris would get some news before the press and he'd faithfully pass it on to Rosie.

It was just before the 4th of July celebration that Chris came home with a long face.

"Rosie, we got word today that Amelia and Fred left Lae, New Guinea on July 1 for Howland Island and they did not arrive. The Coast Guard Vessel that last heard from them feels that they've gone down somewhere around the Phoenix Islands. A search is now being formed for them. It doesn't look good."

Rosie stared at Chris in shock. She couldn't speak although her mouth moved to try to say something. A low moan came from deep in her throat.

Chris took her in his arms, hugged her close and then sat her in a chair. He ran to the bathroom sink and wet a towel with cool water. He bathed her head with the towel and said "Go ahead Rosie. Let it loose. Don't try to hold back."

And she did. She cried, grieving the loss of her role model.

Weeks later the search was called off with no physical evidence of Earhart, Noonan or the Electra ever found.

Rosie went through a bad period after the disappearance of Amelia Earhart and Fred Noonan. She followed the many theories that emerged in the ensuing months. Two possibilities seemed to prevail. Many researchers felt that they ran out of fuel in their futile search for Howland Island and crashed into the sea.

Others thought that they may have found an island on which to set down and survived. Rosie hung on to that theory and prayed that they would be found on some deserted island and returned home.

But months passed without anything further on their fate and Rosie, in her wisdom accepted it. Chris continued on his job at Lockheed getting busier each day with the threat of war looming over their heads.

Rosie went back to the flight school, teaching young men and women how to fly. She had now adjusted to the fact that Amelia Earhart was gone.

In the spring she asked Chris if he could get some time off and they could visit the folks on the farm.

"Sure thing honey. I'll put in for a weeks vacation and we'll drive to Kansas. I think a little Midwest leisure will do us both some good."

And so on the Memorial Day weekend they started on the leisurely drive across country to Kansas. When they arrived, the folks were ecstatic. After a few days back on the farm Rosie was her old joyful self and for the first time in a year she was perfectly relaxed.

Summer was upon them and the weather turned hot and humid. A little early in the season but in Kansas you can expect anything.

When Mr. Sterling came in from the fields, wiping his brow he said "Well we should get some relief later today. The weather man says that a cold front is coming through late this afternoon."

"I'll welcome that" Rosie said "It's too early for 90 degrees and 100% humidity."

They suffered through the early afternoon and sure enough it started cooling down later. By the time the dinner hour came around the skies clouded up with thunderheads and the wind picked up considerably.

"Chris, come help me get all the stock into the barn. Looks like a real thunder boomer brewing." Mr. Sterling said.

"I'm right behind you pop" Chris said.

"Be careful you two" Mrs. Sterling said "things are starting to blow around out there."

The two women anxiously watched out the window as their men hustled the agitated horses and cows into the barn. The horses were wild eyed and very nervous. Chris had a particularly hard time with the gelding. He reared and bucked and almost knocked Chris over. But Chris prevailed and soon all animals were under cover. The chickens and pigs needed no coaxing or guidance. They went into the coop and the pen without any need of direction or suggestion.

The men ran back to the house soaked to the skin and shivering from the suddenly very cold rain.

"I wish I could have tied down a few things but this thing came up too fast. I don't like the looks of it either." Mr. Sterling said as he started stripping off his dripping wet shirt.

"Both of you get in the bedroom and get out of those wet duds and into some dry ones." Rosie said. "Mom's putting on a fresh pot of coffee to help you warm up."

After they changed clothes and were drinking steaming hot coffee around the kitchen table Chris said "Look out doors, its black as pitch and sunset isn't for another hour."

"And it sounds like the wind is really picking up." Mr. Sterling said. "I wonder if we shouldn't put on a slicker and head out to the storm cellar."

"I'm all for that" Rosie said. "Better safe than sorry."

They all agreed and put on slickers. The storm cellar was only 50 feet behind the house and sheltered somewhat by a huge oak tree in between. It had a good solid door and had weathered several tornados over the years. When they opened the back door it seemed like all hell broke loose. The door knob was yanked out of Chris' hand and slammed against the house breaking the glass window. The shattered glass cut his hand and was bleeding profusely.

They were half way to the storm cellar when Mrs. Sterling noticed the blood dripping from his hand and she said "Oh Chris, you're hurt. I'll get the first aid kit." She spun around and started running back to the house with the wind pushing her forward.

"Where's that crazy woman going?" Mr. Sterling said. "Come back here woman. There's no time to go back." And he also ran to catch her and get her into the shelter of the storm cellar.

Chris and Rosie had reached the storm cellar and they raised the heavy door. He guided Rosie down the ladder and started down himself when a distant roar became audible and steadily got louder until it sounded like a freight train right over head.

"Oh my God" he yelled. He screamed his loudest "Mom! Dad! Hurry! It's a tornado." But his loudest scream was lost in the cacophony of the wind and rain in the storm.

"Rosie, I've got to go get them."

"No Chris! No! It's too late. If you don't close the door it will pull us right out of here. I saw them go into the house. Maybe they will lie down in the center bathroom and be okay. Close the door."

Chris closed and latched the door and just in the nick of time. The tornado hit with a fury. Even as heavy as the door was, it was almost ripped from its hinges. It shook and rattled in a deafening din.

Chris and Rosie huddled together and silently prayed that mom and dad were unharmed.

It seemed like forever that the storm raged on but the worst was over in a short time. The rattling door settled down and Chris slowly raised it. They were greeted with a steady rain and a stiff breeze and semi-darkness prevailed.

There was enough light to see the mass destruction that the storm had left. There was no doubt that this had been a direct hit. There was a huge path of rubble leading from the southwest. It looked like Mother Nature had taken a huge broom and swept a 100 yard swath for a couple of miles.

The house was gone. In its place stood a fireplace with half a chimney and a pile of rubble. The barn was a shambles and dead animals lay strewn about.

Rosie raised her head up through the door opening and jumped out of the cellar, running headlong towards the pile of rubble that was where the house had stood. She was screaming "MOM! DAD! Where are you?"

Chris followed close behind. "Honey. Honey. This might not be good. Stay here and let me look."

He started peeling away debris and soon found what he hoped he would not. Mr. Sterling was lying across Mrs. Sterling's body as if to shield her in the last act of love for his lifelong partner. He cleared away a spot and gently laid their bodies side by side.

He walked back to where Rosie was standing under the stripped branches of the huge oak tree that somehow had survived one more tornado.

He said "I'm so sorry honey. They…they didn't make it. Come with me. I'll take you to them and you can give them one last hug."

"OH NO, NO." she screamed "I didn't want them to go back. I just knew it! I just knew it! Oh please, I want to see them and tell them how much I love them….I must see them one more time" Rosie said through her tears as she staggered towards the rubble.

While she was with her parents, sobbing and grieving over her loss, the Sheriff and a deputy drove up the winding driveway. As they got out of the cruiser, Chris walked down to meet them.

"Hello Sheriff. I'm Chris Conner, Rosie's husband."

"Yes, I remember when you and Rosie got hitched. Looks like you folks caught the brunt of it out here. Is anyone hurt? I can radio for an ambulance."

"Well I'm afraid the Sterling's didn't make it." Chris said. "Rosie's with their bodies now right over behind that mess of rubble."

"Oh no. Oh my God no. They were such good folks. Damn, seems like it's always the good ones. Let's walk over and talk to Rosie. I'm sure she can use a kind voice at this terrible time." said the Sheriff.

"Thanks Sheriff. I think we're both still in shock."

The Sheriff turned to his deputy. "Go back to the cruiser and radio the hospital to send two ambulances. One for the two dead folks and one for the young couple. Looks like this young man needs some work on that cut hand. Probably needs stitches."

"Yes sir. I'm on it." said the young deputy.

"It's the law that the dead folks go to the hospital for cause of death. And then Rosie and you can determine which funeral home you'd want to pick them up."

"Sure. I understand." said Chris.

They walked to the bodies and Rosie looked up as they approached. She stood and Chris enveloped her in his arms. She sobbed, buried her head in Chris' chest and cried. After a few minutes she contained herself and turned to the Sheriff.

He said "I'm so sorry for your loss Rosie. My wife and I will do all we can to help you through this. We've known you all your life and your folks for most of theirs. We'll miss them. For now, let's get you and your husband to the hospital and get you checked out. I'll take care of your mom and dad."

"Thank you Sheriff. My head's in a whirl and I just feel drained. I'm not sure about the animals. I think I saw some cows run off and maybe a horse. Can you…?"

"Let me take care of all of that. I'll get the vet out here and a crew to round them up. You go into town and we'll talk about everything when you're a little stronger."

CHAPTER NINE

......my folks were gone. I had to go on with my life as I knew they would want me to. As a direct bearing on the future an Electra airplane became available. It was the duplicate of the one flown by Miss Earhart. We bought it......

After the funeral Rosie went to the offices of her father's attorney. He had approached her in the funeral home and told her to stop in at her leisure, and when she felt up to it, to tie up all the legal odds and ends.

He, too, was an old family friend and had known her since she was born. He hugged her as she and Chris entered his office and seated them at his desk.

"Rosie, as you know, I was friends with your mom and dad since high school days. Your dad trusted me with all his legal affairs and kept me up to date with his financial status. They updated their will several years ago and in the event of their demise you are the only heir and inherit the entire estate. Their assets include the farm and all equipment, a savings account, a few stocks and life insurance policies on both."

Rosie said "Well I guess the farm and equipment are not worth very much now."

"Yes it was pretty well wiped out by the tornado but that's what insurance is for. Your father was not only a good farmer but a wise business man. He had more than adequate insurance on the property and all equipment. I've contacted the local agent, also an old class mate, and he is making a request to the insurer to pay you the full amount of the market value and they will acquire the property. You don't have to make up your mind until you hear their offer. I'm assuming that you'll take a reasonable offer rather than try to work the farm yourself. Am I right?"

"Yes, of course but how will I know if it's reasonable?"

"I'll be happy to advise you, if you choose, but you could also get other legal help."

"Oh no, I trust you and I'd be very happy if you'd help me."

"Thank you Rosie. Also with the savings account, stocks and life insurance alone you'll be financially independent and can live quite comfortably. I'll have the final figures in a few days."

"Wow. I didn't even think about all this. I also was surprised when the funeral director told me that dad had prepaid all the funeral expenses. They were so thoughtful and loved me so much that they didn't want me to worry about anything. I'll miss them so much."

"They were the best." said the lawyer. "And now why don't you two relax for a few days. I'll have all the required paperwork completed and you can go back to California and get on with your life."

The next few days were spent tying up some loose ends, the settlement was made and the funds were transferred to their bank in California. They made contact with a financial planner, recommended by the attorney, and would make some decisions on what best to do with the inheritance.

After they got home they decided to discuss their future plans. Now that they had the funds it might be time to think about buying a house and raise a family.

"I think I'd like to do that eventually Chris" Rosie said "but let's go about it slowly. I don't want to make a mistake."

"Of course honey. I know that the loss of your mom and dad has caused some deep wounds and you need some time to heal."

So Chris went back to his job at Lockheed where he was in the midst of engineering state of the art fighter planes. He was deeply involved in the work that he loved and time passed quickly.

Rosie got back into instructing at a local flying school and was in great demand because of her tremendous experience and the ability to get her point across to very eager students, some of which had the same boundless desire that Rosie had as a teenager.

She immersed herself in her students and after a while, the hurt of loosing her mom and dad lessened but would still always be a part of her.

It happened that one day shortly after her last daily lesson, and she was planning the schedule for the next day while at her desk, her boss came in and said "A visitor is flying in this evening. He's an old friend of mine and he wants to park his plane here while he's got it up for sale. You might want to meet him. He's an old timer and has a raft of stories about the old air races. You two might have some mutual friends."

"Oh yes. It would be nice to reminisce about the days of the powder puff races. I still follow them. What kind of aircraft does he fly?"

"As I remember it's a Lockheed L-10E. Your husband is probably familiar with it."

"Well yes he is but so am I. It was a version of that model that Amelia Earhart flew when she was lost in the Pacific."

"Oh, I'm sorry I forgot that you and Chris had a history with her. It completely slipped my mind."

"That's okay boss. You didn't mean anything. Did you say it was for sale?"

"Yes it is but I'm not sure of the condition if you had any thoughts that way."

"Probably not, but you never know. At least I may take a look at it just for old time's sake."

That night at dinner she told Chris about the plane.

"I hope it doesn't stir up any old memories sweetheart. But go ahead and take a look. I've never seen a stronger more well adjusted person than you. It should be fun for you and I'm sure the old gentleman has some interesting tales to tell you."

Rosie went to bed that night looking forward to the next day.

****

When Rosie arrived at the airfield the next morning, a little earlier than she usually did, the L-10E was parked adjacent to the hanger. She slowly sauntered over and gazed up at the cockpit. She ducked under the wing and side stepped along the fuselage to the tail section, eyeballing it all the way.

She was deeply engrossed and was startled when a deep gravely voice said "Ain't she a beaut?"

"Oh my" Rosie said as she jumped "I guess I wasn't paying attention."

She laughed nervously and said "Yes she is a beauty and it brings back some memories."

"I know" he said "your boss told me that you knew Earhart."

"Well I can't say that I really knew her. I only met her once but I guess she was kind of my role model. My husband did meet her through Lockheed. He also met her at Purdue and worked with her at Lockheed when they modified her L-10E."

"Well this one doesn't have all the modifications that Lockheed did for her, but it is the exact same basic model. In fact as I understand it the serial numbers are only a few away from each other."

"Would it be too much trouble for me to look inside?" asked Rosie.

"Not at all. Are you interested in buying a plane? I've reached the point in life and with health issues that I'm forced to sell her....as much as I hate to admit it."

"I'm not sure what I'd do with my own plane. And I'm also not sure what my husband would say. It's more nostalgia than anything else."

"That's okay little lady. You go ahead and make yourself at home. I've got to meet that boss of yours for breakfast and he's buying so I don't want to miss it. See you later." he said as he walked away.

Rosie hoisted herself upon the wing and opened the hatch. She squeezed herself into the cockpit and settled into the pilot's seat. She sat there eyeing the instrumentation and she slowly reached up and gripped the control wheel.

As she gazed out onto the airstrip she relaxed her tightened shoulder muscles that had been knotted up like a couple of major league baseballs. A wonderful feeling of tranquility seemed to settle throughout her whole body and she shot both arms into the air and bellowed "YES".

She exited through the hatch, jumped to the ground and ran into the office. She sat at her desk and called Lockheed.

"Chris, this is Rosie."

"Yes honey" he laughed and said "I know your voice. You sound excited. What is it?'

"Darling I'd like to talk to you tonight about an airplane."

That night when Chris got home he said "You never cease to amaze me Rosie. What's this about an airplane?"

"Well first of all, I know we are planning to buy a house soon and we've looked at a few that would be just right for us so after I tell you what I would like to do, if you say 'No' I won't be mad and I'll do what ever you think is best."

"Wow! Now I'm really curious."

She took his hands and looked him in the eye and said "There's an L-10E Electra at the field that's for sale. It's the duplicate of Amelia's except for the circumnavigation modifications. I'd like you to take a look at it and see if we should buy it."

"Well sure I'll look at it. Price shouldn't be a factor. I know we have the money from the inheritance but honey what would you do with so much airplane? It's not something you just tool around in."

"That's the next question for you. Could you make the modifications that were on Amelia's plane?"

"What? What in the world would you do with an airplane that is built to fly around the world?.........Oh Rosie...... don't tell me"

"Chris. I want to complete Amelia's flight, *the unfinished flight*. I want to start at that same field in New Guinea and end up in Oakland going the same route that she had planned."

Chris sat there with his mouth half open and his eyes bugged out "I....I....just don't know what to say. Is it okay if I have a shot of scotch?"

The following Saturday found Rosie and Chris at the air field pouring over the Lockheed L-10E Electra. Chris took the entire morning examining everything that he could twist, turn or open. He kicked on the engines and listened with a trained ear.

"Well Rosie, I must say that our friend has taken good care of this old baby. It's showing a little age but that's only the natural progression of things. Let's go in the office and talk to him. I have just a few questions and I saw him go into the office with your boss."

"Do you think he'd let us take it up for a trial run?" Rosie said.

"I'm sure he would but he'd probably want to ride along or get some assurance that we won't run off with it. If I get the right answers to my questions, we'll ask."

They entered the office and approached the two gentlemen sitting at the boss' desk.

The older gentleman said "Well whatta you think of old Bessie?"

"She looks like a venerable old gal but I have a few questions." Chris said.

"I would expect as much" he answered "Why don't we grab a bite of lunch and talk this over. I'll be happy to answer anything that I can but I may have to refer you to my mechanic for some of the more technical answers."

They adjourned to the diner, had a light lunch and Chris had satisfactory answers to his questions. He got the phone number of the mechanic in case he needed more information.

"I can tell you that we are very interested in the plane" Chris said "I guess the next step is to fly her. Do you think we could take a test flight tomorrow?"

"Absolutely. Why don't you and your wife come by in the morning and take her up for a spin. No need for me to go along. I've been assured that you both are exceptional pilots and extremely trustworthy. I'll have her gassed up and ready to go. Come at your leisure. I won't be here until later in the day. I've prepared a spec sheet which includes my asking price for you to take home and study."

"Thank you sir and we'll be here first thing in the morning."

On the ride home Rosie excitedly asked "What do you think honey? Can we buy it? The price isn't so bad."

"Just hold on Rosie. You're right about the price but don't forget, if you want to do this hair brained trip from New Guinea, there are quite a few modifications like fuel capacity and much more to consider in the cost. Also timing is a factor. Some modifications must be done by experts and we don't know how long that will take. We don't want to do it in suspect weather conditions so we might have to wait. And the biggest 'if' is my job. I've gotten to be well thought of by management and I don't want to toss that into the dumper."

"Oh you're right Chris. You've always been the level headed one in this arrangement. Maybe it is a little too hair brained. Maybe we should just scrub the whole idea." Rosie said with a long face and the glint of a tear in her eye.

"Now, now dear, we'll take the flight tomorrow. I'll talk to my boss. Then you and I will talk about it"

"You sweetheart. No wonder I love you so much. You're so good to me Chris."

The next day's test flight went very well. Both felt right at home with the controls and when they landed they left word with the owner that they would be in touch before the week was out.

CHAPTER TEN

*.....now I could fulfill my dream of finishing Amelia's flight.
Chris engineered the rebuilding of the Electra and we started
our flight from New Guinea but alas as with Amelia we ran
out of fuel. We were lucky to ditch at an atoll....*

IN THE YEAR OF 1940

Chris was true to his word and talked to his boss about the possibility of
the purchase and the reason for it. His boss also had been involved in the
L-10E that Earhart had flown so he was very cooperative in releasing the
specs. He agreed to talk to upper management about a one year leave of
absence for Chris, but he mentioned they would be skeptical in the timing
since the war in Europe was ramping up and they were very busy with a
large order for the new double fuselage fighter plane P-38.

"Thanks boss. But this is not cut and dried yet. We're still in the
planning stage." Chris said.

Later that week, Chris and Rosie sat down to go over everything they
had compiled to date.

"Things have pretty well come together at this point." Chris said.
"Lockheed has reluctantly agreed to a leave of absence. They have also
given me a price on the modifications that I can't do myself and delivery
time is not great but it's doable. I've come up with a ballpark figure which
includes the plane and all modifications, the loss of one years salary for

both of us, the cost of the trip itself, which by the way we haven't tied down yet, and Rosie we're talking close to a couple hundred thousand dollars. That's almost your whole inheritance. Honey, this must be your decision."

"I've thought about it Chris and I want to do this more than anything. When it's done we can start from scratch and raise our family."

"Okay. But before we make him an offer, have you given thought as to how we're going to make this trip?"

Rosie laughed out loud and said "Sweetie, I've had a plan of how I'd make this trip in my mind for years. I've already done the preliminaries for shipping the plane to New Guinea, plotting the course from Lae to Howland to Honolulu to Oakland. I've got all the paperwork completed to submit for getting all necessary clearances and permissions so when we get the plane ready, I've got the rest lined up. I've even set up an itinerary. All we have to do is fill in the dates"

"As I said before Rosie, you never cease to amaze me."

And so the die was cast. The happy couple spent the next few months bringing to fruition all their carefully laid out plans. It involved some hard work and some frustration when things didn't go quite right or delivery promises that were not met. But it soon became time to load the completed L-10E on a freighter for shipment to New Guinea.

They were able to book passage on the same ship which was a freighter rather than a passenger type ship. The accommodations were very comfortable and since it was a freighter there were very few passengers. The service, as well as the food, was great. It was kind of like a second honeymoon for the happy couple. They took advantage of the leisure time, slept late each day, enjoyed the balmy weather and relaxed for the first time in several months.

Rosie said "This is just like that new song 'I'd Love To Get You On A Slow Boat to China' and I love it."

They eventually got to New Guinea and made arrangements to have the plane transported to the airfield where it would be restored to flying condition. Every step of the way had Chris' supervision and sometimes he had to get a little harsh with the way he wanted it done.

When it reached a point where he was satisfied enough to make a test flight he called Rosie over and let her double check everything.

"Since you're going to be the pilot on this venture, I think it's only right that you take over as of now. Tomorrow we'll take her up and you'll be in command. I'll be the copilot as well as the navigator. We'll put her through her paces, make any adjustments, take one more test flight and plan our get away day. I'd like to make a tentative flight plan to give to the Coast Guard right away so they can make any suggested changes or alterations before we submit the final flight plan." Chris said in a very business like tone.

Rosie was cognizant of the seriousness of his tone and she nodded her head while looking him in the eye. "Yes" she said.

Chris drew a deep breath. He looked directly at Rosie, took her hands in his and said "This is it Rosie. We still have time to back out. The really hard part is yet to come. We can sell the plane, go home and resume our lives. The best woman pilot in the world was not able to complete this flight. I'm with you all the way in any decision that you make."

"We are about to embark on the greatest adventure of our lives and I'm doing it with the one person I love with all my heart and with whom I have the greatest confidence to help me complete this journey." Rosie answered.

One week later this young adventurous couple left Lae, New Guinea, the same air field, in the same type heavily loaded airplane, en route to Howland Island just as Amelia Earhart and Fred Noonan did on July 2, 1937.

The take off was not an easy one with the overloaded plane. But they made it.....with very little runway to spare. After clearing the coast of New Guinea they headed east northeast for the first stop at Howland Island. They were over open water on a clear, calm day and had a spectacular view of the Solomon Islands when passing over. A few hours into the flight took them over a long stretch of open water. This would be the case until they reached the first destination.

This first landfall would be their most difficult. Howland Island is only about 1¼ miles long, 3/10 of a mile wide and worst of all only about 10 feet high. They were traveling 2,256 miles to try to locate this flat sliver of land. It will take superior navigation on Chris' part with not much room for error since fuel or lack of fuel will be a factor. But they had good radio equipment....better than Earhart's....and they were in communication with shipping along the route.

However the weather was good and weather reports showed nothing to be concerned with. They left before first light in the morning so with a flight time of 14 to 16 hours they should enjoy day light, most of if not, all the way. Daylight on the equator is about 12 hours but they were traveling east which will shorten their day. All was going well for the first 8 hours or so.

"Well hon, this is a piece of cake, so far." Rosie said.

"Let's hope it keeps up" Chris said "I'm going to catch a quick nap so I'm nice and fresh when we get close to Howland. I'll need to be alert to find that little spec of land. You okay with that?"

"Sure thing. This baby is practically flying itself." Rosie said.

Chris nodded off and Rosie relaxed until she felt some slight turbulence. It quickly got her attention since the skies had been clear and she passed it off as clear air turbulence.

But a little later it got choppy and off to the north she could see storm clouds building. She didn't want to alter her course to the south since finding Howland would be difficult enough as it was.

Maybe they could beat the storm as long as it wasn't moving southeast to intersect them.

She decided to stay the course.

After ten or fifteen minutes she could see that they were going to head right into the eye of the storm. That's when she woke up Chris.

"Looks like our luck has run out on the weather, Chris."

"Holy mackerel" he said anxiously "where did that come from?"

"I don't know. It just seemed to come from nowhere and its growing. Those black clouds look fierce."

No sooner did she say that and the bottom seemed to drop out and they hit heavy turbulence that rattled their teeth. The sudden downdraft was almost more than they could handle. Rosie was fighting the controls. The plane side slipped and Rosie brought it out but now the side forces caused it to fall into a spin whirling downward in a sickening spiral.

"Help me with the controls Chris."

Chris grabbed hold and they worked together to pullout and regain some semblance of control. She leveled off at a lower altitude and they bumped along for 30 minutes or so, maintaining a good course. She heaved a sigh of relief and smiled over at her spouse, relaxing a little.

"Never again will I use the old phrase 'piece of cake' Rosie said.

Suddenly after a few minutes of minor bumps the storm grabbed them, tossed them up and then the most violent turbulence yet tossed them around like their Electra was a paper toy. Rosie fought from going into a stall and Chris applied all the power he had cut back to regain some control.

The increase in speed caused a vibration that shook so badly Rosie could hardly hang on to the wheel.

"Power back, Chris, we're going to shake the rivets loose. The wings are almost flapping."

With decreased power again they took the storm a little better but surged violently up and down.

"Honey I would have taken us south if I would have had any idea of this storm." Chris said.

"Not your fault. It seemed to form out of nowhere. Nothing we can do now except fight our way through it. We'll be okay if it doesn't get any worse......Whoa...Whoa....Whoa....It's a bad one" yelled Rosie as they hit another air pocket that felt like they hit a brick wall. She struggled to right the plane's attitude. She fought off the increasing vertigo brought on by the twisting and turning of the gyrating Electra.

"I'll help you all I can Rosie" yelled Chris above the shrieking wind noise.

They leveled off and the clouds seemed to close in on them. It was pitch dark and visibility was non existent. They strained to even see past the nose cone. It was a monsoon.

"I'm going to climb higher and see if we can get out of this mess and it may be a little smoother air. Give me a little more power I need both hands on the wheel in this turbulence." she said.

The Electra nosed up and bounced along but slowly climbed out of the turmoil. Suddenly they seemed to hang there and almost stop in midair.

"We're going into a stall...POWER...MORE POWER." She yelled as she righted the plane and nosed down to break the stall. Chris increased power to give her the ability to get response from the plane and soon they were back on an even keel.

Her voice quavered "Wow that was close. I think we're getting out of the worst of it now. Better ease off we've used way too much fuel getting through this mess. We still have about 300 miles to go at last check."

"Speaking of fuel, I swear that I'm getting a suspicious odor like gasoline. I hope we didn't spring a leak in all that turbulence. We put some pretty good stress and strain on this baby." Chris said.

"What's the gauge say?" she asked.

"Oh boy. Not good. It seems to be quite a bit lower. Let me switch tanks. Oh no, that one shows empty." He answered.

"Of all the damn luck. We were going to be close anyway. Well at least the storm is diminishing. I see some breaks in the clouds up ahead and not near as much lightning. I'm going to go down lower and see if we can get a visual of an island or something. We should be pretty close to the Phoenix Islands."

"I don't know Rosie. That wind pushed us all over the place. I'm not sure of our position and Howland's going to be tough to find at best. Seems like we should be west of the Phoenix Islands.... maybe closer to Tuvalu. I don't think we have enough fuel to make it much further." He said.

"Okay, I think you're right. We better look for a place to set her down. See if you can raise anyone on the radio and let them know our situation. Maybe some ship is close enough if we have to ditch."

Chris grabbed the radio microphone and started transmitting a mayday. He gave the coordinates as close as he knew them. Suddenly they broke through the cloud layer. It was still raining but at least they had some visibility and both scanned the horizon for a spot to put down.

The starboard engine suddenly coughed, sputtered and shut down. Rosie hit the starter and it started back up for a short minute and then it quit for good. The port engine kept running but they knew it would also give up the ghost.

Finally it did and the Electra went into a glide. The relative quiet was eerie and the two passengers sat silent, both staring off into the now clearing skies looking hopefully for something other than a vast expanse of ocean.

They entered a cloud bank.....so thick it seemed like cotton rushing by the windows. When they broke out, the sunshine was brilliant. Chris shaded his eyes and looked off to his right.

"Rosie look to starboard, I see something."

Rosie banked the quickly descending plane and headed to a small atoll. She lengthened her glide as much as possible and kept it in the air just long enough to reach the small island.

A coral reef surrounded the island and formed a lagoon with a spot wide enough to give them a shot at belly flopping in. Rosie aimed for the likely spot, glided just clear of the reef, used the flaps to slow her down without dropping like a rock. When she reached the wide spot she gave it full flaps and pulled back on the wheel all the way. The plane hit the water tail first and then the nose dropped with a jolt. They submerged about half way, plowing through the surf and then stopped. They popped back up for an instant and then started to settle. The empty tanks would keep them afloat for a short time. The upper part of the plane was above the water line but it would soon slip under and come to rest on the bottom of the shallow lagoon.

"Rosie, you did it! You saved us. Hey are you okay? You forehead is bleeding. Let me take a look."

"I'm okay. Just a little bump on the head."

"Can you swim to shore? This baby's going under shortly."

"Yes. Grab what ever you can especially the waterproof pouch of survival gear. I'll try to grab what ever food I can. I think we have time to inflate the rubber life raft and be able to salvage more than by swimming."

They quickly worked to salvaged everything possible and pushed off just before the Electra disappeared from view.

This was a very small island but it was a God send to them because nothing else was in sight. They rowed into a wide sand beach and pulled the dinghy up to the tree line. One of the things they did in preparation for this trip was to take instruction for survival in a situation just like this.

They used the dinghy to make a lean to when they found a suitable spot to set up camp since it was now approaching sun set. They needed their rest so that the next day they could explore a bit and see what their situation was. It was very unlikely that an atoll this small was inhabited but they needed to know.

They settled in the lean to, both exhausted and both soon dropped off to sleep.

Several hours later, Rosie shook Chris and said "I hear something."

"What? What do you hear?"

"Sounds like something crawling and kind of clicking."

"I'll take a quick look but it's probably some kind of nocturnal animal. There's bound to be something on this rock."

Chris could find nothing unusual, just a couple of ugly crabs down by the water. He told Rosie about the crabs and they both drifted off in a restless sleep.

CHAPTER ELEVEN

......life on the atoll was difficult but we could survive. We were so happy to see a ship and be rescued. Little did we know what awaited us......

Chris and Rosie had been on the island now for three days and found that there was not much more than what they had seen when they crashed. It's very flat so they can't find a high spot to have a signal fire if they spot a ship. They collected palms and sticks and piled them on the beach a different points. Part of the survival gear had a fire starting kit so they were ready if it was needed.

So far food was no problem. They had some rations but also Chris caught a couple of those ugly crabs that come out at night and they tasted pretty good when roasted over the fire but they would be even better if they could be boiled or steamed. The problem was a lack of fresh water.

"I think these are called coconut crabs" Chris said "they really have strong pincers. I saw one breaking open a coconut this morning. I'd sure hate to have one latch on to my finger."

"They give me the creeps" Rosie said "I never saw such ugly crabs. It's a good thing they're not any bigger."

"Well I didn't catch the biggest ones. They scooted off pretty fast and I didn't want to mess with those strong claws. And believe it or not I saw one big one climbing a tree. He got up to the coconuts and knocked one to the ground. That's the one I saw breaking the shell to dig out the coconut meat."

A few more days passed by and things were getting pretty boring. No ships were spotted and they were keeping a constant watch. They decided to take turns watching at night since spotting a light might be even easier.

Rosie was taking her turn on watch. It was a calm balmy night and she was having a problem staying awake under this peaceful starlit sky. The only sound was the surf on the other side of the reef when she noticed a stirring on the beach. The only light was from the stars since the moon had not yet arisen so she stood and walked towards the slowly moving object.

She screamed "IT'S A HUGE CRAB! OH MY GOD IT'S HUGE" and she ran to the lean to screaming all the way.

Chris leaped to his feet, heart beating so hard it threatened to jump out of his chest. "ROSIE! ROSIE WHAT'S WRONG?"

She leaped into his arms. She was shaking like a leaf. "Oh Chris it's awful. A huge crab and I walked right up to it. It raised a huge claw and snapped it over and over. It looked at me with those ugly eyes and I thought it was going to attack me right there."

"Now, now just relax. It probably was more scared than you were and just going to defend itself. Let's go find it and we'll have him for breakfast."

"Chris, I'm not kidding, this one was huge. He'd probably be a week's breakfast."

They walked out on to the beach and tried to find Rosie's monster crab but to no avail.

As they turned to go back to the lean to they heard a clicking sound and suddenly there he was. The monster was at least three feet wide from claw to claw. His body length looked to be 15 or 16 inches long. They both stopped to gaze in wonder and the crab gazed back.

Chris said "Holy mackerel."

"What should we do?" asked Rosie.

"I don't think I have anything big enough to battle this ugly freak, but you can bet I'm coming up with something for the next time we meet."

As they stood and watched the crab slowly turned and slithered away back to his underground den among the rocks. Chris took note of where he disappeared.

The wide awake couple returned to their humble abode. They sat and talked of rescue for the rest of the night.

The next morning Chris gave some thought as to some kind of weapon. He noticed that the top of the crab shell was quite hard but the bottom under belly was very soft. This is the part were the good meat came from. He found several straight long sticks and fashioned a point on them with a part of a small crab shell that they had previously eaten. He then made a stronger, thicker pole that the crab could grab with his pincer but not snap in two. If he could entice the huge crab to grab the thick pole and use the leverage to flip him over he could spear him with the sharp sticks in the under belly.

Tonight he'd find out.

"Do you think it will work Chris?"

Chris didn't have the opportunity to find out since the monster decided not to emerge from his lair that night and Chris decided not to bother after a few nights of no sightings.

A welcome cold front came through one day and with it came the rain. It rained for two days and they filled every thing that could hold water. They hydrated themselves thoroughly.

As Chris was walking by the rocky area where the monster disappeared he noticed that the huge crab was half emerged from his hole, probably to get some of the needed moisture in the humid air. He ran back to get his weapons and felt his chances were better in the daylight than at night.

He approached his prey and teased it with the thick rod. The crab leaped fully out of the protection of his burrow and snapped at the branch but missed. Chris teased him some more until the quarry was on a flat hard surface. Perfect for what Chris wanted to do. He offered the leverage rod at the right angle and the crab grabbed on.

"Holy mackerel this thing is really strong" yelled Chris as he pried up but the claw just twisted. The body did not raise up to expose the underside. Chris worked his way around so the lever was now across the body and the crab snapped at the lever with the other claw a forth of the way up from the end from where the first claw was. PERFECT. Chris now had a solid grip and he used all his strength to slowly turn the crab up on its side and then suddenly over on its back.

He grabbed his spears and buried the first one in the belly until it bottomed out against the inside of the hard shell. The crab still writhed. Chris did the same with the second spear and then the third and finally the fourth one. The crab gave a final shudder and then lay quietly.

Chris stood staring and panting, completely spent. Suddenly he heard a very feminine voice call "Oh my great white hunter you are so brave. Bring your kill to my cave and I will prepare a feast for you."

He turned and his giggling young wife ran into his arms.

"Go ahead and laugh but you were the one that came running and screaming the other night. And besides this was not an easy kill."

"I know honey, I'm only kidding. But it was kind of funny even if it is a big ugly monster of a crab."

They walked back to the lean to arm in arm to get some tools to cut up their dinner. Tonight they'll boil the crab meat."

They both stopped short. Steaming into the lagoon was a small ship. It looked like a Japanese flag was flying from the mast. After it cleared the inlet which led to the lagoon they could hear the sound of an anchor chain banging through the hawse pipe and the splash of an anchor.

"How did we miss seeing that ship, Chris?" Rosie was aghast.

"I don't know" he answered "it must have approached from the other side of the island. But it's here and we're saved."

"YAHOO...YIPEEE" they both yelled.

They hugged each other and jumped up and down, laughing and cheering all the while. They ran down to the waters edge waving their arms and screaming at the tops of their voices

WE'RE HERE....WE'RE HERE! COME GET US!

There suddenly was a lot of activity on the ship. The anchor detail made fast the anchor chain and the port side of the bridge was crowded with men, all with binoculars trained on them.

"I think they are very surprised to see two human beings on this desolate piece of real estate." Chris said.

"I don't doubt that a bit" Rosie said "After all we went down without much warning and that May Day of yours was not exactly a long, lasting notification."

It appeared that a motor whale boat was being lowered over the side with several crew members aboard and when it hit the water they immediately kicked on the engine and headed towards them.

"Oh honey we really are going to be saved" Rosie said filled with excitement.

"I hope so" Chris said "That looks like a military vessel and don't forget Japan is at war with China. I don't think it should affect our standing. At least the last I heard the U.S. and Japan hadn't started shooting at each other......yet. Let's not mention that I'm an engineer with Lockheed. We're just a couple of unlucky tourists whose plane crashed."

"I'm sure it'll be okay. Its international law that they must give aid to shipwrecked people. And we certainly qualify as such." Rosie said.

The Japanese sailors beached the whale boat and two armed, uniformed men jumped out and quickly approached them while the rest secured the boat.

Chris walked towards them and said "Hello! We're Americans and we're stranded here. Can you take us to your ship?"

The sailors both stopped and trained their rifles at Chris and one spoke a loud command in Japanese.

Chris raised his hands and said "We come in peace. Do you speak English?"

More Japanese commands and gestures to move back.

"Okay! Okay!" Chris said.

The obvious officer in charge then slowly approached and spoke to the sailors who answered.

The young officer turned towards Chris and Rosie and said "My men tell me that you are English. Is that so?"

"Oh thank the Good Lord you speak English. No sir, we are Americans."

"Ahhh Americans. So how do you happen to be on this island?"

"Our plane crashed in the lagoon during a storm several weeks ago. We were en route back to the states. Can you take us somewhere that we can arrange passage back home?"

"That will be up to the Captain, of course. We are doing research on these islands and will be anchored here until we have explored and charted this island and others."

"I understand. Can you take us to your Captain so we can see if arrangements can be made? Or if not would it be possible to contact the U.S. authorities to send a rescue party for us?"

"We will take you to the Captain. Please board the whale boat."

Rosie said "You speak exceptionally good English. May I ask where you learned it so well?"

"Of course you may. I am a graduate of Stanford University in your country. My degree is in engineering. Where did you matriculate?"

"Oh I didn't go to college but my husband is a graduate of Purdue."

"Ah yes, the Big Ten. I believe you beat us in a football game." He said to Chris.

They boarded the small craft and motored out to the anchored ship where they disembarked at a gangway that had been rigged on the port side.

They climbed to the quarterdeck where they were treated very politely, after the young officer spoke to the officer of the deck.

"Please follow me to the ward room where the Captain will meet with you. I must first brief him on your status." said the young officer.

The couple followed the officer down the passageway and Chris noticed that the ship was spotless. Not one sign of rust. This was a regular Navy vessel and not an every day merchantman. The sailors were all in uniform and clean shaven. They soon reached the officers ward room and were ushered inside where they were seated at a dining table.

"I imagine that you would like some refreshment after being on that island for awhile. Would you like some tea and cake until we can offer something more stable?"

"That's very kind of you and yes I'm dying for a cup of hot tea." Rosie said.

The officer called a steward and ordered in Japanese. The steward bowed and scurried off to the galley.

"Please enjoy your tea and cake. I must give my report to the Captain. I will return soon." he said.

After a short wait the steward retuned with a tray of tea and an assortment of cakes.

"This is a first class vessel" Chris said "it's not a man'o'war but I'm guessing some kind of research ship. Not much armament and some of the older men looked like educated civilians. The crew looks well trained."

Rosie was enjoying her refreshment and said "It sure doesn't appear that they're roughing it."

Soon the young officer appeared and with him was a very distinguished looking high ranking Japanese officer in full regalia. He pulled himself to his full height and said "Mr. and Mrs. Conner, I have the pleasure to introduce you to our commander, Captain Yamaguchi."

The captain made a slight bow and spoke in Japanese. The officer said "Our captain speaks only a little English and has asked me to translate so there are no misunderstandings."

"Of course. We understand. Tell the captain that we are honored to meet him and thank him for rescuing us from the island." Chris said.

The officer did so and the captain answered in Japanese.

"Our captain welcomes you and will instruct the crew to see to your comfort."

"Thank you again. We would be most pleased if he could somehow contact or take us to somewhere where we could contact the authorities to return us to our country." Chris said.

Again the officer did so and the captain answered somewhat abruptly.

"The captain asked that you have patience. We have duties to perform here and radio silence must be observed. He reminds you that we are at war with China and certain restraints must be observed."

"I understand" Chris said "it's just that we are anxious to be home."

The officer did not have time to translate before the captain spewed out a long Japanese order, turned on his heel and left the room.

They stood silently for a moment and then the officer said "We have vacated a cabin for you and your wife. I will take you there and the captain wishes that you rest and remain in the cabin until he has made a decision on what action we will take."

With that he turned and abruptly said "Please follow me."

Later in the small cabin with an upper and lower bunk, a sink with a hand held shower nozzle and a compact toilet, the couple refreshed themselves. As small and somewhat crude as it was it was a lot better than what they left.

"It may be awhile before we get to civilization honey but it's a start." Chris said.

"I know, but I'm just a bit uneasy. Something's not quite right. I hope we hear something soon" said Rosie.

"Yes, it seems the initial friendliness has worn off" said Chris.

CHAPTER TWELVE

......the Japanese ship took us to Tongolo, a beautiful island but under Japanese control. The brutality began. We thought we were rescued but in reality we were captured and imprisoned....

EARLY IN THE YEAR OF 1941

After a short but anxious wait, a knock came on their cabin door. Chris anxiously opened it but it was just the steward with a tray of food. They were happy to get it but they longed for some word.

It was the following morning when the English speaking officer knocked on the door and asked them to follow him to the ward room for breakfast, after which the captain wanted a word with them.

They ate breakfast at a table with several officers none of which spoke English and there seemed to be an air of tension in the room.

Soon the captain entered and all the officers rose and stood silently until the captain barked out an order whereupon the whole group filed out of the room.

The captain and his translator approached their table. Chris stood but Rosie remained seated.

"Captain Yamaguchi has asked me to pass on to you his decision and will remain here in case you have questions." said the officer.

"Please give him my thanks." Chris said.

"Ah so. We will research this island for just one more day. It does not offer the potential that we are looking for at this time. We will get underway at first light tomorrow en route to an island that we previously researched and found to be very desirable for a supply depot and possible runway. It is a long days travel and is known as Tongolo on our charts. It has a natural harbor and currently we have a detachment of soldiers with a preliminary construction crew on the island. It is unique in that it is not a part of an archipelago. The base commander will make his decision on your next move. Neither I nor my ship will be involved in the decision after that. Do you have questions?"

"No. None that I can think of now. Will you be available if we do?"

"Of course, however we request that you stay in your room. Your food will be delivered to you. If you need me please ask the steward for Lt. Nakamoto."

They were again alone in their room and feeling very uneasy.

When they awoke the next morning the ship was already underway. Shortly after they were dressed, a steward delivered their breakfast.

"I guess he really meant it when he said to stay in our room. It's almost like we're in the brig. Hopefully things at Tongolo will be different." Rosie said.

"Maybe they are just being cautious since it's a government research vessel and after all they are at war even if it's not with us." Chris said.

"Gosh, I hope so. It's such an eerie feeling when you're under control of a foreign government, I really long for the good old U.S.A." Rosie said.

Since they couldn't leave the room and they had no porthole to see when they reached land, time passed slowly.

After they were served their evening meal they could sense a slow down and eventually they heard the anchor dropping and soon the ship was motionless.

They eagerly awaited the arrival of Lt. Nakamoto which never came. In fact all was quiet and they became even more nervous when it became very late and no one came to their cabin. They decided to try to get some rest.

They were sleeping soundly early the next morning when a loud rapping on the door awoke them.

"Just a moment." called Chris as he pulled on his trousers and made his way to open the door.

In the passageway were two armed sailors. One said, in very broken English "Please to get dressed to leave ship NOW."

"Okay, okay give us a moment" and he tried to close the door but was blocked from doing so by one of the guards.

"My wife would like some privacy." Chris said sharply.

"No privacy. Get dressed NOW!" he said.

The two of them hurriedly dressed and were led away by the guards. They climbed to the quarter deck where they were met by Lt. Nakamoto.

He said "The captain has received orders to transfer you to the base commander's office immediately." And he turned and walked away.

They were led down the gangway to the awaiting small craft and as soon as they were boarded, it pulled away and headed towards shore to a small makeshift dock.

When they arrived and the boat was secured to the dock they were instructed by sign language to disembark. The area looked to be a small Polynesian village but strangely enough there were only a few villagers in sight. The bulk of the men were soldiers and a few Japanese civilians.

They were led to the one building that looked newly constructed and not in the fashion of the other Polynesian type huts. They entered the building and when their eyes adjusted to the dim interior they found themselves in a small windowless entry room with a door leading to perhaps another room or office.

After a long uncomfortable wait, while standing, facing the door with an armed guard at their backs, the door opened. They were ushered into an office of the base commander, he was sitting at his desk, staring down at some documents. The officer that showed them in turned and said, "Colonel Soto will now speak to you."

The Colonel looked up after a long pause. The silence was deafening. Finally he abruptly said "Names please."

"I am Chris Conner and my wife is Rosemarie Conner and we are Amer....."

"QUIET! I only asked your names. Please listen to instructions." Again, there was a long pause.

"How long were you on the island before you were captured?"

"About three weeks. But I didn't think we were captured. We were rescued." Chris explained.

"When spies are found we consider them to be captured and will be treated as such" the commander said.

"Wait a minute. We're not spies. Our plane crashed due to a storm and we ran out of fuel." Chris further explained.

"In the report there was no evidence of an aircraft. We know that you were under orders from Roosevelt to spy on Japanese activity and you were placed there by U.S. Coast guard."

"NO! NO! That's not true." screamed Rosie.

"QUIET WOMAN. YOU ARE AS GUILTY AS THIS MAN WHO YOU CLAIM TO BE YOUR HUSBAND."

"Please sir, you must believe us. I AM her husband and we are just tourists trying to get back home. Will you help us?" asked Chris.

"You will both be interrogated separately and then a disposition will be made." he said.

He spoke in Japanese to the officer who opened the door and called instructions to the armed guard. The guard answered and entered the room where he roughly shoved Chris out the door. When Rosie started to follow, the officer said "NO, you wait."

Chris was led to a guarded enclosure where a group of Tahitian villagers were confined. He was ushered into a small hut and roughly shoved onto a hard wooden chair.

In the hut, was a uniformed Japanese officer and a muscular man with a bare torso and an evil sneer on his face. His hands looked strange, a darker shade of brown. Maybe calloused? He flexed his fingers continuously.

"Now American pig, we will ask you questions and if you cooperate you will not be harmed but if you don't it could be painful."

"I don't know what I can tell….."

WHACK! The enforcer hit him flush in the mouth and knocked him backwards out of the chair. Chris painfully raised himself to his knees and spit blood from severely damaged lips. It happened so fast he had no time to react.

They both pulled him back upright and slammed him into the chair.

"That is just a very small sample of the pain my assistant is capable of inflicting on you if you do not cooperate."

"What were you doing on the island?" he continued.

"As I told the Colonel, our airplane crashed in a storm." He spit out through bleeding lips.

WHACK! Another punch, but even harder, with the blow landing in his rib cage. Chris flew backwards, landed on his back and he lay gasping for breath, the wind knocked from his lungs.

They let him lay there until he could again draw painful breaths.

Chris groaned as they roughly dragged him back to the chair and propped him up in a sitting position.

"Please to cooperate, American pig" shouted the officer.

Chris raised his head and whispered "I'm telling the truth. I don't know........."

WHACK! A severe blow to the head meant for the face but Chris had turned his head.

He again flew off the chair and lay there unconscious.

"You idiot" said the officer "you hit him too hard. Now we must wait until he's conscious again...if ever. Drag him out to the compound. He may be more cooperative later."

Chris was dragged out and thrown in a heap on the bare ground. When the interrogators left, two of the Polynesians turned Chris on his back and one of them tried to give him a drink of putrid water.

After a few moments Chris stirred and when he opened the one eye, that was not swollen shut, he instinctively lashed out.

The Polynesian who helped him jumped back and said "Whoa, Whoa boss. We help."

Chris tried to sit up but got sick and gagged on his own blood. He moaned. "Why did they do this?"

"These very bad people boss. They beat and kill many of our villagers. They want us to work like slaves for them."

"What about my wife? What will they do to her?" Chris said.

"Very bad. They are monsters. They have defiled our women. Maybe your wife will be lucky. The new commander reprimanded the soldiers for making the women unfit for work. They were brutal and now it only happens outside of the camp. If they put her in the women's compound and she does good work they may not harm her."

"I've got to see her and make sure she's okay." muttered Chris through swollen lips.

"When we go out on a work party tomorrow you may see her but don't try to talk to her. They may kill you both."

That night they all slept on the ground and they were roughly awakened at sunrise. A pot of some kind of mush was carried in and scooped out in tin cups for breakfast. They were lined up and marched out to an area that was to be leveled. Chris and his group were told to remove some tree stumps. It was hard work and there were few tools. What tools they had were very crude and progress was very slow. It was a long day and on the march back they saw a group of women also marching back from a work detail. Rosie stood out from the darker Tahitian women and when she saw Chris and the condition of his face she let out a stifled scream. A guard roughly shoved her forward.

Earlier when Chris had been shown out of the Commanders office and Rosie was held back, the Commander barked an order to a sergeant who had entered the room. The sergeant answered and then turned and leered at Rosie, muttering some Japanese obscenity.

The Commander jumped to his feet and screamed an order to the sergeant who turned, bowed and muttered an answer to the Commander.

He then turned, took Rosie by the arm and ushered her to the women's compound.

The compound was much like the men's and the women were expected to work as hard as the men.

Rosie tried to communicate but could find no one who knew English and most of the women shunned her. The women were aroused at sunrise each day also. There was no communication with the men except during kitchen detail where both men and women sometimes crossed paths, and only then some quiet words were passed.

A young girl approached Rosie late one evening and said "My name is Kellea. I can speak some English but the others have told me not to talk to you. They don't trust you because you are different and they think you may be a spy for the Japanese."

"Oh no, tell them that I am an American and we don't like the Japanese either." Rosie said.

"I will try." She said and then scurried off.

Weeks went by. Luckily Chris was not interrogated again. Probably because they really knew their circumstances and determined they were more valuable on work details since labor was in short supply. Some of the villagers had escaped to the hills and the others did not put forth their best effort.

Chris' face was healing nicely but it was still painful to breathe. He probably had gotten some cracked ribs in the beating and the last few weeks were miserable. Even though the pain at times was almost unbearable he did his best to work and kept from getting beaten any more. The Polynesian that spoke some English helped bathe the wounds to try to keep infection down, and he helped Chris during the work day when he struggled with the pain in his rib cage. Without the help from this kind man named Maunea, Chris may not have survived this ordeal.

One night a group of the villagers were quietly but seriously engaged in a closed group conversation. When it broke up, Maunea sidled up to Chris and said. "Good news. Tomorrow night the hill people will attack the camp and give us the opportunity to escape. Not all of the men want to go since many may die in the attempt. Do you want to go?"

"Yes, but what about the women? Can we take my wife?" Chris said.

"It will be very dangerous but there is a plan to free some of the wives. As with the men some do not want to take the chance."

"Rosie will. I know she will. I'm in. Just tell me what to do."

CHAPTER THIRTEEN

…...Chris and the villagers devised a successful plan to escape. We have joined a group who previously escaped and are living in caves at the twin peaks. There is still some mistrust of us since we are different. I have befriended a young girl named Kellea. She speaks broken English and has explained that we are Americans. Some of the young Polynesians want to retaliate. I'm so frightened that it will provoke them to attack us. The latest rumor is that the Japanese have attacked Honolulu and wiped out the entire U.S. Fleet. They claim that they will conquer the Americans before the year is out….

The next day just crawled by. The guards seemed to be extra brutal at the work site. One of the villagers, who was old and sick, wasn't moving fast enough and the same ruthless sergeant that leered at Rosie decided to punish him. He hit the man with the butt of his rifle on the back of his head. It sounded like he hit a melon. The man fell in a heap with his head split open. The other guards dragged him off to the side and just left him lying there. Chris was sure the man was dead or at least dying. He retched with nausea. The sergeant swung around at the sound and Chris' new found friend stepped in front of him to shield him from the guard.

"Keep working. Don't even look up. They use any excuse to punish us" said the big Polynesian.

Chris dropped to his knees and started digging around a rock with vigor. His eyes were watering and his stomach was churning. He wanted out of this horrible situation. Tonight was his chance to find Rosie and leave. What ever happens couldn't be worse than these conditions. His mind was made up.

After a few hours two of the guards showed up in a truck. They loaded the old man's body into the back and drove off. There was no doubt that he was dead.

Finally the work day ended and the crew was marched back to the compound. They passed by the women who were also on the way back. Chris saw Rosie but made no sign of recognition or signal since this was a very dangerous thing to do. The guards welcomed an opportunity to punish anyone that tried any kind of communication.

After they were locked up in the compound they were given their slop for the evening meal. All eagerly ate it even though it was hardly edible, they needed nourishment. After the meal, the men who were planning the escape gathered in a group. The prisoner that worked in the galley told them that about six women wanted to go with them and the white woman was one of them. Chris smiled.

"There would be no moon tonight so it would be very dark. The hill people will attack after all is quiet in the camp. Each of the Japanese sentries will be subdued and beheaded with machetes except for the two guards at each compound. It will be up to us to kill all four of them. We have two machetes hidden" explained Maunea.

"As soon as the attack is on, we should act. Most of the action will be on the other side of the village so all the guards except for the two guarding our compound and the two at the women's compound will go where the action is to defend against the attack."

"As soon as we subdue our guards we must rush to the women. By that time the guards will be alert as to the attack so we must move fast and carefully."

"Anyone that stays behind must realize there may be repercussions so it will be wise to all gather in a group away from the action and beg their mercy when it's over. Even to the point of agreeing to help hunt for us by telling them that we are camped in the hills. Don't worry about us. We will protect ourselves."

"Some of us may be killed or wounded but at least we will die fighting for our freedom. Anyone that does not want to go should say so now" he continued.

They all mumbled their assent to escape.

Everyone went to the normal sleeping spot so as to cause no suspicion. The camp became quiet except for the usual moans and some quiet weeping from both women and men.

Soon all that could be heard was an occasional rustling in the brush by some night creatures hunting for a kill for their nightly meal. But tonight a few extra rustlings were evident. Not enough to cause the suspicion of the guards because of the slow stealth. Men, who had been born and raised in this jungle, were silently creeping up to their assigned prey.

On a prearranged signal that had the sound of a night creature, four figures rose up from hidden view and machete blades flashed in the star lit night. The only sound was a few muffled grunts and the sound of four headless bodies slipping quietly on to the ground. A blood curdling battle cry rung out and shiny painted bodies rushed out of the bush and charged into the camp swinging machetes and throwing spears. They created as much pandemonium as they could to draw the troops away from the prisoner compounds. This must be a hit and run tactic since the Japanese firepower out matched theirs by a great deal. Timing was so important.

As soon as the battle cry was heard the men prisoners reacted. The two designated to subdue the guards with the machetes were the first to move. The closest guard didn't even see the flashing blade coming. His head hit the ground before his body. It was a clean, hard blow to the back of the neck.

The second guard was off to the side and he turned toward the advancing Polynesian when he heard the sound of the battle cry and of running feet. He fired off a shot which hit the man but he kept running towards the soldier. Another shot and the man went down. As he stood over the prone figure, a flying body struck the soldier from behind and sent the rifle flying from his grip. A screaming young Polynesian scooped up the fallen machete and swung it mightily at the guard. The Japanese raised his arm to ward off the blow and lost his hand from the wrist down. As he lie screaming and looking in disbelief at the handless arm, the young native boy finished the job with his second swing. The tip of the blade hit the soldier in the throat. He knelt on the ground and drowned in his own blood.

While this gory scene was going on Chris and four others ran to the women's compound. The first machete wielder was among them. When they reached the compound they found only one guard and he was looking off to where all the noise and fighting was going on. He looked frightened and confused and didn't quite know what to do. He was very young and obviously an untrained rookie. He gave no resistance and was an easy kill. His fellow guard must have run off to join the battle and probably will be severely reprimanded for leaving his post to be guarded by the young trainee.

The women were ready. They ran out of the gate which was opened by the prisoners. They all ran for the protection of the thick jungle. Chris grabbed Rosie by the hand and practically dragged her behind him. They could hear much gun fire now from where the main attack occurred. But by then the attackers had withdrawn back into the bush.

They didn't stop running until they were so spent they had to rest for a moment. They took a quick count. There were six women and ten men. A few men were not accounted for but hopefully they'd show up later. They knew of at least one that died. Some of the main attack group may have also been killed by gun fire.

As soon as they were able they trudged on towards the twin peaks that identified their island home. They knew of caves where they could live and join up with others that had escaped the brutality of the invaders.

After a long, tiring climb they reached the first set of caves. There was a flat pasture where a small garden was planted. In front of the caves were women and a few children. One of them came running out calling the name of one of the men. He also ran to her. Chris found out later that they were brother and sister.

The raiding party had not gotten back yet. One of the women said that they would stay in the jungle for a few days so the Japanese would not follow them to the caves.

The women welcomed them and had some food ready for them to eat. They knew the conditions the prisoners had faced while imprisoned with the Japanese.

Some of them looked suspiciously at Chris and Rosie. They gathered in groups and gestured towards them while talking in their own language.

Kellea was explaining who they were and the suspicion remained with a few, but most of the others accepted them.

CHAPTER FOURTEEN

.....the Japanese patrols are getting closer and closer. So far we've been able to avoid them but some of the younger, aggressive boys are now taking the offensive, luring them with tricks and ambushing them. The boys have a collection of arms now consisting of rifles, pistols and grenades. They have agreed to give a supply of arms to the older men for our defense. The boys released a soldier that was only wounded in the last attack and told him that cannibalism was now being revived here in our compound and that any soldier captured could expect that fate. We hope revulsion will cut down on the patrols. Our men took a beating in this last raid. We drove off the soldiers but next time they are sure to bring more troops. Chris was wounded but thank God it was minor......

They settled in with the other villagers under some very rough, crude conditions but anything is better than what they had just left. At least they were together.

Rosie and Chris decided to pitch in right away and try to make conditions more livable. Both Kellea and the fellow prisoner that helped Chris escape talked to the suspicious villagers to assure them that the Americans were on their side and could offer valuable assistance in their survival.

The acceptance was slow but through their efforts, Rosie and Chris became members of the group.

"Rosie, Rosie" called Kellea "Wait for me. I have something for you."

"Oh Chris, It's Kellea. Yes, Kellea, we're waiting."

"What is it? What do you have?" Rosie said.

"Do you remember when I told you about the missionary priest that stayed on our island when I was a little girl? He was the one that taught me English. Well in the bag of belongings that I was able to save is a diary that he gave to my mother. It has never been written in and I am not good at writing. Do you think you would want it to record these events? Kellea said.

"Oh yes, Kellea. That would be wonderful. But what can I write with?"

"I also have two pencils because he was going to teach me writing but the old medicine man banned him from the island. A sailing ship took him away. I was too young to understand but I was very sad to see him go. He was so kind."

"Thank you Kellea. I'll start writing tonight."

The English speaking Tahitian, called Maunea, became the unspoken leader. The raiding party came back a small group at a time and reported that three of them were killed by gun fire and two were feared to be captured. Both had been wounded and it was not known if they survived. Ten of the original fifteen were back safely. The raiding party's leader was one of the fatalities.

Maunea said "Future raids, if any, needed better planning so there would not be as many casualties.

Chris agreed and said to Maunea "I have had some R.O.T.C. training at Purdue and I would like to assist in any defense of the camp. We need more fire power. Machetes are no match against rifles and grenades."

"You are right Chris. But how can we do this?"

"The Japanese send patrols of three to five men to round up stray villagers and search for escapees. They need laborers. Your men are experienced in hunting in the jungle. Our advantage is in the stealth acquired in this type of hunting. Let's plan to ambush these patrols and confiscate their weapons but we need to create a diversion to take them off guard. Even in a surprise attack they have much more fire power than our men with only machetes and spears…..Hmm. The ladies do their washing of clothes in the stream up here on the mountain. Could we convince four or five of the young ones to do some wash down stream where the patrols are more likely to come across them? I'm sure if those animals found some unguarded women in a stream washing clothes, having a good time laughing and talking, their attention would be diverted enough for our men to move in. The soldiers may even lay down their arms, if they think they could sexually abuse the girls. We can have ample men hiding in the surrounding bush to move quickly. It will be an opportune time for those young warriors to sharpen up their skills with a bow and arrow too. It will put the Japanese at high risk and we can get some weapons for future raids." Chris said.

"Yes. We can do this. We will gather the young warriors in our group and set up a plan. The young women here will cooperate, I'm sure. There are several of them that remember the sexual abuse in the village and will only be too happy to get some revenge." Maunea said.

They decided to try an ambush the very next night. Eight of the young aggressive men went with Maunea with what weapons they had. Some had nothing better than a machete or a spear but three had a bow and arrows and were quite adept in using them.

About eight hours passed when the party returned. They had not encountered any patrols.

"We should probably send our own scouts out in singles to see where the patrols roam and if there is a time of day or night that they go." Chris said.

All agreed. Volunteers came forward and a schedule was made up in eight hour shifts around the clock. They started that very night and success by several scouts allowed them to plan an ambush.

The same men, three women and Maunea left for battle early in the evening. They returned before midnight with three rifles, a pistol and several grenades.

"It went exactly as planned" Maunea said "We waited along the bank of the stream at the bottom of the other mountain where we knew they would stop to drink and refresh themselves. When they got there, the women were washing clothes. They laid down their rifles to harass the women and were completely vulnerable to our attack. The three foot soldiers had rifles and the leader had a side arm. The leader was the only one that could have resisted us so we got him first. I think he was supposed to be watching while the others harassed the women but he was too busy relieving himself and watching what he thought was going to be a rape. He didn't hear Paola sneak up from behind and slit his throat with his blade. The only sound was a gurgling escaping from his bloody lips. One of the soldiers looked up at that instant and was immediately dispatched with a machete blade. The other two yelled and stood to retrieve their rifles but it was too late. We were upon them before they could take more than a step or two. The bows and arrows were not even needed. We now have some fire power in case of attack to our camp."

"That was good execution, Maunea, but they probably won't fall for that one again. We'll have to get them in a different situation. Surprise is our biggest weapon." Chris said.

"We have already thought of that Chris, but we should wait a day or two. They will be extra careful as soon as they find these bodies and they know that we now have a few guns." He answered.

One of the young warriors came up to Maunea and said that he and his brother wanted to go on the next ambush. They wanted revenge for their family. They were the only ones left of a family of seven. Their mother, father and three sisters were brutalized and then killed.

"We have all lost family members to the Japanese" Maunea said "but you and your brother can go to gain some revenge. You must follow orders though. They are soldiers and do not go down easily if something goes wrong."

"We will follow orders for the kill. But after the kill we will practice what our ancestors did when they killed an enemy."

"We cannot revert back to cannibalism" Maunea screamed "our village decided long ago that this practice was banned."

"But grandfather said it gives you their strength if you eat the heart of your enemy."

"Do you want the heart of those beasts? The very ones that raped your mother and your sisters? Do you want to be like them?"

The two boys cowered and said "We just want revenge. We want them to hurt as bad as we do." The younger one was crying. Rosie tried to comfort him.

"I understand but that is not the way to do it." Maunea said.

All was quiet while the two boys settled themselves.

"I'm not familiar with past practices of your ancestors" Chris said "but maybe the Japanese are. Maybe we could set up a scam that would make them think we are cannibals. We could leave one alive and allow him to escape after we take one of the dead bodies away using sign language or some words, that he might understand, that we are going to eat the body or at least part of it. Then we could bury the body so they couldn't find it. It may fill them with enough revulsion so the desire to hunt us down would not be so great."

"I don't know Chris. Let me think on this. Tomorrow we go hunting again. But we only go for guns."

Everyone returned to their sleeping spots and relaxed. Rosie asked Chris to come for a walk. She wanted to tell him about the diary.

IN THE BASE COMMANDERS OFFICE

"What is it, Sergeant? What news is so important to disturb me at this time?" the Colonel said.

"Sir, those contemptible escaped prisoners have ambushed one of our patrols and killed four of our honorable soldiers."

The Colonel leaped to his feet and shrieked "How could this happen? How could our imperial troops be defeated by those rebellious dogs?"

"They were ambushed while refreshing themselves at the small stream at the mountain base. Those dogs hacked them to death."

"We must annihilate them. We cannot let such rabble overrun our troops. Where are they camped?"

"We know there are caves on the twin peaks sir but we are not sure exactly where they have set up camp."

"Find out! I want a detachment of your men led by you to ferret them out and show no mercy. If you can capture those two American dogs I want them brought back for some special treatment."

"Yes sir. I will gather a detachment of my best men. We should be able to subdue them without a struggle. But first I must try to locate them with a patrol so we can swoop in and take them by surprise. We should have them eliminated before the week is up."

BACK AT THE CAVES

"Kellea told me today that two women who worked in the galley were able to escape when they were sent to dispose of garbage. They told her that the Japs were celebrating because they bombed Pearl Harbor in Hawaii and destroyed the American Pacific Fleet. They said Americans are weak and they will invade California and defeat us in a year. How could this happen?" asked Rosie.

"I was sure we'd be at war with them sooner than later. And I'm also sure there is some exaggeration on the attack." Chris said.

"Do you think we'll ever get back home? Rosie said.

"I don't know honey. Let's just concentrate on staying alive.

The days dragged on. More ambushes were made and a small arsenal was accumulating. Chris had heard that a few aggressive young boys had staged their own raid and really hacked up the bodies so they would be found and appear to be cannibalized. They left the mutilated bodies headless and took the heads as trophies.

Maunea was furious and reprimanded the boys but they just laughed.

"No matter what those evil men have done, we cannot become as evil as they are. What have you done with the heads?" Maunea said.

The leader of the young warriors replied "We have them hidden in an empty cave. We were going to smoke them over a fire to preserve them like they did in the old days."

"No" said Maunea "bury them in the jungle. We cannot have human heads in our midst. I completely forbid it. It is only for survival that we are doing what we must do."

The young men shuffled nervously and agreed. They had great respect for their leader and promised Maunea that they would not become evil monsters. They would be proud Polynesian warriors and fight for survival of their people with honor.

Several days later, on a quiet evening a lookout came running into the camp bellowing "They're coming. They're coming. Lots of them."

The men ran for their rifles and hastened the women and children into the caves. The men had set up a battle line away from the caves to keep the fighting away from the women and children and keep the living quarters hidden.

They set up behind the felled trees and rocks in anticipation of such an attack and waited until the Japanese detachment were clear of the trees and visible. They opened fire with rifles and grenades and the Japanese detachment was taken by surprise. They had expected the encounter to be further up the side of the mountain and were lax and not prepared for such an assault. Chris' idea to set up away from the caves was ingenious. About half of the enemy fell during the first ten minutes. They fell back and regrouped. The sergeant was livid.

"Fall back into the trees and six of you crawl unseen to attack from the south side." said the sergeant.

Chris expected this maneuver, to try to out flank them, and when they showed up on their left, his group was expecting them and cut them down.

The sergeant was aghast that these untrained Polynesians could beat them so decidedly. The few that were left scurried back to the village.

"How can I explain this?" he mumbled under his breath. "Maybe I can convince him that we have a spy in our midst. That's it. I will execute the spies. It will somewhat appease him but I know he won't be happy. I must defeat those dogs before he'll forget this embarrassment. I WILL GET MY REVENGE."

The escapees had won the first skirmish but not without casualties. Thankfully only one was killed but several were wounded. One of the wounded was Chris. It was only a slight wound on his upper arm but Rosie was beside herself with worry.

Chris was now a hero. It was his battle plan that saved the village and he was now looked to as one of the leaders.

"We cannot rest on our laurels" Chris said "they will be back and with more of a force. I think we should move the main camp higher on the hill into the bigger caves."

All agreed and the move to safer grounds began.

CHAPTER FIFTEEN

......living up here in the high caves is more peaceful. It helps since I'm pregnant. Chris is worried but I told him that Kellea and the other women have promised to take care of me. Things have gotten better, its cooler and the caves are bigger. Chris made me a nice shelf for a bed. The midwife checked me and she thinks I'm further along than we thought. Well she was right.....my beautiful baby girl was born two days ago. We named her Eva. She was early so she's small but healthy. Kellea did most of the delivery with instruction from the old woman. Chris is very proud of our daughter. Since I don't know the exact date I will record the birth in this diary as being October 12, 1942......and more excitement today. A U.S. Navy pilot that had been shot down was found off the west end of the island. The men brought him back to the caves and we are nursing him back to health......after a few days the pilot was able to tell us that the war has reached a turning point. We are starting to turn them back. Thank God.....

IN THE YEAR OF 1942

The move to the higher caves was a wise one because the raids became more frequent. The women and children are safe on this higher ground but they miss their men. The men have stayed on the lower levels and are able to hold off the Japanese troops.

Last night seemed to be an even more furious fight from the sounds of gun fire. Chris was wounded again and he made his way up to Rosie's cave for some aid.

Rosie nursed his wounds and asked him if this would ever end. He said "Even though we took a great many casualties, the enemy took more. I feel that we may get a little respite since they have found that we don't give up easily."

"You need some rest darling. Sleep for awhile and I'll make some soup for us to eat later."

She left the cave and stood at the entrance feeling nauseated.

"What's wrong Rosie?" Kellea said.

"I don't know but I'm always feeling sick, especially in the morning."

Kellea smiled and said "I've noticed that you've put on a few pounds also Rosie."

"Oh Kellea, do you think I'm pregnant?"

"Oh yes I do." laughed Kellea "let's go see the midwife."

After a visit to the midwife, a wise old woman, it was a foregone conclusion that Rosie was going to have a baby. The surprising thing to Rosie was how far along the midwife thought she might be. According to the old lady she's probably in her second trimester. Rosie is obviously one of those women who doesn't show her pregnancy up front. When Chris wakes up she'll break the news to him.

As Kellea and Rosie walked back to her cave one of the men from below met them with good news. Chris was right.

He said "The Japanese soldiers all seemed to have left the area. Maunea has sent a scout to the village area to see if there is any activity there."

"Thank the Good Lord" Rosie said.

As she turned, Chris was walking towards her. He heard the news and said "Maybe now we can relax awhile."

"Well I have some other good news too honey." Rosie said.

"I hope it has to do with dinner. I'm starved." Chris said.

"Not exactly but I think you'll be happy."

"Well don't keep me in suspense any longer lady. Out with it."

"Okay, but sit down. You're going to be a daddy."

"What?"

"Yes honey. We're going to have a baby."

"Are you sure?"

"Ya wanna feel my belly?"

He took her in his arms and said "Oh honey I am happy but are you going to be okay with this? These are not the best of conditions."

"Too late now, honey, these women have been birthing babies for hundreds of years. I'll be fine."

"Do you know when it will come?"

"The midwife thinks maybe in about four months, sooner than I thought. But I'm in pretty good shape so that may be why I'm not showing as much. She said I'll get bigger pretty quick now."

"Oh Rosie, I wish we were at home. I'm worried about you and the baby both."

"We'll be okay. Kellea said she would give me all the help I need."

As time went on, things got better. The conditions on this higher ground and living in the larger caves was much more tolerable. It was definitely cooler and with the fighting of the Japanese now nonexistent, Chris had the time to make a comfortable, homey nook in the cave.

Rosie now wrote in her diary regularly.

The women had planted a garden so fresh vegetables were now available. Rosie helped harvest but soon found it too difficult to move up and down the hill.

One warm day she felt a different pain in her stomach and sat on a rock to rest. She thought she felt it getting wet under her.

Kellea walked by and said "Oh oh. We'd better get you inside on your mat."

"I don't feel well Kellea." Rosie said.

"It looks like it's time Rosie. You lie down while I get the old mother."

By the time Kellea and the midwife returned Rosie was writhing in pain.

"Isn't it too soon? Will my baby be okay?"

"Just relax Rosie. Old mother will take care of everything."

It was a difficult birth and the baby was small but the end result was a beautiful little girl. She was all cleaned up and resting in her mothers arms when Chris walked through the cave entrance.

"What's going on here?" he chided.

He stopped suddenly and stared at his wife lying on her bed holding an infant.

Rosie managed a weak smile and said "Come see your little girl, daddy."

"It can't be" he said "it's too soon."

"She decided it was time to make an appearance and although she's kind of small, she seems strong and has a loud, lusty cry so I guess its okay." Kellea said.

"Are you okay Rosie?" Chris asked.

"I'm very tired and pretty weak but the midwife seems to think it all went well and I'm doing as well as expected. Do you want to hold the baby?"

"Sure I do." Chris said as he reached out "Oh my, she really is tiny. Have you decided on her name?"

"Yes I have if it's okay with you I'd like to call her Eva."

"That's a beautiful name. Certainly it's okay with me."

The happy little family admired the newest edition to the group and soon the tired little mother drifted off to sleep for a well deserved rest. Soon little Eva did the same and the happy new father left to spread the word and do some bragging about his beautiful new daughter.

The next month or so was a peaceful period with no intervention from the Japanese soldiers. There were still some patrols but closer to the village. It was more defensive rather than offensive. It seemed as though there were not as many soldiers from the occasional news that they got from the village

One of the ways to get fresh food was to fish the far side of the island away from the village. This was done daily by different groups of men. One day the fishing group came back early carrying a wounded U.S. Navy pilot.

"We saw him in a life raft floating off shore so we swam out to see who it could be. At first we thought he was dead."

The pilot was badly dehydrated and had some wounds, possibly from shrapnel. He opened his eyes and eagerly drank some water before he passed out again. They took him into a cave and laid him in a bed of straw. Kellea took charge of nursing him back to health. She didn't mind at all. He was quite a handsome young man.

It was a few days later when he awakened and found out where he was, he was very thankful. He said "Our squadron had just returned from a sortie where we knocked out a Japanese airfield. My plane took some shrapnel and I tried to make it back to the carrier but I had to bail out. I was lucky to locate the raft that I had deployed at bail out."

"How is the war going. We haven't heard much." Chris asked.

"Since the battle of Midway, where we beat up the Jap navy pretty bad, it's been going more our way." He said.

"Lieutenant, you need your rest. You can fill us in later when you're stronger." Kellea protectively said.

Chris smiled and said "I'll come back tomorrow and maybe we can talk further."

As he left the cave he met Maunea. He said "There may be other reasons we haven't gotten more visits from the soldiers, Maunea. It seems that the war has taken a turn for the better and maybe they have other priorities than a bunch of renegade villagers. They don't seem to be working on that airstrip now either."

"Yes, you may be right. I'm anxious to talk to Lieutenant Taylor and find out more."

Kellea guarded the Lieutenant from any outside distractions. She hand fed him soup and soon he was able to sit up and his wounds were not as swollen. Finally after a few days and he was able to eat some solid food and she allowed some of the men to enter and ask questions about the war.

"What can you tell us Lieutenant? We are starved from lack of information." Chris said.

The Lieutenant answered "First of all I want to thank everyone for saving my life. When I was floating around out there with no land in sight, things looked pretty bleak. I'm still not sure where I am. If we are in the area that I think we are in, an island of this size is not supposed to be here."

"That may be the reason the Japs picked this place and why we don't see any ship or air traffic." Maunea said.

"Anyway, the war has taken a turn in our favor. There now is heavy fighting around Guadalcanal and everyone is hopeful that the Marines can take it back in a month or so."

"That sounds wonderful. It may take a while to work their way north to us but at least we know they're coming this way. How about the war in Europe?"

"That also looks better. The whole world is at war with Germany, Japan and Italy. It's not easy and there are many men being killed on both sides. We've heard of some terrible atrocities against the Jews in Europe."

"Thank you Lieutenant. This is the most news that we've had in a year. Get well and we'll try to figure out what to do with you."

"Kellea's taking pretty good care of me so I've got no complaints." Taylor said as Kellea blushed and gave out a tender giggle.

The next few months passed without incident. Rosie was now an attentive mother, Eva was growing like a weed, Chris and Lieutenant

Taylor tried to plan a way to return him to his squadron and the group of villagers lived a quiet, if a bit uncomfortable, life.

One day a squadron of U.S Navy Corsairs flew in sight of the island but didn't come their way. Lieutenant Taylor was excited. This meant that a Navy Aircraft Carrier was somewhere in the vicinity. Another reason that things were going well.

Rosie called to Kellea "Could you watch Eva for a few hours? It's my turn to go down to the garden with a few of the young girls and harvest some vegetables."

"Yes, of course. I hope you're taking some men with you."

"No Kellea, they have enough to do. There's no danger now."

"Please be careful. There are still a few patrols."

"We'll be okay. Just watch Eva and tell Chris where I went."

CHAPTER SIXTEEN

…...the garden is a great help to our food supply. The women in our camp make regular trips to harvest vegetables, and tomorrow is my turn to go down with two other young girls and harvest. Usually two or three of the armed men come along in case we run into a patrol but it's so seldom now and the last patrol just disappeared without any retaliation after a few shots were fired. We'll leave early and Kellea will watch Eva for me since Chris has his duties to perform. He has become a leader in the group. We are looking forward to some fresh produce…...

EARLY IN THE YEAR OF 1943

Rosie and the two young girls walked down the hill with their empty baskets to gather as much produce as they could carry. They were laughing and joking all the way. Attitudes had improved considerably since the threat of attack had lessened.

It was early and the heat of the day was not yet upon them. They wanted to start back up the hill before it got too hot so they worked happily and quickly.

They had just filled their baskets and were about to leave the garden when three Japanese soldiers walked out of the bush. They had evil smiles on their faces and were making crude remarks in a fractured Polynesian tongue. The patrol was led by a sergeant who laughed loudly at the crude remarks from the two unkempt soldiers.

The two of them carried rifles and the third, the ruthless sergeant who was now sneering, carried a sidearm.

The two young Polynesian girls screamed and dropped their baskets. Rosie stood her ground and glared at the three taunting monsters that were now making obscene gestures.

"Leave us alone" Rosie said in a strong authoritative voice.

"Aha" the sergeant said "we have lucked on to the American pig. We meet again white woman. This time it will be different. I am in charge and you will do as I say."

He glared at her and slowly his lips curled into a lustful grin.

Both of the young girls bolted from the garden and ran as hard as they could to get away from these evil men.

The sergeant yelled a command to the soldiers in Japanese.

They both dropped their rifles and gave chase to the girls.

"Leave them alone you monsters" screamed Rosie as she tried to follow them but she was roughly grabbed and held firmly by the sergeant.

He laughed in his sinister way and said in a voice dripping with evil "They will become grown up women now."

Rosie struggled, trying to free herself from the strong grasp of her captor. She wanted to give assistance to the girls but the sergeant roughly threw her to the ground, face down, and put his foot on her back to hold her down. "You will stay here until they return and then we will go to the village" he sternly commanded.

And then changed to his oily, sinister tone of voice and said "don't worry I will not let them harm you. They are crude and don't know how to treat a woman. We will wait until we return to my quarters and you will see what a real Japanese man can do."

Rosie could hear screams and grunts from the bush and she covered her head with her arms and sobbed.

Eventually the two soldiers returned laughing and even more disheveled. They picked up their rifles. The sergeant spoke to them, they answered, and then laughed even harder. This cruelty was unbelievable and Rosie retched with nausea.

"It seems that we will return to the village without your two little friends." said the sergeant.

"Oh my God! You are inhuman. They were just young girls."

The sergeant pulled her to her feet and pushed her ahead.

"Walk. We return to the camp."

They had no mercy and pushed her along the jungle path. When she fell, they roughly yanked her to her feet. She had bruises and scratches on her arms and legs. Her clothing was torn and they laughed at her modesty.

When they reached the camp she was not confined in the compound which now seemed to be empty. The prisoners were probably on a work party.

The sergeant walked her to a hut on the edge of the village and roughly shoved her inside. He bound her hand and foot and chained her to a pole in the center of the room. These chains and this pole had been used in this fashion before.

He left the hut and she was alone. Her eyes adjusted to the semi darkness and she could see that it was not a hut used as living quarters but rather a place for confinement.

"Oh why didn't I listen to Kellea and take some men with us. Those poor girls, how they must have suffered" she muttered to herself.

Several hours passed and the room got dark. It must be after sunset. She was thirsty. Suddenly the door opened and a form walked through the door. It was him.

"I have brought a bucket of water and a canteen. Clean and refresh yourself. I want you to be clean. My aide will bring a bowl of rice soon and then I must attend to other duties. Tomorrow I am free for the day. That will be our day" he leered as he spoke.

The door opened and a bowl was handed in to him. He passed it over to her and commanded "Eat. I will bring you more in the morning when I come to stay with you."

He freed her hands and left the hut. Rosie rolled over and sobbed and sobbed uncontrollably.

After a while she drank some water and ate the rice. She cleaned the scratches and washed her face. She was exhausted and fell into a troubled sleep.

She awoke the next morning dreading what could happen today. She ached both physically and mentally. Even though he had freed her hands last night, which made it a little more comfortable, her feet were still bound in leg irons and she was still chained to the pole.

She heard footsteps outside and voices. One she recognized as the sergeant's and the other seemed strangely familiar. They were arguing but it was in Japanese and not understandable. Even if she understood some

Japanese she doubted if she would recognize what they said. The argument gained even more in volume. They were shouting now. And finally there was one last adamant command, so loud and forceful, it almost hurt her ears. Definitely it was meant to finalize the argument.

She heard hard footsteps stomping off on the hard ground and a voice fading away that she was sure were Japanese obscenities.

All was quiet and then the door slowly opened. A figure quietly entered and softly said "Mrs. Conner. Are you alright?"

"Ye...yes. Who is it? Please who is it?" she quavered.

"It is me, Lieutenant Nakamoto. We met on the research vessel that rescued you and your husband."

"Yes, I remember you. Your ship brought us to this horrible place. We've been prisoners as is everyone on this island." Rosie said.

"Most unfortunate Mrs. Conner. It is not always pleasant to perform your duty and do as you are commanded but this is war and my country needs me." Lieutenant Nakamoto said.

"That sergeant and his men are the most brutal monsters I have ever met or even heard of." she said while sobbing.

"I am aware of the brutality that has gone on here, even though the base commander has somewhat curtailed it, I'm afraid that it still happens. Here let me free you from these chains. My orders are to take you to the base commander's office where Captain Yamaguchi and two civilians from Tokyo await us."

"Oh thank you so much. These chains are inhuman and really hurt my ankles. Will they let me go? I'm not a threat to them."

"They will explain. It is not for me to say. I am only to free you and take you there."

Lieutenant Nakamoto removed the chains and said "Now wait here. I will leave you for a few minutes while two women come in and clean you better, comb your hair and give you another smock to wear. It will be better for you to look nice. They will call to me when they are done and then we'll go."

When he left he called to the women who entered and busily attended to Rosie. She recognized one of the women and asked "What's going on here? Why are they taking me to the commander?"

But the women wouldn't answer. They just went about their business and muttered "No, no missy no, no."

Soon they were done and one of them went to the door and loudly said "Okay."

Lieutenant Nakamoto then reentered, looked approvingly at her and said "Okay Mrs. Conner as they say in the good old U.S.A. 'It's show time' and they walked out the door towards the office, flanked by two armed guards, where a strange meeting was about to take place.

Rosie silently wondered "What is going on? Something is just not right."

CHAPTER SEVENTEEN

BACK AT THE CAVES

"Chris, Chris you must come quick, HURRY" called an excited young boy "something has happened at the garden. Come quick."

Chris threw down the rifle that he was cleaning and ran to where a group had gathered around the prone sobbing figure of a young girl. Her smock was torn and bloody.

"What happened? Who did this to you?" Chris said in a panic.

The girl was incoherent. She was trying to speak through bloody lips while she sobbed uncontrollably.

The boy that called Chris to come said "I went to the garden to see if I could help carry the vegetables back with them. I found her on the path crawling back here from the garden. I could tell she was hurt bad so I half carried her as far as I could. Then I ran to get you."

"Where are Rosie and the other girl? Did you see them?" Chris shouted in a panic stricken voice.

"No, but my father and some of the other men have left and are running down to the garden to see."

"Help me carry her into a cave where someone can tend to her. She's in bad shape. Maybe she can tell us more if we can settle her down. Where are the men that accompanied them?" Chris said.

"I hate to tell you this but I don't think any men were along with them. I heard them talking to Kellea before they left and she warned them that they shouldn't go without some men. But I think they did. That's why I was going down to help."

"Oh my God" Chris said "I'm going down there."

He took off running and stopped to pick up a side arm on the way. He was racing down the path when he heard voices and drew up to a stop. He then recognized the voices to be men from his camp and he called "Hello down there. It's Chris. Where are you?"

They shouted back "Chris we're on the east path leading from the garden. HURRY."

Chris ran towards the voices in a panic. He was getting very worried now. Where was Rosie? He smashed through the brush headlong until he saw the men. They were standing over a body. It was the other girl and her father was cradling her in his arms and weeping loudly.

"She's dead Chris. She was brutalized just like the other one but she was just too fragile to take the abuse."

"Oh my God" Chris said "this is horrible. Have you found Rosie? Where's Rosie?" He started trembling.

Chris turned and ran towards the garden calling "Rosie, Rosie can you hear me? Rosie make a sound if you can here me."

He searched all through the garden to no avail. The other men joined him and they searched the whole area around the garden.

One of the older men who was noted to be a hunter and tracker called and said "Chris come here. I want to show you something."

Chris ran to him and yelled "Have you found her?"

"No, no but look at this trail. To me it looks like tracks of three soldiers and a woman. It's probably Rosie. Their trail leads away from here and towards the old village. I can follow it and tell you for sure. Do you want to follow me? I think only two of us should go. We can stay concealed because I'm sure we will encounter some of the enemy and we'll stand a better chance of hiding from them."

"Yes, let's go. It's almost dark. Can you follow the trail in the dark?" Chris said.

"I'll try. We may have to camp along the way and finish in the morning but I'm sure it will lead to the village. Exactly where in the village may be more difficult."

They went back to the group and Chris told them what they were going to do. He said "Will you please ask Kellea to keep Eva tonight? I have a feeling we may be gone over night and possibly tomorrow."

"Of course, Chris, find Rosie and bring her home. Eva will be fine with Kellea."

The two trackers left and made their way through the brush. In the jungle, darkness comes suddenly, like a blanket pulled over your head. And with the darkness came the night sounds, unseen, but the night creatures were out there.

Occasionally there was a scurrying on the path ahead of them and the glint of green eyes from the trees. The old tracker kept his eyes glued to the ground and went forward on a steady gait. Suddenly he stopped and retrieved a small piece of clothe from a thorn bush, examined it, and then handed it to Chris.

Chris took it in his hands and studied it in the darkness. He sniffed it and said "Yes. I'm sure it's Rosie's."

They went on but the pace slowed. The old tracker stopped and turned to Chris. He whispered "Be very quiet. There is someone ahead. I can hear some quiet talking and the sound of metal against metal. It might be a patrol or guards. I don't think it's our quarry."

They stood very quietly and soon the old man motioned for Chris to follow him off into the brush. He put his finger to his lips for a sign to be quiet.

They stole off the trail and silently found a place to be well concealed.

"We may not be able to make it into the camp tonight without getting caught. I know you want to find Rosie as soon as you can but it won't do her any good if we get caught by the Japanese. Let's wait here for awhile and if it's clear we can proceed.

They hunkered down and waited. It seemed like hours. Chris felt his legs cramping up and he tried to stretch them out. He rustled the brush and the old man frowned at him and again put his finger to his lips.

The rustling brought no response from the spot the sounds had come from. The old tracker slowly raised himself to a semi crouch, sniffed the air and slowly turned all the way around.

He motioned to Chris to follow him. It was now just beginning to break daylight. They must be very careful. But now there might not be as many guards.

They were soon in sight of the village. The old tracker motioned to Chris to drop to the prone position and scoot along under the brush. They crept to the edge of the jungle and found a spot to observe without being seen.

Some activity was beginning. A few women came out of huts and were stoking up cooking fires. Just a few soldiers were visible with the main force still in their bunks.

The pair waited and observed. The tracker was sure that the trail led them to a spot of entry very close to where they lay in hiding.

The camp was now starting to show signs of life with soldiers coming out of huts to start their day of duties. The prisoner compounds also were stirring and awaiting their ration of slop for breakfast.

Chris was getting impatient. He wanted to initiate some action. He wanted to do something to find out where they were keeping Rosie.

The tracker admonished him and said "Patience Chris. We can't move too quickly. We will find out soon. She is not in a compound. She is too valuable a prisoner for that. They need her to find the rest of us. They will be interrogating her soon enough."

They waited a little longer when there was a flurry of excitement. Walking from the center of the village towards them were two men, side by side, one appeared to be a soldier in a sergeants uniform but the other was a young navy officer. Behind them were two women carrying buckets of water, towels and bowls of food and behind them were two armed soldiers.

It was very strange that the conversation between the sergeant and the navy officer was quite animated. In fact as they got closer it got very animated. The sergeant was livid. Soon the officer was just as livid. It almost appeared that they were going to come to blows. The two soldiers were ordered something from the sergeant and they looked at each other in bewilderment. They took a step towards the officer but when the officer quickly turned and adamantly shouted a command they both stopped. They nervously stepped back and stood at attention, confusion etched on their faces.

The sergeant eyeballed both of them and muttered Japanese obscenities. He turned to the lieutenant, glared at him with a look of hatred, spewed some guttural sounding words and turned on his heel and stomped off all the while growling and grumbling.

The Lieutenant relaxed his tense shoulders in a sign of great relief. He turned to the two guards and quietly commanded them to stand at ease.

The two women also seemed to relax a bit and silently stood by.

The lieutenant then turned to the hut entrance and slowly opened the door. He entered while the others stood outside awaiting his orders.

He was inside for ten minutes or so, came back out and spoke to the women. They then entered the hut while the three men stood outside and waited.

It was at least an hour later when one of the women opened the door and said "Okay."

The lieutenant reentered and within minutes the women, the lieutenant and the prisoner exited the hut. Yes it was Rosie.

Chris breathed sharply and started to rise up but the tracker grabbed him and whispered "No. Not yet."

"Oh thank God she seems to be okay." Chris muttered.

"Yes she is okay. So let's figure out how we can safely get her out of there. If we rush in now they'll kill both of us."

"You're right. Of course we must wait. That navy officer was the one that helped us on the ship that rescued us off the atoll. Maybe he's still helping. I think he saved Rosie from that brutal sergeant."

"Let's see where they are taking her. It looks like they may be going to the headquarters office down by the dock." The tracker said.

They made their way around the village and got as close to the waters edge as they could without being seen. They were prone in the thick brush.

"Okay now we must wait again" said the tracker "if they take her back to the hut we can make our move after dark."

"I'll get my Rosie back no matter what." Chris said with an anguished tone.

Hours later Chris' muscles were cramping from lying in one position. He shifted and as he did a guard caught a glimpse of movement. The guard cautiously approached with his rifle barrel parting the thick brush. When he was close enough to smell his body odor, the tracker leaped up and slit his throat with one swipe. The only sound was a gurgling cough and a body hitting the ground.

But the sudden movement was enough to cause the guards partner to come and investigate the disturbance. He was cautiously approaching the two insurgents and would soon be on top of them.

The tracker grabbed Chris and said "Let's go. Quickly."

"I've got to get Rosie." Chris said in panic.

"Not now. We must go or we'll never get her."

They scurried out of the camp and into the jungle just before the guard found his companion with a slit throat and rushed back to set off a general alarm screaming all the way "They killed Noshi. They are in the jungle. Hurry! Hurry!"

A squad of armed soldiers quickly ran with the guard towards the spot of incursion.

"Did you see how many there were?" breathlessly asked the lieutenant in charge.

"No, but I heard them running off into the jungle. There must have been at least five or six heathens."

"Let's split up. Sergeant, take eight men and follow the path to the north. I will take the rest of the men and go to the west. Keep in touch by radio."

They cautiously plowed through the jungle expecting to encounter a formidable group of natives.

Chris and the tracker heard the alarm and took a course away from the paths leading to the caves. They zigzagged through the jungle trying to lose their pursuers. They could travel faster since there were only two of them and didn't leave a noticeable trail.

On one occasion they guessed wrong and unknowingly doubled back into the path of the splinter group of eight soldiers. They hid in the thick brush, burrowing deeply into the underbrush so they couldn't be seen.

The soldiers passed so close by they had to hold their breath and came very close to being discovered. But fortunately they weren't and soon the soldiers were in the clear. They tried to be more cautious now and waited until they knew they were safe.

After several hours of picking their way through the thickest part of the jungle they were able to make their way back to the relative safety of their mountain hideaway without any further encounter.

They were exhausted and flopped on the ground in front of the caves. The women brought them some soup while they reported the findings to Maunea.

CHAPTER EIGHTEEN

.......My name is Chris Conner. My wife Rosie Conner has started this diary and is not here to finish it. I will try to continue it. The last time I saw Rosie was in the Japanese camp. I'm afraid to think of what may have happened but I think they took her off of the island. I don't know where or what they are doing to her. I pray that she is not suffering. I will spend the rest of my life searching for her but for now my resources, to do so, are very limited. I have our daughter Eva to care for and I promised Rosie to always protect her. I will. My plan is to try to contact the English speaking Japanese officer. Maybe he will help me. This diary will be hidden in the alcove that was once the home of my little family.

After leaving the hut Rosie was escorted to the headquarters office. She entered the office and stood facing the camp commander's desk. The commander was sitting in his chair with several Japanese standing to the side. She was sure one was the Captain of the research ship that had brought them to the island. The other two were in civilian clothes.

"Good morning Mrs. Conner." Captain Yamaguchi said in broken English.

Rosie looked around. She didn't quite know what to make of this latest development. "Good morning" she uttered.

"Don't be concerned or apprehensive Mrs. Conner, we have a proposition for you that you may be interested in hearing." said the base commander.

"I don't understand" Rosie said "whatever proposition could I be interested in? Please let me go back to my husband and my baby."

"Mrs. Conner, sit down and we will explain" he said.

Rosie sat in a chair provided for her and gave a puzzled look at the group of Japanese men. She was very much on her guard. All of a sudden she was being treated like a human being. Like someone who had something to offer or to be bargained with.

One of the very polite, well dressed civilians turned to her. "As you know Japan is at war with your country. Being a civilized nation, we want to do all we can to promote a peaceful transition in your country after we have defeated you. One of the things that we feel we can do is communicate with your fighting forces and attempt to promote good feelings as well as give them news from their homeland. This communication might not be well received from a Japanese military man or even a Japanese civilian, neither male nor female. We wish to employ your help in accomplishing this and at the same time give you the comforts that you are not now enjoying."

"I have no idea what help I could give you, but if the atrocities that I saw by your soldiers are any indication of your country being a civilized nation I will have no part in anything you plan for me." Rosie had risen up sitting tall in her chair and stated this very clearly and adamantly.

They were not dealing with a shrinking violet.

The military men all shuffled nervously as the civilians looked at each other knowingly.

"Please Mrs. Conner, you must understand that certain types of men under the mental strain of war and the tensions of facing death every day sometimes snap and may do things that under ordinary circumstances they would not do" said one civilian.

"I understand exactly what was done to two young girls, hardly out of puberty, by two of your soldiers and under the guidance and authorization of one of your non commissioned officers….just yesterday……acts like that are not caused by the mental strain of war and that does not count all of the previous acts of inhumanity which were overlooked by that man. RIGHT THERE." Rosie screamed as she leaped to her feet and pointed at the base commander.

The commander jumped to his feet and said "This is not true. I have forbidden any mistreatment of prisoners. A few men under my command have already been punished for unauthorized abuse. If an atrocity has happened it is without my knowledge."

He apprehensively looked from face to face. A look of guilt was obvious.

The room grew quiet.

The older civilian spoke to the young English speaking civilian who turned and faced the commander.

"Do we know which men that Mrs. Conner is accusing of these acts?" said the English speaking civilian.

The commander answered in Japanese.

The older civilian spoke harshly to the commander who immediately turned and left the room. The room grew quiet. No one spoke but the air was filled with tension.

The two civilians drew into a corner and whispered to each other. They seemed very disturbed.

When the commander returned after an agonizingly long time, he again spoke to the civilians in Japanese.

The young civilian turned to Rosie and said "Mrs. Conner you will be pleased to know that the two perpetrators are being confined as we speak and will be punished harshly. The sergeant will be reprimanded and reduced in rank for allowing this to happen."

"That still will not bring back the innocence of those two little girls and does not help the living conditions of all those poor people who are hiding from your soldiers up on those mountains." Rosie said.

"Hmmm. Yes I see." he said.

He gathered the group around him and they had a lengthy discussion in Japanese. Some were in agreement and others obviously not. But the meeting took a strange turn and ended abruptly with very loud exclamatory remarks from the older civilian that had been very quiet up until then. He had prefaced this final order with some questions for the commander. He seemed to now be in charge and carried much more respect that the other English speaking man. This became very obvious when they all drew back to their original positions and again the room became very quiet.

The English speaking man asked a question in Japanese, to the man now very obviously in charge, who answered in a low tone.

He then turned and addressed Rosie.

"We certainly understand your concern for the others in your party Mrs. Conner and of course for your husband. Do you have other family there?" he said.

"Yes I have a daughter. She is only 4 months old." she said.

"Ah so. If you cooperate, and will just listen to a plan with our communication and promotion experts, we can assure you that the people now living in the mountains will not be harassed by our forces. As long as they do not exhibit any aggression to our soldiers or try to promote an escape of workers here at the base they will enjoy a peaceful existence. Any abuse, either sexual or physical by any rogue soldiers would be judged with harshly."

"I still don't understand. What would I have to do?" Rosie asked.

"You will leave the island on the research ship at first light tomorrow. You will be transported to a larger port where you will be transferred to a ship, probably a military troop ship that will be bound for Manila and then eventually end up in Tokyo. It is there that you will join several other English speaking women and be given instructions on your duties. You will live in comfort and be in no harm."

"But I'll be away from Chris and Eva. How can I leave them?"

"You will be leaving them with the knowledge that, because of your actions, they will be safe and likely survive this war. You also will very likely survive, and after we have defeated your country we will do all possible to reunite you with your family."

"And if I refuse?"

"My superior and I will leave the island under the control of the base commander with orders to complete this supply base under whatever force it takes to do so. It will be out of our hands and...... on your own conscience"

Rosie hesitated before saying "To protect my family I will go on the ship and I will listen to your plan but if I find that it involves being a traitor to my country I will refuse."

"That is a wise choice Mrs. Conner and I'm sure you will make the same wise decision when you hear our plan. In the long run it will benefit everyone involved."

The commander's aide came quickly through the door and spoke to him rapidly in Japanese. The commander turned to the civilians and repeated the phrase with even more emphasis and then without waiting for a response he gave a command to the aide who ran from the room.

An alarm sounded and shots rang out with soldiers barking out commands.

The Japanese man gave an order to Captain Yamaguchi who turned to Lieutenant Nakamoto and repeated the order.

The Lieutenant saluted smartly and turned to Rosie.

"Please come with me Mrs. Conner. We will now go to the ship and prepare for departure in the morning." he said.

"What's all the excitement about, Lieutenant?" asked Rosie.

"Nothing for you to be concerned about Mrs. Conner. Just a minor fracas with one of the village men" he answered.

He then took her arm and gently guided her down the dock to the tied up research ship.

After boarding the ship she was escorted below decks to a small but neat cabin similar to the one she and Chris had on the journey to Tongolo.

She sat on the bed and tried to contemplate all that had happened in the last few days. How quickly her situation changed. She raised her hands to her face and sobbed.

"My baby, my baby. Please God protect my baby. I'll give up my life if you will protect sweet baby Eva."

CHAPTER NINETEEN

Chris and the tracker got back to the caves and were met by some of the older men. They were very upset when they saw that Rosie was not with them.

"Chris, where is she? Is she okay? Did they hurt her? The young warriors want to get a raiding party together and storm the camp to rescue her." said one of the senior villagers.

"We saw her and she looks to be okay for now but we ran into trouble with the soldiers. We had to kill one and this set off an alarm. We could not carry out our plan to rescue her but I think it can still be done. Tell the young men not to move too quickly. It may do more harm than good and could be bad for Rosie. I've got a few ideas and with some help maybe we can rescue her without a big loss of life." Chris said.

The villagers all answered at once agreeing to help in any way they could to bring Rosie back home.

"I want to get a few hours sleep and make a trip back to the village after dark. The tracker can go with me again since he is familiar with the layout. We saw the hut where she had been kept and I'm pretty sure she'll go back there under guard. Maybe one of the young men can go with us to offer some support if we encounter some guards. I think a small force will do better than an outright attack. She seems to be under the protection of a Japanese Naval officer. We met him on the trip here aboard the research ship. I some how feel that they will not put her in the compound but that also is a possibility."

"Can we get her out if she's in the compound? That's always pretty heavily guarded." said the old man.

"I don't know. They had taken her to the headquarters office and we had to get out of there. They're probably trying to interrogate her. For what? I don't know. It's all so strange. They seemed to be treating her well. Even feeding and clothing her. Maybe it's a ploy to get some information but I don't know anything more than that. There were two village women that attended her. Maybe we could find them and question them before we make a move. Anyway, for now the plan is to go back tonight. Hold off the young warriors."

Chris then went to find Kellea to see his little baby girl and ask Kellea if she could keep Eva until he brought Rosie home.

He found her in her cave and she broke out in tears when she heard that Rosie had been captured by the Japanese.

"What will you do, Chris? Can we get her back? Oh I'm so sad. I love Rosie. She is like my big sister." Kellea said.

"I know Kellea. Yes I will find her and get her back. She is my whole life and I will not rest until I get her back."

"I know that she misses Eva too and little Eva sure misses her. She cried herself to sleep last night."

"Can I see my little girl? Is she taking a nap?"

"She's awake now. Just laying in her bed and cooing. She's such a good baby. I love her too."

Chris went into the cave and picked up his baby. He hugged her and said in a tender voice "Oh Eva I wish I could have brought your mommy back but I couldn't sweetie. I will though. Just be patient and I'll bring mommy home."

He turned to Kellea.

"I'm going to need your help Kellea. It may take some time and a lot of planning to bring Rosie home. I won't be able to care for Eva. Can I count on you to watch her while I get a rescue mission together?"

"You know you can count on me Chris. You go ahead and do what ever it takes to bring Rosie home. I will care for Eva 24 hours a day for as many days that you need me. And any time you want to see her just come to my cave. I will be her nanny."

"Thank you Kellea. You are a dear and loyal friend. Someone I know is there when I need help."

He handed the baby to her and said "Now I've got to rest and get my strength back so I can try to bring Rosie back home."

He walked back to his cave and lay in the bunk. The cool atmosphere of the cave felt refreshing after being in the heat of the day. He lay with his eyes wide open and his body as taut as a stretched rubber band even though he was exhausted. Soon his body relaxed and as he was almost asleep he was startled with a spasm. All part of his exhaustion. And he again relaxed and finally fell into a deep dreamless sleep.

He awoke when he heard someone calling his name. He sat up and rubbed his eyes. It was twilight and the cave was losing light. He saw a figure standing at the entrance.

"If we are going back to the village tonight Chris you will need some food. I brought you a meal for the strength you will need tonight."

Chris then focused as the figure moved in out of the glare and he saw that it was the tracker. He arose out of the bed and greeted his companion.

"Come in my friend. Come to think of it I haven't eaten since yesterday. Let me splash some water in my face and you can share the meal. It looks like you brought enough for two."

"Yes" said the tracker "and we can lay out our plan for tonight. A young warrior will join us. He will be here shortly."

Chris was famished and he dug right in as did the tracker.

When they had finished and were starting to devise the plan a young Polynesian entered the cave. He was certainly formidable and Chris was sure he would add strength and stealth to their small force.

"We can leave before it's completely dark. There are no known patrols in the area." said the tracker.

"Yes that should put us at the village well into the night. I'd like to scout out the hut Rosie was in and hopefully she still will be there. If she is I'm sure there will be a guard close by. If not hopefully she'll just be bound or chained up. If she's guarded, we'll subdue the guard or guards quietly so as not to raise an alarm. Then we'll check out the hut. If she's not in the hut, we'll attempt to find the women who assisted her. I saw which hut they went into after they left Rosie. They must be some sort of trustees. Hopefully they will help us and give us the information we need. Then we'll have to play it by ear. If we can't find her tonight I don't want to raise an alarm so we can give it another try the next night. We may even find out some information by observing during the day."

"Okay Chris. I think that's as close as we can plan until we know more." said the tracker.

"Let's get our packs ready and hit the trail." Chris said.

They quietly stole off the mountain just in case they were being observed by a Japanese patrol and made their way through the jungle towards the village.

It was well after midnight when they reached the edge of the village grounds. They had encountered no Japanese at all the whole way. Not even a random patrol.

The village was quiet and they made their way to the side where Rosie's hut was located. They lay quietly in the bush and just observed for awhile. There was no guard other than the normal sentry making his rounds. Even he seemed a bit lax.

The tracker whispered "I have more experience than either of you in sneaking upon a prey. I will enter the village and steal up to the hut in a round about way so the sentry will not notice me. When I get there I'll attempt to enter and see what's inside. If Rosie is in there I'll bring her out but I have a feeling that it is empty."

Chris and the young man nodded their assent.

The tracker left them and disappeared into the bush. Time passed slowly. All was quiet. The sentry passed by again within 30 yards of where they lay. No sign of the tracker yet. More time passed. Chris then noticed movement at the side of the hut. It was the tracker.

He was prone and as still as the night. He waited until the sentry made another round and then he stole around the front where the entrance was located. There was a rickety door which he pushed open and slowly entered the hut and the door closed.

Again all was quiet. Time passed. The door slowly opened. Chris drew a deep breath and held it. The tracker slowly emerged. Would Rosie be with him? NO. The tracker was alone. Chris loudly expelled the breath and the young Polynesian gave him a sharp glance.

They waited again while the tracker made his way back to the two men.

When he finally got there Chris asked "Did you see any sign of her?"

"No." the tracker said "just the empty chains that I imagine they had bound her with."

"Okay. We've got to ask the servant women what they know."

"Are you sure you remember the hut they went into?" said the tracker.

"Yes, I'm sure it was on the other side by the compound and close to the edge of the village." Chris said.

"Let's go. We'll go around through the jungle. It's longer but safer" said the tracker.

They back tracked and made their way to the other side. Again they met up with no Japanese patrols. When they reached the spot where Chris had a view of the hut, they hunkered down in the bush and observed for awhile. All was quiet.

He whispered to the tracker "Okay it's my turn. This looks easier since it's close to the edge."

"You'll have to hurry. I'd say we have a little over an hour of complete darkness and then we've got to get deeper into the jungle. We might be able to sneak a peak after daylight if we find a good spot. There doesn't seem to be a lot of activity from patrols."

Chris made his way through the bush until he was close to the compound. The fence offered some concealment. He scooted along the fence towards the hut. He could see a sentry on the other side of the compound that, luckily, was walking the other way. The sentry was a good distance away when he stopped and slipped into a hut. Chris waited quietly and then he heard a female giggle coming from the hut. He was pretty sure that the sentry would not be coming out of the hut for a while.

Chris then crawled to the servant women's hut, cautiously looked around, and pulled himself up to the window. Inside he saw one of the women sleeping on a mat. He recognized her as one of those that was in Rosie's hut. He stole around to the entrance. There was no door. He crawled in and silently pulled himself along side of the woman. He placed one hand firmly over her mouth and held her body down with his other arm. She gave a muffled cry and her body writhed, trying to get out from under Chris' strong arm. She was a small delicate woman and offered very little resistance against this much stronger man.

Chris said "Sh, sh be quiet. I won't hurt you. Be quiet." She stopped struggling when she saw him but stared at him with frightened eyes. He slowly removed his hand from her mouth but continued to pin her down.

"You speaky English?"

"Scoshy bit."

"Where is the white woman? My wife. Where did they take her?"

"Don't know where. Only see sailor man take to ship."

"What ship? Japanee ship in harbor?"

"Not in harbor any more."

"Japanee ship gone?"

"Yes. Japanee ship go bye bye early today."

"Was she still on ship when ship go bye bye?"

"Think so. No see her come back. Stay on ship"

Chris was devastated. Where did they take her? He thought the Navy Lieutenant might be friendly enough to help him but if the ship was gone then so was he.

He slowly released the woman and crawled out the door. He made his way back to his two friends.

"What did you find out Chris?" said the tracker.

He stared at the tracker, downcast.

"She's gone. She's gone." moaned Chris.

"Gone? You mean they killed her?"

"No, no they took her away on that research ship. I don't know why or where they are going. She's gone. I don't know what to do."

The three just laid there for awhile.

Chris silently wept and was drenched in sweat. The two Polynesians moved quietly away a short distance giving him some privacy.

They had deep respect for this man and shared in his grief.

Soon the tracker approached him and gently said "We have to go Chris. It will be light soon. Let's go back to the caves. I don't know what else we can do here."

They stole away from the edge of the village into the hot, humid jungle. The going was slow or at least it seemed much slower than before. The attitude of the small party was down beat plus Chris' deep depression. He also was feverish. At about the half way point he asked to stop and rest. The tracker felt his forehead and said "You are burning up with fever. We must get you back into the coolness of the caves. It could very well be Malaria. I've seen it before and you have all the symptoms."

CHAPTER TWENTY

The Japanese research vessel, Noshi Maru, left Tongolo at first light en route to New Guinea where Rosie was to be transferred to a Japanese troop ship bound for Manila.

She had fallen into a troubled sleep and thought she was dreaming when she was awakened by a galley Mess Cook who had placed a breakfast tray on her small table.

The galley Mess Cook left saying something in Japanese that Rosie did not understand. She picked at her breakfast and thoughtfully contemplated her future. What did they have planned for her? Her only real skill was flying but surely that would have nothing to do with it. They mentioned communication. She rose and tried the door. It was not locked. But then where would she go? They were out in the middle of the ocean. She decided to take a walk. She made her way down the passageway to a ladder that looked like it might go topside. It did, and she found herself out on the deck on the starboard side of the ship.

She walked forward to the end of the superstructure and out on the open deck forward of the bridge. When the lookout spotted her it caused quite a turmoil on the bridge. Shortly thereafter a messenger came down to meet her and through sign language conveyed to her a request to follow him up to the bridge.

When she got to the bridge, the officer of the deck motioned for her to sit in a deck chair. She did and shortly after she sat down, Lieutenant Nakamoto entered the bridge.

"Good morning Mrs. Conner. Did you sleep well?" he said.

"Good morning. Yes as well as I could sleep, under the circumstances." she answered.

"Please, come and walk with me where we can talk about your situation. We want you to be comfortable."

They left the bridge and walked to the stern of the ship where the wind was shielded by the superstructure.

He turned to her and said "You are aware of my education in America. Most of my formative years were there. My father was a Naval Officer in the Japanese Navy and it was my duty to follow in his footsteps. I love my country and I will do my duty. But I sometimes shudder at some of the horrors of this war. I am fortunate that my duties do not include combat and entail mostly research. Now as far as your status, I will tell you as much as I know."

He continued "First of all, you are not a prisoner and you have complete run of the ship. Except, of course, some restricted areas for your own safety and certain sensitive research cabins. This ship is only a means of transportation to New Guinea where you and the two civilian operatives will be transferred to another ship. I will not be seeing you after that."

"What happens after that?" she asked.

"All I know is that your next stop will be in Manila where you may undergo some training for your mission." he answered.

"And just what will this mission be? I don't quite get what this communication promotion is all about."

"Yes. Well I understand that you have spent the entire war up to this point on an island with little or no contact with the outside world. Is that right? You didn't have any radio or other means of information gathering?" he asked.

"That's right. The only word we got was hearsay from your soldiers and we did rescue an American pilot who gave us some news on the progression of the war. But no radio was available. Tongolo is a very remote island and the villagers are quite antiquated. They have no modern conveniences."

"Yes, that is as I understood it to be. Of course you would have no knowledge of the radio broadcasts that beam out to your fighting forces from both Manila and Tokyo. These broadcasts are in English by Caucasian women. Do you know of this?" he asked.

"No. What kind of broadcasts?" she asked.

"Mostly they play popular songs. Many of your sentimental love songs and they talk to the men, sometimes on a one on one type of one way conversation. Asking about their loved ones back home and how much their women must miss them while they are away fighting the superior Japanese forces." he mused.

"I don't think that would make them feel very good. In fact it probably makes them homesick and anxious." she said.

"That is true. And of course that is the whole object of the broadcasts."

She looked at him incredulously "And they want me to do this?"

"That is the idea. Your forces have even made a name for the woman. They call her 'Tokyo Rose'. But of course the broadcasts have grown to where we must use more than one woman and broadcast from several locations to get better coverage. It is quite well thought out. That is the job of the two civilians aboard. They were quite impressed with you and that is why they insisted on the terms you more or less dictated. You will start in Manila but I think they have you eventually destined for Tokyo. You may become famous."

"I can't partake in Japanese propaganda. I can't become a traitor." She spoke in an adamant tone.

"Please Mrs. Conner don't speak this way to the two civilians. It could go very badly for you. Wait until you see the program. When Japan wins this war you could be in a very good position."

"And what if America wins this war? From what I hear the tide has turned and the U.S. Marines have taken Guadalcanal back from Japanese forces."

"This is only a temporary setback." He bristled.

"I'm not an expert on war or how it's fought but I know Americans are proud and capable people. You must know that since you were educated in America. Don't count us out yet."

Lieutenant Nakamoto was strangely quiet and Rosie thought she noticed a strange watering in his eyes. Was his confidence wavering?

He looked her in the eye and said "Please do not do or say anything to cause harm to you or to your family back on Tongolo. It would not bode well for any of you. Show your cooperation as much as you can. Many things can change and it will be some delay until you get to Manila. You must understand that no matter what my personal feelings are, I am still an officer in the Japanese Navy. Please heed my advice and I will make my report to the operatives, that you are in complete cooperation. Can you do that?"

"If it means protecting my family I'll go along with their requests up until the point of outright treason. So just tell them that I'm cooperative but apprehensive."

"Very well, I'll do that. You may go to your cabin or stay out on deck as you choose. I may see you at mealtime. I believe the plan is to have your meals in the wardroom with the two civilians. One speaks English very well as you know. You may learn more about the program. He also received an education in America. I'm not sure where he went to school. Somewhere in the Ivy League I believe. Someone will come to your cabin and instruct you."

He turned and left her standing on the fantail. Her situation was a little clearer now, but she didn't know what awaited her in Manila or how she would handle it. At least she could relax with the knowledge that Chris and Eva had a good chance to survive this hell.

She had plenty of time to think about it. It would be a week before they reached New Guinea and no telling how long before she caught a ship to Manila. Then a long voyage on a troop ship to her destination. She would use this time to get strong and somehow come up with some sort of a plan to get back to her family.

She mused "I must use my wits to stay alive without becoming a traitor......I must......It's vital to my family and my country to be cunning and outwit them."

CHAPTER TWENTY ONE

BACK ON TONGOLO

Chris collapsed just before they reached the caves. He had to be helped most of the way after the fever was discovered and now he could go no further. He lost consciousness as the tracker tried to help him to his feet. The two men lifted him by his arms and carried him to the caves.

When they reached the garden area others were there and they devised a litter to transport him to his own cave.

When they laid him down, they swabbed his head with wet rags but he started shaking uncontrollably. They sent for the old medicine woman who came right away.

"This is very bad" said the ancient woman. "There is an herb in the jungle that will help with the fever but sometimes it is too late, the fever consumes the body and it just shuts down. I will send my oldest son to find the herb but we can only hope that we are in time."

"We must try to keep him cool even if he is shaking like a leaf. If the fever gets too high he will suffer greatly and even if he does not die he could become slow witted."

Chris became delirious and called for Rosie. He cried and screamed and finally fell unconscious again, still shaking and trembling.

Hours later the boy returned with the plants for which the ancient one had sent him. She took them back to her cave and mixed a potion. When she got back to Chris' cave Kellea was there and she said that her mother was watching Eva and she would tend to Chris.

The ancient one awakened Chris. He barely opened his eyes and he was shaking even more violently when awake. She tried to make him swallow the bitter herb but he resisted and spewed it out.

She said "He must swallow this or he will die. Help me Kellea."

She put another dose in his mouth and Kellea firmly held his mouth closed. He clawed at her arms but was so weak he couldn't muster enough strength to do so. He finally gave up and lapsed back into a deep sleep.

"I must go" said the ancient one "give him a dose at sunset and another at sunrise. I will come back tomorrow. If he lives through two nights he may survive."

She left and Kellea stayed by his side swabbing his head with wet cloths. He still trembled but not as violently as before.

Chris was in a troubled sleep. He thrashed around and tried to fight off who ever it was holding him down but he had no strength. Those demons were trying to poison him. Finally they let him go and he slept.

They came back. The demons tried to poison him again. I can't fight anymore. They are too strong. And he slept.

"I'm so cold" he thought "where is Rosie? She should be here. Eva needs her. Eva. Eva. Where is Eva? Those men....they're coming after her... leave her alone....Rosie...Rosie....take Eva and run. Run away as fast as you can....Oh why can't I see them."

He awoke and rose up screaming "ROSIE...EVA." He tried to get off his mat and fell.

Kellea awoke and said "Chris, Chris lie down you are dreaming. You must lie down.'

She grabbed him and with all her strength she pushed him back onto the mat. He looked wild eyed and fought her screaming "You demon. Leave us alone. Leave my family alone."

He was weak and she lay across his body to hold him down. He started a violent shaking again and tearing at his clothes trying to get cool but she finally subdued him and he laid there shivering.

She again got some wet towels from a cool spring and swabbed his head. He fell back into his troubled sleep.

Again he was dreaming and would flail his arms like he was trying to fight off something. Kellea stayed by his side the rest of the night.

The sun came up and she knew she must give him another dose of the herb. She tried to gently awaken him and when he opened his eyes he looked at her and said her name. She opened his mouth and gave him the medicine and he swallowed it without a struggle. He then closed his eyes and fell back asleep.

The ancient one arrived. She said "He is still in danger but not as much. The medicine is working but sometimes after an improvement another bad period starts. Almost worse than the first because he is much weaker and cannot fight the fever as well. Give him a dose when the sun is high in the sky and again at sun set. If he makes it through the night give him one more at sunrise. That is all his body will stand. After that he must fight the final effects with his own body. More medicine at that stage will be too much for him to handle. He would surely die."

She left and Kellea did as she was told. There were more periods of delirium, more nightmares, more struggles and violent shivering. He lasted through the night but it was even more of a struggle.

Kellea was exhausted and she had slept in short naps between his rants and ravings. He seemed more settled after the final dose although he was still perspiring and shivering. She tried to give him water and he drank in gulps. She slowed him down because he started choking and gagged. Finally he slept without flailing and she was sure the fever was less.

She laid on the mat next to him and fell into a deep sleep. Hours later she awoke with a start. She had dreamed he said her name and touched her. But it wasn't a dream. As she lifted her head he was looking at her and said "Kellea is that you?"

She quickly stood and said "Yes it is me. Don't try to get up. You are still sick and very weak."

"What happened? My head feels like it is splitting open."

"You are very sick. The ancient one said it is Malaria. You must stay in bed for a while yet. The danger has not passed."

"I'm so thirsty. Can I have some water?"

"Yes, I will give you some and then you must rest some more."

She gave him a drink and wiped his head with a cool cloth with water from the spring and said "Now sleep some. I will go for the ancient one and see what we do next."

She waited until he drifted off and then went for the ancient one.

When she found the ancient one she told her how Chris had awakened and his fever was almost gone.

"That is good. But we cannot rush it. A relapse could occur. Let him sleep as long as possible today and tonight. The herb effects should wear off by tomorrow morning and you can feed him some broth. I will give you the ingredients for the broth. It is part of the cure to get some strength back. He may still have a fever and tremble but not as before. You have done a good job Kellea, as you did when Rosie had her baby. Some day you may take my place as the one to give care to the sick."

Before she went back to Chris' cave she stopped by her mother's cave to see her other responsibility, Eva.

"Mother, mother I'm here."

"Ah Kellea. I have heard that Chris has awakened. Is he going to be all right?"

"I think so mother. The fever has broken somewhat but I'm still needed. Is Eva okay?"

"That child is no bother at all. Do you want to see her?"

"Oh yes. She is almost like my own."

Kellea entered the cave and picked up Eva who cooed and smiled at Kellea. She knew her nanny and missed her. Kellea played with her for awhile and then put her back into her little bed.

"I must go little one. Your daddy is sick and needs my care but I will return. Be a good girl now."

She returned to Chris' cave and found that he was still sleeping. This would give her the chance to collect the ingredients for the broth and make it tonight. Then she would be able to feed it to him in the morning.

She had to go into the jungle to collect some of the roots needed so she asked the young Polynesian that helped bring Chris back to go with her for needed protection.

"I will be most happy to go with you Kellea and you need not worry about any harm coming to you while I'm with you."

"Thank you Nomea." she shyly said.

They trekked off into the bush. Kellea picked and dug the herbs and stored them in the pouch the ancient one had given her. It was hers to keep and to be used as her herb pouch.

After she got back to the cave Nomea asked if he could stay in case she needed help.

She agreed. Nomea was very nice and helpful too but he was so young. Oh well. It had been a pleasant day.

CHAPTER TWENTY TWO

Rosie was standing by the fantail rail, gazing out at the tranquil Pacific Ocean. She was lost in thought as she absently watched the wake left by the twin screws of the ship. Two distinct foamy trails with a rolling wave extending out from each side.

Her meditation was suddenly broken and she was startled by a female voice. She jumped and twisted around to see a young blonde woman standing behind her.

"Well, I had heard through the grapevine that another 'Tokyo Rose' was going to join me." She said with a wide smile on her face.

"Oh my God" Rosie said "where in the world did you come from?"

The woman laughed "And obviously they didn't tell you about me. I've been aboard for about two weeks. I'm an Army nurse. They picked me up on Tarawa where I was captured with a bunch of soldiers when the Japs took the island. Those poor guys are all headed for a P.O.W. camp. How about you?"

"They put me aboard at Tongolo, the place we just left."

"I figured that but I didn't know where we were. They locked me in my cabin until just now. I'm right next to yours. How did you happen on Tongolo? I don't know about that island."

"It's a long story" Rosie said.

"Well tell it to me honey, 'cause we have plenty of time. What's your name?" she asked.

"My name is Rosie Conner. What's yours?"

"June Beck. Let's go sit in the ward room. It's the most comfortable place where we're allowed to go."

When they got to the ward room they sat at a table and Rosie told her tale.

"My husband Chris Conner and I, are pilots. We flew a Lockheed L-10E, which we bought in California, and had shipped to New Guinea, where we embarked en route to Howland Island. We were going to duplicate the flight that Amelia Earhart was taking but we hit some bad weather and crashed on a small atoll."

"Sounds to me like you duplicated Earhart's flight a little too closely. Didn't she also crash in that area?" June said.

Rosie hesitated and said "Yeah, she did and yeah, we did."

"Hey you know what? I think I remember hearing about you guys. There was a story in the press about some woman pilot trying to complete Earhart's flight. Honey, everyone thinks you're dead. Is your husband okay?"

"Let me tell you the rest. We survived a crash on an atoll and spent a month or so on it. And then this very ship rescued us or at least we thought it was a rescue. They took us to Tongolo and the Japs imprisoned us. We escaped with some locals and hid in the hills for over a year. I had a baby while we were there. Through my own carelessness, I was recaptured and I thought I was doomed to abuse and torture when the two civilians that are on board decided to put me in their program. And here I am."

"That's quite a story. Is your husband and baby okay?"

"That's part of the reason that I'm here. The Japs promised no more reprisals to my family and the rest if I would cooperate."

"Oh that's so typical of these animals. I made a similar deal but mine also included no more sexual abuse to me or my fellow nurses. These people are monsters. Did you know they executed several of Jimmy Doolittle's pilots that were captured after his air raid on Tokyo? Even though they were prisoners of war."

"I met Jimmy Doolittle when I was racing. I didn't even know he was back in the military let alone bombing Tokyo. We got no news at all while on Tongolo. Can you bring me up to date?"

"Sure I can honey. But let's talk later. The officers are coming in for the noon meal and we'll probably eat with our two Japanese hosts.......if that's what we should call them."

As she said that, the two Japanese civilians entered the room and sat at a table set for four. The English speaking one arose after conferring with his superior and walked over to the two women.

"I see that you two ladies have met. I had sent a messenger to your cabins to invite you to join us for lunch but of course you weren't in. I'm glad you were here. Please come to our table."

He politely escorted them to the table and introduced his superior.

"We of course know your names but we have neglected to tell you ours. I am Mr. Ito and this is Mr. Yamato. Unfortunately Mr. Yamato does not speak English well. He knows a few phrases and prefers not to use them and appear to be backward. He is a very proud man."

"Please sit ladies" he continued.

Yamato spoke in Japanese to Ito and Ito answered.

"He wanted to make sure you understood why he would not be speaking directly to you. He will speak through me and I will ask him any questions that you will want answered." Ito said.

"Mrs. Conner and I were wondering where in New Guinea we are going and how long before we get there, Mr. Ito."

"Ah yes. We have changed our destination to Jayapura on the northwest coast. There are reports of some battles going on in the south and we want to keep you out of danger. We should arrive in about a week."

He translated this to Yamato.

"Do you have any idea when we will embark for Manila after arrival?" Rosie asked.

"No unfortunately we must depend on the schedule of troop ships or possibly another class of vessel that would accommodate all four of us." Ito said.

With that the food arrived. Both women had a problem handling chop sticks but each had some past experience with them and Ito helped them. They soon adapted to them knowing full well that this will be standard procedure from here on out.

After lunch Ito said "Ladies feel free to relax and enjoy the fine weather we are experiencing. It is not always so pleasant. We will see you at the dinner hour at 6:00 P.M. Please be prompt."

After they left the table June said "Let's go to my room Rosie where we can talk. I'll try to fill you in with what I know."

When they reached the room and closed the door June said "I asked them about New Guinea for a reason. Before I left Tarawa we had heard that the Yanks were about to recapture Lae-Salamaua. Maybe they already have. I know they took Buna and Sanananda on New Guinea. The war's starting to go bad for the Japs."

"Tell me more June."

"Here's really a good one. Admiral Yamamoto who was the guy in charge of the Pearl Harbor attack was flying in a bomber near Bougainville and eighteen of our P-38's caught up to him and shot him out of the sky. End of one bad guy. I guess our code breakers pin pointed him for our guys."

"Oh Chris will be happy to hear that. Those are Lockheed planes." Rosie said.

"We still have a lot of revenge to get. Those animals torpedoed the Centaur, an Aussy hospital ship, and 299 people were killed. Can you imagine what kind of a submarine commander would sink an unarmed ship with wounded men aboard. They had to know. It was painted white with a big red cross on each side. I had a good nurse friend aboard that ship. She didn't make it."

"That's so sad, June. I know what atrocities they executed on our little island. I agreed to come with them hoping that they will stop."

"I pray that they do, Rosie, but some of them are plain animals and they just do what they please."

"Well it sounds like we're turning them back. Have you heard anything about the war in Europe?"

"Yes and that seems to be swinging our way too. There was a huge invasion of mostly U.S. and British troops in France. They called it D Day. But there's horrible fighting going on. We're winning but at a tremendous cost of lives." June said.

"Before we left, we had heard that the Nazi's were persecuting the Jews. Did anything come of that?" Rosie asked.

"Yes. There have been some terrible things reported and I'm sure there will be much more when this thing is done."

"What's this world coming to? Our lives have changed so much. Here I am. I have a husband and a little girl that I cannot be with and they probably don't know if I'm alive or dead. It all seems so futile."

"Now Rosie, you just hang in there. We're going to come out of this thing okay. You'd be so proud of our troops. I tended many of the wounded and they all had so much spirit. Some of them couldn't wait to get back in action. We've got a good bunch of soldiers, sailors, marines and airmen. We're going to win this mess and you'll be back with your man and your baby before you know it."

"Oh June I'm so glad that I met you. Just talking to you makes me want to live again."

"That's my job honey. I've talked to guys that are a whole lot worse off than we are and they look up at me and smile. Some of them even wisecrack and I just give it back to them. They love it. Now why don't we try to find out what these oily dudes have planned for us while we're eating some dinner. If we're going to break bread with them three times a day we might as well use it to our advantage. Let's think of some questions to ask."

"Okay. I'm all for it."

CHAPTER TWENTY THREE

BACK ON TONGOLO

Chris stirred and opened his eyes. He had slept for 12 hours straight and the fever was now sporadic but he still got chills. He was extremely weak. The malaria had taken a toll on his body.

Kellea was by his side when he awoke. Now was the time to feed him the broth that she had concocted. She raised his head on a makeshift pillow and offered him a tiny bit of broth with a spoon fashioned from an animal bone. He accepted it hungrily. She gave him a bigger portion and again he gulped it down. This was good. It was the first real positive sign that he was really on the road to recovery.

She fed him the entire bowl and saw that it exhausted him.

"Please rest Chris" she said "you need to get your strength back."

He closed his eyes and again drifted off. His sleep was more tranquil now. The demons no longer troubled his sleep probably because the fever had now diminished.

When he awoke four hours later, he was alone. He lay there trying to process what happened to him. He remembered the agony of the raging fever and the horrible dreams. How long had he been sick?

He tried to separate the dreams from reality but it was so difficult. Was Rosie really gone? Did he dream she had been captured? No. He was pretty sure that was true. But….something about a ship…the research ship. Was she on it?.....It left the island?

"I must talk to the tracker and Nomea" he muttered. The sound of his crackling voice startled him.

"….so thirsty…" he rasped.

He tried to raise himself up to look for water but a wave of vertigo overcame him and he slammed back on the mat. He lay there for a minute until his head cleared and then looked around at his surroundings.

He remembered Kellea being here earlier. Maybe she would come back.

He mustered all his strength and called "Kellea. Kellea."

Kellea and Nomea were on the path leading to the cave when she stopped and said "Nomea did you here something?"

Nomea pulled up short and anxiously looked around "What is it Kellea? Is something wrong? I heard nothing."

"I thought I heard something in the cave. Let's hurry. Maybe its Chris or something is in the cave." she said.

Nomea took off in a gallop towards the cave and when he burst in through the entrance it startled Chris and he crackled a weak scream.

"Chris, are you okay?" Nomea anxiously questioned.

"Nomea…Nomea. Oh you scared me."

"I'm so sorry. I thought something was wrong. That something or someone was in here."

Kellea then entered "Chris, are you okay?"

"Yes Kellea" he rasped "But I need some water and I'm too weak to get it."

"I will get it and I have more broth. Both will do you a lot of good." she said.

She gave him a drink and fed him a large bowl of the medicinal broth. He devoured both.

When he finished Nomea fashioned a backrest for him so he could sit up.

"Nomea" he said "I'm having a problem separating dreams from reality. I don't remember anything about the trip back from the village."

"No, you were pretty much out of it all the way. I think the fever even started before we left. You were in a heavy sweat when you came back from seeing the old servant lady" he said.

"Oh yes, that's coming back. I remember now how incredible it sounded when she told me that Rosie was on the ship and it left. I was devastated. So that wasn't a dream after all." Chris said thoughtfully.

"I'm afraid not Chris" he answered "the tracker and I have been trying to figure out a way to find out where the ship was headed and why they took her, but we're up against a stone wall."

"I'll figure out someway to get my Rosie back even if it takes me a lifetime." he said.

"Do you want to see Eva, Chris?" Kellea said.

"Yes. Please can you bring her to me?" he answered.

"I will, but she should stay with me and my mother until you are strong. She misses her mommy" she said.

"So do I" he said with a catch in his voice.

As each day passed, Chris grew stronger and soon he was able to walk around the cave. One day Kellea brought Eva and he sat outside in the sunshine on a mat and played with the baby. She brought back his will to exist. He had to get well and be strong for her.

Living on the mountain, without the harassment of the Japanese soldiers was pleasant. Chris spent many hours with the Navy pilot who had been shot down and traded stories about their exploits with airplanes.

"I'm really getting itchy about getting back to my outfit since I'm all healed up" the pilot said one day "do you think there's any way I could get off this island?"

"I've thought about that many times" Chris said "but I don't know where we'd go with the Japanese occupying everything around here."

"I guess you're right" he said "If only we had a radio or some means of communication we could ask for a sub or even a P.T. Boat that we could swim to at night."

"Wow, that's a pretty wild thought. But we don't have a radio so no one even knows we're alive let alone on this island."

As they were talking, some excitement was going on down on the flat ground between caves.

"I'll go down and see what's going on" said the pilot.

Chris watched as he saw the pilot talking to the group and then looking up and gesturing his way. Soon he started walking towards him with a Polynesian man that Chris did not recognize.

When they got there the pilot said "Chris this man just walked out of the Japanese camp. He's been working with them as kind of a trustee and had the run of the camp. Security is very lax now so he left to come see his mother and sister here on the mountain. He said that he will return to the camp because his wife and children are there. As long as he returns before sunset he won't get in trouble. But the important thing is he seems to know something about your wife."

Chris stood and faced the man "What do you know? Where did they take her?" he asked firmly.

"Easy, Chris, easy. He's on our side. He'll tell you what he knows" the pilot said.

"Go ahead fella, tell Chris what you told me" he continued.

"Okay boss. When Japnee sailor man take nice lady away from bad sergeant, he take her to boss man at headquarter office. My job that day is fix window of boss man office. Many big time Japnee in office. I hear not very much except hear nice lady very mad. Japnee man say lady come to ship and Japnee be nice to husband and baby. Go to Manila and maybe Tokyo. Lady do much work to help Yankee troops. Then soldier come and make me do another job."

"What else? What kind of work to help the Yanks?" asked Chris.

"That all I know boss." he answered.

"Was she hurt? Did she look okay?" Chris asked.

"Nice lady not hurt. She look okay. That's all boss. I go back now or big trouble for me and family."

The man scurried off.

"At least I know she's okay. And you might know she'd agree to something to protect Eva and me" Chris said.

"It apparently carried over to the rest of the group too. Have you noticed the extreme lack of Japanese presence lately? I think Rosie was responsible for all of this peaceful tranquility we've all been enjoying lately" said the pilot.

"Wow, Manila and then Tokyo, if they take her there it's going to be a long time before I'll get to see my sweet wife" Chris said as he dejectedly turned to go back to his cave.

CHAPTER TWENTY FOUR

BACK ON THE NOSHI MARU

The Noshi Maru continued on its altered course to the northwest coast of New Guinea. The women noticed a definite change in the demeanor of the two Japanese civilians and even some of the crew. It was just a feeling but both women sensed it.

"What do you think June? Do you sense the same type of apprehension that I do?" Rosie asked.

"I sure do. Let's ask some questions today about the increased speed and additional lookouts." June answered.

They made their way to the ward room and found it much harder to negotiate the walk since with a rough sea and the increased speed the ship was pitching and rolling. They finally made it and when they reached the ward room they saw that the two Japanese gentlemen were already at the table. The older one had a distinct pallor on his oriental face.

When they sat down, neither one rose, and only the one who communicated with them nodded with a grunt. The girls gave a knowing look at each other both having had experience with motion sickness but neither was bothered by it.

"My we certainly have picked up speed. I would have thought they'd slow down in the rough seas. What do you think Mr. Ito?" June asked.

Suddenly Mr. Yamato leaped to his feet, exclaimed something to Ito and rushed out of the room. He was holding his hands to his mouth as he half ran to the exit.

"Oh dear" Rosie said "I think Mr. Yamato may be feeling ill. Are you also bothered by this pitching and rolling Mr. Ito?"

"No, I am fine" he snapped.

"Oh that's good" said June. "Gosh I'm starved, I hope they have something good today. That dish they had the other day was pretty good. I think it had some raw eggs in it and some of the marinated octopus that seems to slide down so easily. I guess that's why they make it slippery."

"Ooh yea. I'm famished too" said Rosie "something about this salt air and this invigorating ride just builds my appetite."

Ito was getting paler by the minute.

"Oh what about it, Mr. Ito. Why have we increased speed?"

"I don't know" he answered with obvious agitation "something about enemy submarines in the area."

He then arose and quickly said "I must go and check on Mr. Yamato." And he also hurried from the room swaying as he ran.

Both ladies chuckled and almost burst into an outright belly laugh as they knowingly looked at each other.

"Well its a little 'pay back' and it sure felt good." June said.

Their food was served and thankfully it was neither of the foods June had mentioned. However it was limited, due to the rough seas, and they were served uncooked items, but it was palatable.

While they were eating Lieutenant Nakamoto stopped at their table. "I see that your two hosts are not feeling well. May I join you?"

"Certainly Lieutenant" said Rosie.

"Our two hosts didn't seem to know why we increased speed in these rough conditions Lieutenant. Can you tell us anything?" June asked.

Nakamoto didn't speak right away. He hesitantly said "Don't worry ladies. This ship is very safe and capable of this speed."

"Oh we're sure it is. It seems to be a very modern vessel" she said. "But why hurry so? Has something happened?"

"Of course not. A little extra precaution, just in case enemy submarines may be in the area" he nervously answered.

"But since you are not a man o' war would a sub torpedo you?" she asked.

"Of course they would you naïve woman. This is a Japanese naval vessel and we have some armament. Do you think that this war is child's play?" His tone had changed and was a bit louder. Several other officers at adjoining tables glanced at him.

"Oh well we just wondered" she said.

Rosie had been quiet during this query and then she asked "Have you lost some other ships in the area?"

"Certainly there are always casualties in every war. I've had enough of this conversation. I must report for duty on the bridge. Good day ladies." He stood in a huff and quickly strode off.

"I think we touched a nerve honey" June said.

They finished the meal and made their way back to their cabins to lie in their bunks during this bumpy ride.

It was two days later that they arrived in New Guinea and they dropped anchor since there was no dock available. Several hours later Mr. Ito knocked on her door, looking better than the last time she saw him. Both he and Mr. Yamato had taken their meals in their cabins since that day in the ward room.

"Please be ready to disembark in one hour, Mrs. Conner" he said in his restored oily tone.

"I'll be ready Mr. Ito. I hope you're feeling better." Rosie said.

"I am fine. I had many reports to write and opted to stay in my quarters to do so. Please be prompt and make sure Miss Beck is with you. The barge leaves in one hour." he replied as he turned on his heel and stomped off.

Some time later there was a light knock on her door. When she opened it she was surprised to see the lieutenant.

"Oh Lieutenant" she said "I was expecting June."

"Mrs. Conner, I just wanted to say that I respect you for the brave thing you are doing for your family. I wish circumstances were different. I'm sure that I could become friends with you and your husband if I lived in America. I hope you and your family survive this war. I'm not sure that I will be so lucky. I have been transferred to a cruiser and we will be operating in the Leyte Gulf. We will fight to the end. A very wise Japanese Admiral has stated 'I think we have awakened a sleeping giant' and I think we are starting to see that come to pass. I will be leaving for my new ship as soon as I pick up my duffle bag. Good bye and do what you must to stay alive."

She watched as he walked away down the companionway.

She sat down on her bed and contemplated what he had said. We must really be beating them back for him to have that attitude. I'm sure he must be a good person down deep but his patriotism and duty is foremost. That poor man.

The next knock on her door was June. She opened the door and June said "Okay honey let's head out to our new adventure on this cruise. I can hardly wait to see what our sea sick buddies have in store for us."

Rosie would tell her about the lieutenant's visit later when she had more time.

They carried their few belongings and went topside to the quarterdeck. The two Japanese civilians were already there and directed them to the gangway where they clamored down to a motorized barge.

The trip in took about a half hour and they docked at what looked like the city dock. There was much activity on the docks with both Japanese and locals hustling and bustling with dockside activities.

Several Japanese ships were tied up. Mostly freighters either being loaded or unloaded with cargo. One was unloading military vehicles and what might have been boxes of arms and ammunition according to June.

Across the jetty was what appeared to be a troop ship sitting high in the water, indicating that it was not loaded with troops.

"I wonder if that's ours" said June.

"All right ladies" said Ito "disembark and you will be assigned to your temporary quarters while we wait for our transportation to be assigned."

The girls stood waiting on the dock until a military vehicle pulled up and a young officer got out and spoke to Ito. Then Ito handed him some paperwork and he looked it over and then again spoke to Ito in Japanese.

Ito turned to the girls and said "You will go with adjutant's aide. He will show you to your quarters. Unfortunately you will not have run of the base. You will be confined to quarters for obvious reasons. You will be escorted to the dining hall by the aide. Your room should be comfortable and you will have the company of each other. It may be as long as one week before we leave or possibly sooner. If you have needs you can ask for them through the aide. He will communicate them to us. You will be given some written matter to study. Please do so. It will be important to learn it to perform your duties in Manila. Questions?"

The girls looked at each other and shrugged their shoulders.

The aide turned to Rosie and June and said "please follow me."

He turned and walked briskly to a row of barracks. They entered the first one and were shown to a private room.

He said "my name is Sergeant Namara. I will take you to your meals and at that time if you have needs, you may ask me." And with that he left the room and closed the door. They heard an ominous click as he turned the lock.

"Well it could be worse" June said "we could be in one of those work camps or even dead."

"You're right" Rosie answered "what's in this propaganda material that they gave us?"

"You said it, honey. Propaganda."

"It looks like one big separate section that's a transcript for an actual broadcast, including breaks for music and names of songs. Pretty thorough."

"Let's read through this crap and see if we can pin point what they want us for."

They read all they could stomach and it was plain that they wanted the two women to be propaganda artists and to destroy the morale of the American forces. The women now doing it tried to make the troops homesick and they would intimate that their wives were dating other men and they probably would be getting 'Dear John' letters telling them that they want a divorce.

They would play all the latest love songs by all the famous artists and of course this caused much nostalgia with the troops.

"We've got a decision to make here honey. I don't think either of us want to be traitors and in spite of what they tell us, I don't think the war is going well for them." June said.

"You're right, June. Let's play it by ear for now. We'll make a decision on how we can delay taking part in it while we're in Manila."

The week dragged by.

Finally, one afternoon, Mr. Ito stopped by to tell them to prepare to leave on a troop ship the next day. They will board in the morning and probably get underway by late afternoon.

Both Rosie and June were happy just to get going. They were starting to go stir crazy in this small room.

CHAPTER TWENTY FIVE

Early the next morning the aide came to collect them for the morning meal and told them that they would board right after breakfast. On the walk to the mess hall they noticed much activity around the empty troop ship they had seen earlier. Soldiers were boarding and some of them didn't look in very good condition. Some Japanese civilians were also boarding. There seemed to be a down and out attitude with all involved.

The sailors directing the boarding were yelling at the boarders and the boarders were yelling back. No one seemed happy about their situation.

In the mess hall they saw Mr. Ito and he told them that their departure would be delayed until the next morning in order for them to join up with a convoy of other ships and with an escort of destroyers.

"We heard that there were American submarines in the area between here and Manila. Is that true?" Rosie said.

"No questions" he screamed and seemed quite agitated.

Some Japanese officers at nearby tables turned to look at him. He seemed embarrassed and rose to his feet.

"The aide will escort you to the ship and show you to your cabin. I will meet with you before we reach Manila and brief you on the proper ways to act when you are interviewed by the authorities. It will behoove you to listen and do as instructed."

He turned and left.

"Touchy, touchy" June said.

The rest of the day went as planned and the next morning they were allowed on deck as they left the dock. The ship steamed out of the harbor for a rendezvous with other ships and an escort.

By the end of the day they had met up with one other ship but no others and no escorts were in sight. After heaving to for a short while, the two ships took a northerly course together.

They became acquainted with an Indonesian businessman who spoke English.

June asked "Hey do you know what's going on here?"

He answered "Apparently there has been a snafu in getting the ships into the passing convoy. Typical of Japanese planning lately. I think the two ships will try to catch up to the convoy in a day or two."

"Well at least the weather is good. That ocean's as flat as a mill pond." she said.

The girls decided to go to the cabin and rest.

That night was filled with nightmares and weird dreams for Rosie. She thrashed about all night. She awoke and had no idea of the time but it had to be in the dead of night. There were no portholes so she couldn't see outside. She could sense the ship turning so it must be following some sort of zigzag course to avoid a submarine attack.

Suddenly the piercing alarm of General Quarters sounded followed quickly by a deafening explosion and a shocking upheaval that threw her and June from their bunks.

She landed hard on the steel deck from her lower bunk and screamed "JUNE! Where are you?"

No answer. She crawled around the deck in the pitch black cabin feeling for June and finally found her lying limp and obviously unconscious. She lifted her head and her hand was sticky from the blood gushing from a deep scalp wound.

She said to herself "Oh June. My God, she must have hit head first when she was thrown out of the upper bunk. I think she's still breathing. I must get her out of here."

Rosie opened the door and tried dragging June. The ship was listing badly and it was even more difficult dragging June on the pitched deck.

Alarms were blaring loudly everywhere. She could hear men shouting orders and others moaning.

Suddenly came another deafening explosion that seemed to lift the whole ship upwards in the water and then followed by two rapid explosions deep within the bowels of the ship.

The ship slowly settled with the stern sliding silently under the surface. It was almost impossible to pull June up the steeply canted deck but she was almost to the ladder to go topside. Could she make it? Her arms felt like they were pulling out of her shoulder sockets but she must go on….she must.

She hesitated as she heard a sound from forward and slightly above her. Oh my God….a wall of water was cascading down the companionway towards them. Before the torrent hit them she hooked her arm around a rail of the ladder and grabbed her wrist to get a good hold. She hooked June's arm inside of hers and also wrapped her legs around June's waist.

Tons of water hit them and tore June loose from Rosie's grip as easily as if she was a rag doll. Rosie hung on for dear life and was able to struggle up a few steps higher on the ladder. June was gone.

The flow of water lessened slightly and Rosie inched her way up. It seemed to take forever to reach the watertight hatch leading to the main deck. When she did, she found it to be dogged down in a closed watertight condition. She was so weak but she must find the dog wrench and loosen the dogs to get the hatch opened.

It was her only chance to survive and she could hear the ship creaking and crunching as it settled into the black sea.

She stood and felt around the perimeter of the hatch and finally found the dog wrench hanging on its hanger. She slid the wrench down on the first of six dogs that held the hatch tightly against the bulkhead. She pulled with all she could muster but to no avail. She tried again but she didn't have the strength to loosen it.

She needed something to hit it and to get it started. She put the wrench on the bottom dog. She was able to use her foot to stomp down and got that one started. ONE DOWN.

The two lower ones on the sides might be low enough to reach with her foot to try the same thing. She tried it. IT WORKED. Only three more to go.

She leaned up against the bulkhead and her hand fell upon a small fire extinguisher. Just what she needed to strike the other wrench and get it started. She reared back and smacked one of the upper dogs on the side. It broke loose and the other two gave no further problem. She was able to swing back the hatch and then tumbled out on to the canted deck.

She was amazed at what she saw. Light was just appearing in the eastern sky and in the semi darkness she saw mass confusion. Black smoke was pouring out of every opening that was not under water and the rest of the ship was slipping under very quickly.

She must move, and fast, there wasn't much time.

She pulled herself to the edge of the deck and grabbed the lifeline. As she stood she could see that she had to get off now. This part of the ship was only about 10 feet above the water and the stern was settling even more quickly now. She saw only one life boat in the water and she yelled at them before she climbed the rail and jumped in.

When she hit the water it was almost refreshing. She stopped herself from sinking and kicked for the surface. When she broke the surface she looked for the lifeboat but it was no where in sight. She swam to where she thought it might be and when on the crest of a swell she spotted it.

She waved her arms and yelled "Here I am. Help me."

The coxswain turned towards her and gave an order to the oarsmen. They dipped their oars in the water and started rowing.

Rosie couldn't believe it! They were rowing AWAY from her. They were going to leave her to drown.

She started swimming. She didn't know why or where she would swim to but she knew she had to do something to survive.

She spotted some debris. It looked like a wooden crate so she swam to it and found that she could hang on to keep afloat.

Soon she regained enough strength to pull herself halfway on top of the crate. At that point exhaustion took over and she lapsed into a semi conscious state.

When she regained full consciousness the sun was beating down on her. Her mouth was crusted and she needed water. It was so tempting to scoop up some sea water and drink. But she knew this was an invitation to disaster.

She lifted her head and gazed around at the empty sea. As she dropped her head back down she thought she saw something out of a sidelong glance, but had to wait a moment to get strength enough to raise her head up again.

After a few moments she looked up and could see there was something out there. It was yellow and reflecting the sun.

She found a loose board on the side of the crate floating freely and barely attached. She ripped it free and used it as a paddle trying to get closer to the yellow object. She paddled fiercely but made very little headway and soon stopped to rest. But she was closer even though it was still a long way off.

She paddled, paddled and rested. Again paddled, paddled and rested. She was exhausted but she couldn't give up. If she could save herself she could get back to Chris and Eva.

She paddled way into the night and thankfully there was a bright full moon and she paddled until she fell into a deep sleep which may well have been her savior.

She awoke as the sun was peeking over the horizon. She thought she was dreaming because the yellow object that she was chasing was bumping up against her crate. The wind or tide or some miracle had brought them together.

"Oh thank you God". She preferred the miracle.

It was a rubber life raft. Only half way inflated but still floating. She pulled herself up to peer inside and there were two people in the boat.

She very cautiously said in a low crackly voice "Can you help me? Can you give me some water?"

There was no response from either of the Japanese men. She stared. She could only see the face of one of them. His eyes were open and his jaw was slack. He was dead.

The sleep had given her renewed energy. She pulled herself into the raft and lay for a moment until she caught her breathe.

It gave her the willies being with two dead men but it sure was better than the crate. She looked around and sure enough the boat was provisioned for survival. She unsnapped the canvas bag strapped to the gunn'el and inside was two cans of water and some crackers. She opened one water can and drank deeply. She stopped herself although she was not near satisfied.

She opened the crackers and munched eagerly. She allowed herself one more swig of water.

The next job was going to be very distasteful but it must be done. It took several hours and many rest stops before she was able to dispose of the two dead men over the side. She said a prayer for each as they slid into the water.

It was quite late in the afternoon when she had finished this grizzly task. She decided she better take an inventory. There were flares and she found another canvas bag of water and crackers. The Japanese must have died from wounds or burns because they used none of it.

She also found a piece of canvas that she could rig for shade tomorrow using the two oars as props.

She wondered why she didn't see other survivors but perhaps the other ship did not get torpedoed and they were able to pick them up. She preferred being where she was.

"Poor June" she mused "I wish I could have saved her. She was such a good person. Just being with her gave me hope. She must have been a wonderful, caring nurse to our servicemen. I feel so badly."

She slept through the night and the next day set about doing all she could to stay alive. She just knew she would be rescued sooner or later.

A week went by. No rain. The sun beat down unmercifully. In spite of rationing as much as possible she ran out of water and crackers.

She stayed awake as long as she could but soon lapsed into unconsciousness. She was close to death and it was sure to come in another day or so.

Unknown to her the USS Cod, an American submarine was scouting the area for Japanese shipping. The captain was scanning the horizon for a prey when he spotted this yellow life raft.

He almost said "Drop periscope and let's get out of here." when he had second thoughts.

"Let's go ahead and surface. We need to charge the batteries anyway. And if someone is aboard that raft, it could be one of our own airmen."

They surfaced and the skipper went up to the conning tower and looked at the raft through his binoculars.

"Yes. There is someone on that raft. Bo's'n, take a couple men and bring that poor devil aboard."

"Aye aye sir" and they deployed a boat and motored to the raft.

When they got there they couldn't believe their eyes.

The Bo's'n said "Oh my God. It's a woman. The skipper will go nuts trying to figure this one out."

"Get her aboard." He yelled.

They gently lifted her unconscious body into the boat.

The bos'n said "Yeah she's still breathing, but barely. Let's get moving and get her into sick bay or she's not going to make it."

CHAPTER TWENTY SIX

When the rescue boat got back to the sub, and the slight feminine body was lifted aboard, the skipper had already gone back below. He had left orders with the officer of the deck to have the survivor from the raft taken to sick bay and attended to as well as possible.

The sailors gingerly handled this frail young body like it was a precious piece of glass. As typical with this class of submarine space is very limited and sick bay was nothing more than a small compartment with two bunks and a work area for the two non com medical people that consisted of a Chief Pharmacist Mate and his assistant, a Third Class Pharmacist Mate.

Both were very capable men for what they were required to do but what faced them now was completely foreign to them. The Chief who was the older and more experienced of the two took charge right away.

After the rescuers carried her in and placed her gently on a bunk, he ushered them out and with help from the assistant he did his best to examine her.

"Okay" he said "let's get busy. This little filly is pretty far gone. She needs hydrated first of all and probably hasn't eaten for a week. That sun did a real number on her delicate, fair skin too. Let's cool her off first. See if Cookie can spare a little ice. I'll see if I can rouse her and get some fluid in her."

They worked diligently for hours. After she cooled down a bit Rosie opened her eyes for a minute and took some sips of water but she sank right back into oblivion.

The Chief said "I don't think she really was awake at all. It was just a natural reaction of survival. This is one tough little cookie."

There was a knock on the hatch and the Third Class opened it. It was the skipper.

"Chief I had to come down and see if this is really true. A woman?"

"More like a young girl skipper. Can't be more than in her twenties or so. She's been through a real tough ordeal but is putting up one hell of a battle."

"Do we know anything about her? Has she said anything at all?"

"No, she's been unconscious except for one brief incident when she opened her eyes and took some water. She'll need constant care for awhile and maybe she'll make it."

"The raft that she was floating on was Japanese. What did her clothing look like?"

"It was definitely Oriental but she's Caucasian. I'd say maybe American or European. No I.D. or papers."

"Okay Chief. Keep me up to date. I can't break radio silence until we get further south but I'll try to locate a larger vessel with better medical facilities than we have. Hopefully we can transfer her to give her more help. Looks like she can use it."

"We'll do all we can skipper. If we can just keep her alive for the next 24, she's got a chance."

The captain left and the Chief swabbed Rosie's head with a cool towel.

He looked at her with his soft brown eyes and said "Keep fighting little princess. Just hold on and we'll get you home."

The U.S.S. Cod was finishing its successful assignment and had expended all its torpedoes so it was heading back to friendly waters to rendezvous with a sub tender to refuel, replenish and rearm. It probably had two or three days run before it would reach the tender and it would probably be the best place to transfer the survivor. Also there was always the chance of contacting a Man of War, either of these would be better for her. Not probable though, unless they were headed back to base in Australia.

The Chief hardly left Rosie's side. He was treating her just as if she was his own child. There was something about this little girl that was special.

On the third morning she stirred gently and opened her eyes. She looked around and knew she was on a ship. She saw a young American sailor sitting at a desk reading a book.

In a weak squeaky voice she said "Hi"

The sailor jumped up and his book went flying "Oh my God! She's awake and he ran from the room yelling "Chief, chief she's awake!"

Soon an older man in a khaki uniform entered the room. He had a huge smile on a friendly face that had seen its share of wind and sea.

"Well the little princess has decided to join us. Just relax honey. You're safe now and no one will hurt you again."

"Where am I?" she weakly squeaked out.

"You're on a United States Navy Submarine. We found you floating in a raft."

"I'm so thirsty and hungry." She said.

"We've got to start you out easy honey. I'll send for some hot chicken broth for starters and then we'll go from there later."

His mate came in carrying a steaming bowl and gave it to the chief. He fed it to her in small sips at a time and when it was gone she shut her eyes and drifted off into the first peaceful sleep that she'd had in months.

She slept for three or four hours and when she awoke the chief was at her side with more food. It was nothing too heavy but enough nourishment to give Rosie some strength.

When she was finished the skipper entered and said "Well Miss are you up to answering a few questions? We have no idea who you are or where you came from."

Rosie answered "Yes I think I can."

The chief gently raised her head on a fluffed up pillow.

"She's still pretty weak sir so kind of go easy on her."

"Oh don't worry Chief. I'm not going to interrogate her. I just want to find out who she is."

Rosie smiled. She knew that she was being treated special by the weathered older gentleman.

"I'm okay sir. First of all my name is Rosemarie Conner. I'm an American citizen. I was a Japanese prisoner and was being transported to Manila from Tongolo by way of New Guinea."

"Where is Tongolo? I think I've heard of it but it must be pretty small and remote" asked the Captain.

"Yes it is. It's located west of Howland Island."

"Those islands would be under Japanese occupation for now. How did you happen to be there?"

"My husband and I are pilots. We crashed during a storm on an atoll somewhere in that vicinity. A Japanese research vessel rescued us and took us to Tongolo where we were imprisoned. That was in 1940."

"Miss are you aware that it is now 1943?" he quesioned.

"Yes. I know. My husband and I along with some Polynesian villagers escaped and have been living in some caves in the mountains. We have a baby girl now. Her name is Eva."

Rosie's eyes started drooping.

Chief looked over at the skipper.

"Okay Chief. Let her sleep and I'll come back later. Call me when she's awake. This is an interesting story. I've got to hear more."

The skipper left and Chief tucked her in. He closed the door to give her some privacy for when she awoke.

As the chief made his way to his quarters he passed the skipper who said "Hold it a minute chief."

"Yes sir Captain."

"Chief I want to commend you on a fine job with the survivor. I know that you spent many hours spoon feeding her and I'm putting a commendation in your record. You probably saved her life."

"Thank you skipper. I was doing my job and I'm sure that little girl has a story to tell. She's a brave one."

The next day Rosie was able to sit up and take some solid food. But she was still very weak.

Chief and the Third Class Mate were tending to her sun burn when the skipper entered.

"I've been able to make contact with the U.S.S. Dixie. She's about a day away. She's a Destroyer Tender and has a full hospital with two doctors and even a couple of nurses. The Captain is an old buddy of mine and he's willing to alter course to help us out."

"That's great skipper. This little gal could use some comforts that we can't give her."

"Also Chief, I found out that this lady is semi famous."

Rosie looked up and said "Well I've never heard that before."

"Don't be modest now" he said "I understand that you were quite a contender in the Air Races held back in the thirties and you helped KenAire develop an airplane now being used as a fighter. Also the way you ended up here in the Pacific was trying to complete Amelia Earhart's disastrous *unfinished flight*."

"Gosh I never thought anything would be made of all that" Rosie quipped.

"It certainly has and there are many people that will be very happy that you survived that crash. I hate to ask but I must. What about your husband? Do you know if he's still on Tongolo and alive?"

"One of the things I didn't tell you is that I agreed to go with the Japanese if they would not harm my family. I have a little girl on the island also. They wanted me to broadcast Japanese propaganda over the radio. My plan was to hold out as long as possible to protect all the islanders and then refuse when it came time to commit treason."

"So they wanted you to be Tokyo Rose?"

"Yes. I guess that's what they called it. But June and I already had a plan. We would have sabotaged at least one broadcast, more if we could. But poor June didn't make it. She went down with the ship when we were torpedoed. We were on the Sugimoto Maru."

The Chief looked at the skipper and the skipper said "I'm sorry to tell you this Miss but it was our torpedoes that sunk the Sugimoto Maru. You must have drifted for a couple of weeks."

CHAPTER TWENTY SEVEN

The rendezvous with the U.S.S. Dixie was planned for early the next day. The chief felt that Rosie should rest as much as possible today since the day would start early and the transfer at sea might tax her strength. She was still weak.

Rosie felt very badly that June lost her life due to an attack by an American submarine but she knew that it certainly was not the fault of the crew of the U.S.S. Cod. They were doing their job and they did it well. They had expended two of their last few torpedoes to sink the Sugimoto Maru. The other ship escaped.

She tried to sleep but she kept thinking about all the terrible things that had happened in the past few years. Would she ever be able to see her husband and little girl again?

"Oh please God protect them and lead me back to them. I miss them so much."

She drifted off to a peaceful sleep.

Early the next morning the skipper went to the quarter deck and said to the Officer of the Deck "Raise periscope."

When the periscope was in position he scanned the horizon and said "Yep there's the Dixie. Right where she said she'd be. Okay blow the tubes we're going up."

The sub broke the surface and a crew member opened the hatch to topside.

"Signalman, use your light and ask the Dixie how they want to proceed with this transfer."

"Aye aye sir and he aimed the signal light at the larger ship and blinked in Morse code the captain's request."

Minutes later the Dixie returned a message with its signal light.

"Sir, the Dixie said to pull along its port side. They will make turns for 5 knots. Match our speed with his. Strap the survivor in a stretcher. They will drop a hook with a sling to pick her up. Try to position the survivor as even as possible with the sling hanging from the aft port boom. When the stretcher is clear of our deck, swing away immediately. They'll hoist her aboard and take it from there."

The chief was standing by and said "What if they drop her skipper?"

"Don't worry Chief. They've done this before and also have provisioned many tin cans with the same method. They'll have motor whale boats standing by just in case. The stretcher has floats."

"Okay sir, I'll get her ready. We'll have to strap her in after she's topside. We'd never get a loaded stretcher through the hatch."

"That's your department Chief, I've got to snuggle this baby up along side of that behemoth. Get her up here and I'll get astern of the Dixie and ready to match their speed as soon as you're ready."

The chief went below and found that Rosie was up and anxious to get going. He calmly explained how they were going to make the transfer.

"I'm ready Chief and it sounds like it's going to be one wild ride" Rosie said with that adventurous gleam back in her eye.

"Rosie, you are something else. I wish half of my men had your guts."

They went topside where the stretcher was already laid out. Rosie lowered herself into the wire basket type stretcher and the boatswain mate secured her in with straps and line.

He said "Okay skipper, she's ready."

The Captain directed the helmsman to advance along side of the Dixie. When he saw that the stretcher was adjacent to the sling hanging down from a cargo boom he decreased turns to match the speed of the larger ship."

He yelled through his bull horn "Okay Dixie, lower away"

The heavy wire slings dropped to the deck of the Cod. Two seamen each grabbed a sling and slid it over the ends of the stretcher and nestled them into grooves expressly for this purpose.

As they were working Rosie looked up at the chief and beamed a smile while she mouthed "Thank You."

The chief's weathered face lit up and he said "Go with God Rosie, go with God" and he had to look off into the horizon before the rest of the crew could see the tears in his eyes.

The skipper gave the twirling finger signal to raise the stretcher and the boom operator responded immediately. The wire basket cleared the deck and swung in the breeze. The Cod turned to port and was clear of the Dixie quickly.

The boom operator kept a steady pull upwards and the stretcher was soon above the main deck. The boom swung in and he gently set the stretcher down on the deck. You could hear a long loud cheer coming from the Cod.

The signal light from the Cod said "Well done Dixie, well done."

As soon as the slings were removed from the stretcher, two burly seamen lifted it and carried her off to sick bay. It was a well equipped clinic and the two seamen gently removed her from the stretcher and placed her on a hospital bed.

A pretty young nurse appeared and said "Hi. I'm Mary. The doctor will be in shortly to examine you. In the meantime can I get you anything?"

"Hi Mary. I'm Rosie. No I think I'm okay for now."

"Well I can see one thing. We've got to get you some different clothes. Those rags look like they've been through the wringer. Let's get them off of you. Maybe a shower might feel good too, huh?"

Rosie laughed "You'd die if I told you the last time I had a hot shower."

"You poor kid, let's get to work before the doc comes."

The U.S.S. Cod went on to have a distinguished career in World War II sinking 12 enemy vessels amounting to 37,000 tons of shipping.

The Dixie steamed towards Australia where she would go into dry dock for some much needed maintenance.

After a hot shower and some very welcome feminine garments provided by Mary, Rosie relaxed on the examining table.

A middle aged man in scrubs entered and introduced himself. "Hello young lady. I'm Doctor Williams, currently a member in the U.S. navy as a Lieutenant Commander. I understand you've been through quite an ordeal and I'd like to examine you, with your permission of course. Mary will assist me while I'm doing the exam."

"Yes of course doctor. The last doctor I saw was probably 4 years ago, although I had a baby a little over a year ago. She was delivered by a midwife on a remote island."

"Well Rosie you have an interesting medical history. When we have more time I'd like to get the whole story. Now let's take a look."

After the exam the doctor told Rosie that other than some obvious weight loss due to malnutrition and a low blood count she was in surprisingly good health.

"Mainly what you need now is some good meat and potatoes and plenty of rest. We'll keep you here in sick bay for now. In a few days you might be able to move in with Mary and our other nurse Joan" he said.

"Are you ready for a tray of chow Rosie?" said Mary.

"I sure am. I missed breakfast on the Cod."

"I'll get it for you. And then the Exec and the Data Information Officer would like to interview you. Everyone's pretty curious how you ended up here. Is it true that you're the one that tried to complete Earhart's flight and crashed at sea?"

"That's right but I had no idea it made the news."

"Are you kidding? They had a week long search for you guys but I guess some other things got in the way and they weren't able to concentrate as much as they would have liked to."

"Well actually, the crash on an atoll is only the start of a very complicated set of circumstances. Yes I'd like to talk to them to see what can be done about getting me back to my family on Tongolo."

"Wow. I don't even know where Tongolo is. I'm sure the Exec can answer some of your questions but I can tell you that our next stop is at Darwin, Australia."

"Oh good. Maybe the U.S. authorities there will be able to help me. Chris must be so worried and Eva must miss me so much."

The outer door opened and in walked an older gentleman in Khakis and a much younger naval officer.

The older man said "Hello Mrs. Conner, I'm Commander Bullock and this is Lieutenant Unger. Are you strong enough to give us some details on what has happened to you and your husband since the fall of 1940?"

"Yes I think I can give you a pretty good run down but so much has happened it may take a while."

"Young lady it will be 5 days before we hit Darwin so you just take your time. Lieutenant Unger will take some notes and then we may come back to get more detail. When you get to the part on Tongolo we may ask questions. It seems that Naval Intelligence has some interest there. Tongolo seems to be an island no one knows much about."

Rosie started out with the take off from New Guinea, the crash on the atoll, the ill intentioned rescue by the Japanese research ship, the imprisonment in the village, the escape and life in the caves, the birth of her baby, recaptured by the Japanese, the brutality and the Tokyo Rose proposition, the exit from Tongolo, the eventual sinking of the Sugimoto Maru and finally the rescue by the U.S.S. Cod.

They worked through lunch eating at her bed side and up until mid afternoon. She was whipped.

"I can see that you're pretty tired Mrs. Conner. Let's quit for today. We'd like to come back tomorrow and I promise it will not be as tiring or as long."

"Thank you sir. May I ask you a few questions?"

"Certainly. Go ahead."

"The only news we got was through some Japanese gossip. Did this war really start by Japanese planes destroying our fleet in Hawaii?"

"That's true but they didn't quite destroy all of it. It was a sneak attack at Pearl Harbor and they caught most of our battle wagons at anchor in the harbor. I'd be happy to give you more detail tomorrow and a run down on how we're doing now if you like."

"Yes. I love for you to do that."

Lieutenant Unger said "Mrs. Conner I have a copy of President Roosevelt's speech the day after Pearl Harbor. May I read it to you?"

"Oh please do."

Yesterday, December 7, 1941....a day which will live in infamy...The United States of America was suddenly and deliberately attacked. With confidence in our armed forces, with the abounding determination of our people we will gain this inevitable triumph. So help me God.

Unger then said "I carry a copy with me wherever I go. That short message has been an inspiration to all Americans, especially during the early dark days. But now his words are becoming fact and we've got them on the run."

CHAPTER TWENTY EIGHT

The next day Rosie felt stronger so she got out of bed and dressed in the clothes Mary had given her. A medical corpsman entered carrying a breakfast tray.

"Thank you" Rosie said "I feel stronger. Is it okay if I sit up and eat at the table?"

"By all means Miss. I'll tell the doctor that you're feeling better. He'll probably be in to see you after breakfast."

She had just finished eating when the doctor came in and checked her vitals. He said "You're doing well Mrs. Conner. I think we can move you out of sick bay today and into a more comfortable cabin. I'll ask Mary to line one up for you."

"Thank you doctor. I appreciate all that you've done for me. I'm feeling much better now."

As the doctor was leaving, Commander Bullock and Lieutenant Unger came in.

"Good morning Mrs. Conner" they said in tandem.

"We'll just have a shortened interview this morning. But first I think we owe you a briefing on what has happened in the time you've been out of circulation" said the Commander.

He continued "Back in December of '41 things looked pretty grim. The Japanese had attacked us and dealt a crushing blow to our fleet, but just by chance our carrier fleet was out at sea on maneuvers and were not touched by the attack. This sure helped."

"The Japs invaded the Philippines, took Guam, invaded British Borneo and Hong Kong and bombed Manila all before the end of the year."

"We entered the war in Europe and things looked bleak there also. The Germans had already invaded most of Europe and were bombing England."

"The first months of '42 were no better. The Japs were aggressively taking more and more islands down as far as the Solomon's and as far north as the Aleutian's."

"We showed them what we were made of when Jimmy Doolittle's B-25s bombed Tokyo. But it didn't do much more than boost our moral."

"But then in June of '42 the tide turned a bit with a decisive victory for the U.S. in the Battle of Midway. Planes from three of our carriers attacked and destroyed four Japanese carriers, two cruisers and two destroyers. And then in August the Marines invaded Tulagi and Guadalcanal in the Solomon's."

"We've been taking back islands ever since and the rumor is that Emperor Hirohito has stated that his country's situation is "truly grave". We've got them on the run but at a great loss of lives and I'm afraid many more since the enemy has vowed to fight to the death."

"The war in Europe is also looking better. We've taken back North Africa and invaded Sicily. We're bombing strategic positions daily and even into Berlin."

"The real disturbing event is the slaughter of the Jews by the Nazis. Reports have been made that hundreds of thousands of Jewish men, women and children have been gassed and incinerated."

"That's pretty much it in a nut shell Mrs. Conner. Do you have any questions?"

"Yes. Can you tell me if our forces are getting in the vicinity of Tongolo?" Rosie asked.

"Well that's what Intelligence wants to talk to you about. As we understand it, Tongolo is a small remote island just west of the Phoenix Islands and offers some strategic advantages. But not much is known about it. Can you describe it and what the Japs are doing there?"

"Well I'll try. It's not a very big island. Right in the center are two mountains with caves. That's where we lived with the other villagers that escaped from the Japanese work camp. The work camp is where the village used to be. The soldiers invaded the island and took it over. They killed and raped the locals until the commander made them stop or at least tried to make them stop. The only reason he did was to make them work like slaves. Their captors were brutal"

"What were the Japanese trying to build?"

"From what Chris found out, they at first wanted to build an airstrip but found that the terrain was not suitable so they abandoned that project. Now they use it as a supply base but activity had slowed way down when I was forced to leave."

"Tell us about the harbor."

"The harbor is a fairly large well protected lagoon. I heard one of the men say that the village was not even visible from the ocean. I think the land must curve out and around the harbor with an entrance on one side."

"That pretty well is the description that Intelligence has Commander" said Lieutenant Unger.

"Okay Mrs. Conner. We're going to leave you alone for the rest of the trip. As soon as we get to Darwin there will be some further help that you can give us. I understand that a group of Navy Brass will ask that you be brought to their offices after you are billeted. You may be very interested in what they have to say."

The two officers left and Rosie sat there with her head in a whirl. 'What could they possibly mean?' she thought to herself.

It wasn't long after that Mary came in and said "Okay Rosie, let's go to your new digs. The doctor told me that you are to spend the next few days, while at sea, to get all your strength back and to do nothing else but rest."

Several days later the ship docked in Darwin and Rosie was billeted with several women nurses. They each had a small but neat room with a bed and a desk. She made herself at home and the nurses took her under their wing, showing her around the base.

The next morning a messenger showed up and asked to see her to give her a message.

An official looking document requested that she report to the Office of Naval Intelligence at 1100 hours.

The messenger said "Ma'am I'll come back and show you where to go if you'd like me to."

"Yes I'd like that very much. Thank you."

After he left one of the nurses said "I don't know what information you're carrying around honey, but they sure want it badly."

Rosie patiently waited and then walked to the Office of Naval Intelligence with the messenger. When she got there she was ushered into a conference room with a long table surrounded by six high ranking Navy officers.

The officer at the head of the table said "Thank you for coming Mrs. Conner. I know you are confused and wondering what this is all about. Please take a seat and I'll do my best to explain."

"Thank you and yes I am confused as to all the attention I seem to have generated." Rosie said.

"I know that you have been out of touch with the outside world but I think you understand that the Allied forces are making great strides against the enemy. As we are moving closer to our goal of unconditional surrender we need bases closer and closer to the point of action. We have the best charts, maps and geographical history of any nation in the world but there are still a few spots that we know little about. One of them is Tongolo. Because of its unique location not many people have been there. But we also understand that it offers some great strategic advantages. We'd like your help."

"Of course I'll help you however I can, but please understand that I was taken there by the Japanese from a remote atoll where my plane crashed. I didn't locate the island myself. I'm not even sure that it was on our charts."

"It probably wasn't. It seems to have been overlooked by many and that's why we need you. You've been there, please describe what you saw."

"I gave a general description of the island to Commander Bullock on the Dixie."

"Yes we have that. In fact it's the harbor we are most interested in. We feel it would be a perfect spot for a P.T. boat base. It's well hidden from the outside, it's out of the shipping lanes and it would give us a big leap forward with a base. We need to know what's going on there. Could we take the island with a small force? Can we count on local help? What can you tell us?"

"From what I saw before I left, the Japanese activity has almost ceased. The soldiers which at one time were many have been shipped elsewhere and there is only a small force left, mostly to guard the villagers. It seems to be more a supply base than anything else and there are less and less ships coming into the harbor. The confined workers number about 40 and the villagers in the mountains are also about 40 including my husband who has some military experience and a Navy pilot that we rescued from the surf after he crashed."

"Would you be willing to work with a cartographer, Mrs. Conner and describe to him the things that you remember so he can create a map of Tongolo?"

"Certainly I will. May I ask what you are planning to do? Are you going to take the island?"

"The final decision is not entirely ours. It's up to us to gather all the data and then turn it over to the military geniuses. But I think I can safely say that there will be some activity there. You must understand that what you've heard in this room is top secret and not to be discussed with anyone not even your roommates."

"I understand that. I worked in the aircraft industry before the war and I know how important that is."

"More so now than ever Mrs. Conner."

"Can I make a request?" Rosie asked.

"Of course you can. What do you need?"

"I really don't need a thing except to get back to my husband and baby. Can I go with our strike force?"

"I'm afraid that is out of the question. But if, and I only say if, we send in a force we will get a message to him for you."

"Just tell him I'm okay and we'll be together again soon."

"We certainly can do that, but there is a lot of planning to do before we can do anything. May we ask what plans you have for yourself at this time?"

"I really haven't had any time to think about anything. I suppose I better get back home and get legal things in order. I guess we're considered deceased."

"We can arrange for a couple of hops that could get you back to the states but it might take several days or so from here. Can I make a suggestion after you get back?"

"Certainly you can."

"You are an experienced pilot. There is a great need for women test pilots. An outfit called Women's Airforce Service Pilots would be a great fit for both you and them."

"Thank you, I'll check it out when I get back."

CHAPTER TWENTY NINE

MONTHS LATER

It was one of those quiet, balmy, peaceful nights in the South Pacific. There was only a small sliver of a moon and a sky full of stars to provide a minimum of light. The surface of the water was calm with only an occasional wake from a dolphin breaking the surface. It was hard to imagine that a terrible war was going on in this tranquil part of the world.

The island of Tongolo was also very quiet. Only a skeleton crew of Japanese soldiers were left at the base to man the supply depot. They were sleeping soundly with only two sentries patrolling and keeping watch over the prisoners. There was no need for more since the island itself was without incident for several months. The prisoners had become docile and some even had the run of the compound during the day.

The other villagers that were peacefully living in the caves on the mountains had settled themselves into a survival attitude and were no longer concerned that they would be harassed by the soldiers. Indeed there were not many soldiers left to bother them and those that were left were told only to keep them away from the base itself.

It was in this setting that a U.S. Navy submarine silently broke the surface of the water 300 yards off the southwest corner of the island, the opposite end from the Japanese supply depot. The sub remained stationary as a lookout emerged from the hatch and scanned the beach with his binoculars.

He then with muted voice said "It looks all clear skipper."

Two seamen then emerged with a rubber dinghy and proceeded to inflate it and launched it over the side. Three darkly clad Navy Seals clamored out of the conning tower and lowered themselves into the dinghy.

No talk was needed. The hefty one grabbed the oars amidships with one Seal in the bow and one in the stern both carrying the needed weapons. As they rowed in towards the beach, the sub slipped silently under the water.

Quickly the surface returned as before, a quiet surf with an occasional dolphin breaking the surface.

The three men beached the rubber dinghy and then pulled it into the bush where they covered it with palm fronds.

The leader checked his map with a pen light and said "Looks like we hit it right where we should. According to the intelligence information, there should be a rough trail leading to the mountains where we'll find the caves and hopefully some friendly's."

They spread out and looked for what might pass for a trail. Finally one of them whistled a signal. The other two joined him and they started out on what could pass for a rough trail going towards the mountains.

The leader said "We should be there in about an hour and a half. Let's move."

The Seals were trained to move quickly and silently and they arrived at the perimeter of the cave settlement in short order. They spotted a campfire and hid in the dense brush while they observed the terrain.

This was the flat area where the gardening took place. There didn't appear to be any sentry and the only people were two teenage boys sleeping by the fire.

Suddenly one of the boys stirred and sat up. He looked around, rubbing the sleep out of his eyes and then he stood up. His friend also stirred and the standing boy said something in Polynesian. The sleeping boy grunted and then lay silent.

The standing one sleepily stumbled towards the surrounding bush and when he reached a palm tree he proceeded to relieve himself. When finished he turned to go back to his mat and suddenly was jerked back into the bush with a large hand covering his mouth and a strong arm around his upper body pinning his arms to his side. At the same time another set of strong arms had pinioned his legs together and lifted them clear of the ground. He was carried in this fashion deeper into the rain forest and then laid on the ground in an open spot. He was still pinned down so he couldn't move or utter a sound.

The man with the hand over his mouth said "Can you speak English? Nod your head if you can."

The boy nodded.

"We are not here to hurt you. We're from America. If I remove my hand will you be quiet?"

The boy nodded.

The Seal slowly removed his hand from the boy's mouth and the boy stared at him with bugged out eyes. He was scared.

"We came here to help your people get back their village. We don't like the Japanese either. Will you help us contact Chris Conner?"

"Y..yes but what am I to do?"

"Do you know where Chris Conner is living?"

"Yes he is in a cave on the other mountain."

"Can you take me there without arousing others?"

"It would be hard to do. It is too far. But maybe I could bring him to you."

"Will you do that without raising an alarm?"

"I will be very quiet. I promise. But what should I tell Chris?"

"Tell him that a Navy Seal has a message from Rosie."

"Do you know Rosie? She taught me English. Is she okay?"

"I met the lady briefly when she described this island to us. She is in good health and is probably back in America by now."

"I am so happy. Chris will be overcome with joy."

"Okay, I'm going to trust you. Go get him."

The boy scurried off and the Seals settled back and hoped that he would not raise an alarm. These people might be distrustful of anyone and you couldn't blame them.

He ran up the trail to the first set of caves. As he passed the cave of his father he paused but thought to himself "No I must keep going. Chris must be the only one to tell. He will know what to do."

He continued on to the second mountain and started climbing to the caves. He was becoming winded from running so hard. His breath was coming in gasps and when he reached Chris' cave he could barely talk.

He threw himself to the ground at the entrance and groaned. Eva heard the noise before her daddy and started crying which awakened Chris. When he went to Eva's side he saw the boy lying in the cave entrance.

"Hey. What's going on here? Is that you Khea?"

"Chris...Chris" he gasped.

"What happened to you boy? What's the matter?"

"Nothing is the matter. Let me catch my breath and I'll tell you."

"Here. Sit up and relax. Now tell me what?"

"Chris, Chris the Americans are here. They woke me up when I was sleeping at the garden. They want me to bring you to them."

"Khea are you sure they are Americans?"

"Yes. They said to tell you he's a Navy Seal and he has a message from Rosie."

"This is not funny Khea. Did someone put you up to this?"

"No, Chris, no. It is true. Please come with me."

"I can't leave Eva. I'll have to take her to Kellea's cave. Help me get her things."

They gathered up the whimpering little girl and some clothes and made their way to where Kellea lived with her mother.

Chris called to her when they arrived and he said "Kellea can you watch her? There seems to be some sort of emergency down by the garden. I'll be back by morning, I'm sure."

"Should I rouse the others to help?" Kellea said.

"No. If I need help I'll send Khea."

The two of them hurried off towards the garden. When they got there all was quiet. Khea's friend was fast asleep and nothing else was stirring.

"Okay young man, where are these Americans?"

A voice from the bush said "We're right here Mr. Conner. We'll come out slowly so no one gets startled."

"Okay" muttered Chris guardedly.

The darkly clad, fully armed, lead Seal emerged followed by the two others.

"Mr. Conner, I'm Lieutenant Donovan, U.S. Navy Seals and behind me is Jones and the big guy is Kowalski."

"Well I've got to admit. This is quite a surprise. Did one of you tell Khea that you had a message from my wife?"

"Yes sir. She's safe. She was rescued by a sub when the Japanese ship she was being held on was torpedoed and she was taken to Australia. That's when I met her and she said to tell you that she is safe and that she is hoping that you and the baby will be back with her soon. You have a very brave and resourceful wife Mr. Conner."

"Oh thank God she's safe. I never gave up hope. What will she do now? Do you know?"

"The last I heard was that she was returning to the states to straighten out any legal entanglements since you were both assumed lost at sea and deceased. Then she may do some test piloting to get reestablished and somehow make her way back to you or you to her. I guess that's to be determined later."

"This is all good news but I'm sure you didn't come here just to tell me that my wife is alive and well."

"Very true sir. Can we get somewhere to discuss a plan? We need your help and we have a military use for this island."

"Let's go back to the caves. First I've got to introduce you to the village leader. It's necessary that he become involved in this"

As the eastern sky grew light, this strange looking group of four men and one boy strode back to the caves and the early risers were taken aback at what they saw.

Some of the men ran for their weapons and some of the women moaned and ran into their caves.

"Chris loudly proclaimed time after time "It's okay. These are Americans and they are here to help us. Be calm. Be calm."

Soon the initial excitement calmed down and the crowd gathered behind them as they approached the village leaders cave.

Chris called out "Maunea come out. We have good news."

CHAPTER THIRTY

Maunea stumbled out of his cave rubbing his eyes and then stopped short when he saw these strange men in black uniforms.

"What's going on, Chris? Who are these men?"

"Relax Maunea. They are American frog men officially known as U.S. Navy Seals. They are here to help us get rid of the scourge that's now on the island. This is Lieutenant Donovan and his men, Kowalski and Jones. Can we go into the big cave where they can explain things?"

"Yes, by all means let's go. It's a short walk and it would be best if we got out of this crowd. He turned to the ever increasing and uneasy group, some of which were carrying weapons."

"People, people" he called "These men are friends. Go back to your caves and let us meet with them. When I find out more we will hold a group session and I will explain everything. Please don't panic."

The group settled down and started to disperse.

As the five of them walked to the large cave the very excited Lieutenant Taylor, the Navy pilot, ran up the trail and exuberantly said "Hey you guys, I'm Navy too. Can you get me back to my outfit?

"Mrs. Conner said there was a Navy pilot on the island. My name's Donovan. You must be Lieutenant Taylor."

"Right. I'm ready to go if you've got room." Taylor said.

"There's a sub standing by off the south end of the island. We can get you aboard after we set up a plan here and return to the sub. We're supposed to rendezvous with them in two days at midnight. It'll be a tight fit in the dinghy but we'll adjust. Now let's get busy here. We don't have a lot of time."

After they settled in the big cave, several of the women led by Kellea brought some food and water for the men. The frog men were especially grateful after a long hard night.

"Tell me what you need from us" Chris said.

"Let me lay it out from the beginning" Donovan said "first of all my crew and I are here to scout the Japanese compound, see what they have in the way of defense and to make contact with you folks to see what your situation is as far as friendliness to us. Hopefully, and I think I'm right on this, it looks like we may get some cooperation from you on helping scout it out and give us what we may need as far as local knowledge. We don't expect you, Chris, or the villagers to participate in any of the actual fighting if it entails that. After my men and I rest today we'd like to get as close to the Japs as possible tonight to see what's left down there. So far our information indicates that they are cutting back on men and visits from ships have decreased. What's your take on that Maunea?"

"It's seems to be so Lieutenant. We sure don't see as many soldiers as we used to. And one of the village men, who has the run of the place, told us that many of the soldiers were shipped out to fight on other islands. We try to stay clear of the camp itself."

"We might have a break here since this is such an out of the way spot, they may be very lax. Can you and Chris, and whoever else who may have a good idea, make a layout of the compound?"

"Sure, we can do that while you and your men catch a few winks. Do you want any of us to go with you?" Maunea said.

"That would be very helpful. But no more than two and whoever knows the layout best."

"I think it should be Maunea and me" Chris said.

"Sounds good. Now where can my men and I sack out for a few hours?" Donovan said.

"I'll take you up to my cave" Chris said "My little girl Eva is staying with Kellea and I have room.

On the walk to the cave Chris asked "What interest would the Navy have with this remote island Lieutenant?"

"We are going to concentrate on these shipping lanes and try to break their backs by sinking as many Jap vessels as we can. This will only be a small portion of the total picture but this little island with its well protected harbor, not visible from the ocean, will make a perfect P.T. Boat base. We think we can come back in here with a small force and take over the Jap base. The Sea Bees can come in here and do a quick job of turning this into a first class base. They will need some labor and that's where we hope your people can help out."

Chris looked a little apprehensive.

"You look troubled Chris. Is something wrong?"

"Well I hope I'm wrong but I know that some of these villagers have been slaves for the Japs and they might be apprehensive about working for any outsiders even after the enemy leaves."

"Well that's a problem for the Sea Bees to solve. My job is to get word to the military on what we have to face here and to help them rid the island of the enemy. I'll include that in my report so adjustments can be made if necessary. Now we'd better rest up. It will probably be another long night."

Chris fixed the men up with sleeping mats and left the cave to find Maunea to help with the layout of the enemy camp.

Maunea was already working on the layout with the tracker who had a fantastic memory and was more than helpful with the detail of the camp. Chris gave his input and between the three of them the finished product was a very good likeness and would prove more than adequate to the Navy men.

"We probably should try to get a few hours sleep this evening Maunea" Chris said "I'm sure we'll be up all night."

"Good idea" Maunea said as they left the big cave.

Later that day as darkness was settling over the mountains the five man party sat and discussed strategy while studying the camp site drawing. They would start the hike to the camp shortly and approach as quietly and as cautiously as possible to get as close to the perimeter as they could. Donovan will call the shots and direct the men. Jones and Kowalski were there for protection and as lookouts to allow Donovan to concentrate on the camp defenses and estimate on number of soldiers that may be encountered. Chris and Maunea were there to answer questions and give what input they could come up with.

"Okay men let's roll" Donovan said.

The five man party of three Navy Seals, one American survivor and one Polynesian islander hiked through the darkened rain forest to reconnoiter the Japanese encampment. There had been enough back and forth traffic between the caves and the old village now populated with Japanese in the last few years that some definite trails had been formed. This made the travel much easier than it was in the early confinement. And although easier it made Donovan nervous.

"Be careful men. What with these well marked trails we could set ourselves up for an ambush" he said.

"When we get closer to the perimeter" Maunea interjected "we should leave the trail and make our way through the bush. We'd be much better concealed and less likely to run into a patrol."

"Good idea. You call the shots, Maunea, of when we should break off."

"Probably in another half hour or so should be safe."

They trudged on and soon Maunea held up his hand for a halt.

"Shh, stand quiet and listen" he said.

Off in the distance they could hear someone talking in Japanese. It sounded like orders were being given. Using hand signals the five of them melted into the bush. They hunkered down and concealed themselves in the thick undergrowth. Soon a three man Japanese patrol passed by but then they stopped. Jones and Kowalski positioned themselves to fire if necessary.

The patrol leader and the two soldiers seemed to be disagreeing about something. The soldiers were gesturing back towards the camp but the leader was arguing and pointing up the trail. This went on for several minutes before the lead man seemed to relent and they headed back towards the camp, the lead man grumbling all the while.

When they had gone Donovan said "I get the feeling that security and discipline here is very lax. Taking this place might be a cakewalk."

"From what we have heard, most if not all, the real soldiers have been shipped off to do battle in other areas where they're more in need. What's left here are mostly young non combatants "Chris said.

"And there also might be a bunch of civilians used to work the supply depot" he added.

They made their way through the brush and soon came to the edge of the village. It was very close to the view of the hut where Rosie had been confined. Chris gave a shudder when he saw it. Donovan sensed it and glanced at him.

"That's where that animal kept Rosie chained up" Chris said.

"Maybe we can have special treatment for such an upstanding Japanese soldier" Donovan said in a low menacing tone.

"This looks like the end of the encampment used for housing. Let's go to our right. I'd like to see the two prison compounds and the headquarters area as well as the loading facilities and docks" he added.

They worked their way around and as they got closer to the docks they heard a great deal of activity.

When they could view the dock they saw a large ship tied up to the main pier.

"Well I'll be darned. They're working a night shift to load a supply vessel. Something must be going on. Let's observe for a while" Donovan said.

They lay in hiding and watched the loading. When the loading stopped a full squad of soldiers boarded the ship.

"My first guess is that these folks are getting ready to shut this place down. Possibly with the advancement of our forces to the south and west of here they may be setting up to make a stand in a spot close by.... maybe in Kiribati or at least in that group of islands. Hmm, I'm sure the military geniuses will be interested in this information. Okay guys let's get out of here. I've got enough to make my report."

And with that they made their way back into the bush and found the trail back to the mountain caves.

All went well and they reached the caves shortly after daylight.

"I'm going to make some notes and then catch forty winks, Chris. We'll be meeting the sub after midnight tonight but I would like to talk to you and Maunea before we leave. This may be easier than we thought but we'll need feedback from you and I need to find out how headquarters wants to handle this. We have some resources on the sub so maybe that's all we'll need. You and Maunea better get some rest. This may be the start of it" Donovan said.

All then bedded down unaware of the horrible atrocity that would take place in the village today.

CHAPTER THIRTY ONE

EARLY IN THE YEAR OF 1944

The day was one of those quiet peaceful balmy days which so often came in this part of the world. Chris rose from a restful sleep where he dreamed that he was with Rosie and they were playing in a grassy meadow with Eva. They were laughing and playing catch with a rubber ball. He awoke and was disappointed that he was alone, asleep in his cave. But at least now he knew that he would be with Rosie again soon.

He blinked his sleepy eyes, got up and had a quick bite to eat.

"I'd better go retrieve my little girl" he mumbled to himself and he struck out, walking to Kellea's cave where Eva was being cared for.

When he got there Eva was playing in front of the cave with two other little girls. When she saw Chris she jumped up and ran to him calling "Daddy, daddy."

"Come here you little sweetheart. If only you could understand that we'll be with mommy pretty soon" as he hugged her.

Kellea came out of the cave and said "As usual she was a perfect little girl Chris. You can leave her with me any time you have the need to."

"Thank you Kellea. I don't know what I'd do without you."

"Oh Chris I'm so happy for you. Rosie is well and I'm sure she's making some kind of plan to reunite with you. I love both of you like my own family."

"Yes, and once we can get this island in American hands we can start thinking about a reunion with all our loved ones."

"Hey Chris" came a call "I wanted to make sure I saw you before I left with the Seals. They're taking me back to the sub with them and I'll be back flying Corsairs in no time. I want to thank you and all the fine folks here for all that you've done for me. I would have been shark bait if those guys hadn't spotted my life raft."

"Well Lieutenant Taylor it's been a real pleasure. When this war is over I think we all ought to get together in Honolulu for a friendly reunion and maybe some relaxing refreshment." Chris said laughingly.

"Let's make it happen" Taylor answered as he gave Chris a bear hug and quickly turned, walking away, rubbing his eyes, looking to find his mates to take him to the sub.

Maunea then came strolling up the path and said "Chris I think we should set up a schedule of observers of the village so we can update the American forces when they arrive."

"A good idea, but first of all let's get some volunteers so we know what to work with. I have an idea who we can ask. Should we start contacting them?"

"Sure, let's do it now before it gets dark. We should send someone tonight."

As they walked through the settlement they saw the three Navy men and Lieutenant Taylor making preparations to start the hike back to the rubber raft and the rendezvous with the sub.

Chris said "Hey it looks like you guys are ready to hit the road."

"Yeah we're about set to start the hike and by the time we row the dinghy out we should be right on time. I have a feeling that we're going to be back pretty quick so stand by for some activity."

"Okay Donovan. Good luck and we'll be here when you need us. I've noticed all the young bucks cleaning up their rifles."

"Hopefully we won't need them but it's always good to know that we have some back up. See you later guys."

The four trudged off and Chris and Maunea went about and talked to the other volunteers, one of which was dispatched to take the first four hour watch of the Japanese encampment.

Hours later, deep into the night, Chris and Maunea couldn't sleep. They sat around the camp fire in restless anticipation, discussing with some of the other men, what could take place in the next week or so. All of them were tense with anticipation.

Suddenly there came a flurry of footsteps. Someone was running and approaching very fast. They all jumped as they heard "CHRIS, CHRIS. Oh my God! It's horrible. It's just horrible"

It was the volunteer that was sent to observe the encampment. He was sobbing and fell at their feet, retching and moaning.

Chris lifted him by his shoulders "Noana what is it? What is wrong? Talk to me!"

Noana looked at Chris and took a deep breath. He said in a quavering tone "They're dead. They're all dead."

"Who's dead, Noana? Who's dead? Tell us what happened."

Noana sat up and was trembling. Someone threw a cloak over his shoulders. With a glassy eyed stare he hesitantly started his story.

"I made my way to the village perimeter as you instructed. I could hear machinery running and saw a bulldozer digging a long trench next to the men's prison compound. It was already quite deep and he soon pulled the dozer aside. I noticed that the women had been released from their compound and were being herded over towards the men's where the ditch had been dug. They then released the men and herded them and the women towards the ditch. The women were crying and the men shouting and started to resist. One man turned and started to make a move towards the sergeant screaming at him. The Sergeant calmly smiled, drew his pistol and shot the man in the head."

"Everybody drew back and the sergeant shrieked an order, whereupon the soldiers pushed and shoved the people until they toppled into the ditch. The monstrous sergeant screamed another order and the soldiers started firing their automatic weapons into the crowd. The ones in the ditch fell where they were and the ones on the edge fell in on top of them. They were screaming and crying and the shooting kept on and on until there was quiet. I laid there sobbing but I couldn't move. I could do nothing. I just laid there in shock for a long time."

"When I raised my head to see if it was clear for me to escape I saw the demon brute who ordered the massacre talking and laughing with the other soldiers. He was gesturing towards the trench and making sounds like the people he had gunned down. I will never, never forget what I saw tonight."

No one spoke. The only sound was moaning and sobbing of grown men silently crying and sniffling.

Maunea choked back the tears and said "It is time for us to do something. We cannot wait for the Americans to do our work for us. It is now our battle and only we can make them pay for the atrocities and suffering that they have brought to our people."

"I'm with you on this" said Chris "let's gather all of the men and every weapon that we have. We must plan an attack. We cannot go off half cocked."

"You're right Chris but I think we should move tomorrow so we can attack at sunset."

"Okay let's work towards that. Start gathering weapons and we still need some information on what we're going to be faced with. There's still some time tonight for me to go down and scout it out. Doesn't Leani understand Japanese?"

"Yes he's one of the guys who came later on was able to pick up some. Mostly understands more than speak it" Maunea said.

"Good that's what I need in case we get close enough to hear something. Go get him and ask him if he'll go with me." Chris said.

A voice from the crowd said "No need to ask. I'm ready to go now Chris."

"Good deal Leani. Let me gather a few things and take Eva to Kellea's and we'll hit the trail.

CHAPTER THIRTY TWO

Chris and Leani had reached the perimeter of the camp. They had only a few hours of darkness left so they had to work fast.

Chris whispered "It looks pretty deserted at this end. Let's make our way to the prison compounds. I think I hear the dozer moving some dirt."

They moved on down to the compounds. The bull dozer had just finished covering up the mass grave and was moving towards the dock area.

The two of them cautiously crept through the thick brush of the rain forest and got as close to the dock area as they dared.

"The supply ship has departed" Chris whispered "and it looks like they're loading what's left of the equipment and other stores on to the dock. Probably expecting another ship in, maybe a cargo ship or freighter of some kind."

"I've tried to count the soldiers and dock workers" said Leani "it's hard to do with the comings and goings but I'll estimate about 20 to 30 men and only half are armed soldiers. Maybe a few more than that."

"Yes and it looks like the man in charge is that brutal, inhuman piece of humanity with sergeant stripes." Chris murmured.

"He's a demon and I think takes pride on what pain and abuse of all kinds that he can inflict on helpless men and women. I saw this first hand when I was imprisoned." Leani spewed in a hateful tone.

"They are obviously abandoning this base and probably realize the enemy is close upon them but it still must go against their nature to give up. We could probably wait it out and come back after they leave. I think we have enough to take back to Maunea. We should make our report and then the group as a whole should decide if we sit back and let them leave peacefully or do we impose our revenge on them and wipe them out. It just boggles my mind, that as long as they had no further use of our island, why murder these innocent villagers? They were good people and never meant any harm to anyone." Chris said.

"I know what I'd like to do" Leani said through clenched jaws.

"Yes. It would be very satisfying to get some closure, wouldn't it?"

They belly crawled back through the brush just as light was creeping into the eastern sky.

They soon got to the, now well traveled, trail back to the caves and made good time since caution and silence was no longer a requirement.

When they got back the others were already busy assembling the equipment and arms for the anticipated raid.

Chris singled out Maunea and asked if he would sit with him for a powwow.

"My friend, there's a decision to be made and I think all of the villagers should hear the options that we have. I am an outsider and I will abide by whatever the final outcome may be. However, you, the people of this island, must decide." Chris stated with conviction.

"You are as much a part of this as anyone, Chris. You are like a brother to me, but tell me what you found and we'll let the people decide."

Chris laid it out as well as he could trying not to sway judgment with his own emotions. It still was obvious that revenge was upper most on his mind.

Maunea nodded and occasionally questioned Chris. When Chris ended with a diatribe on the brutal sergeant, Maunea looked at him and said "Thank you for all you've done. I will discuss this with the others and we will make a quick decision."

They both rose and walked in opposite directions. Chris went to his cave for some much needed rest and Maunea resolutely strode to the large cave where many of the cave dwellers had gathered with weapons in anticipation of what plan their leader was going to describe to them.

"Gather together" said Maunea "do we have everyone who plans on participating in tonight's raid?"

"Most of us are here Maunea" said one of them "but I sent four of them to gather the store of grenades and ammunition in the most bottom caves. They should be back soon."

"Good. Chris has returned and has made his report. He and Leani went to their caves to rest. We have a decision to make."

"What kind of decision?"

"When the others get here, we will take a vote. The Japanese are abandoning the island. It looks like they will be gone within two or three days. Should we wait? Or should we attack and extract our revenge?"

There was a low keyed sound from the crowd, a murmuring, grumbling intonation that seemed to grow in volume and finally a harsh voice that yelled "I want revenge for what they did to my mother and my sister."

Another higher pitched scream cut the air "Kill them! They wiped out our village! We did not deserve this treatment."

And yet another "Don't let them escape! We must avenge our families!"

During this, the four young warriors returned and one said "What's all the yelling?"

Everyone was talking at once. Things were going to be out of control very quickly. Maunea stood on a large rock and screamed "HOLD IT! HOLD IT! I think we all are in agreement. Do we raid the Japanese encampment tonight?"

The resounding answer of a group ready for battle shook the tree tops. "YES! YES! WE FIGHT! WE MUST AVENGE OUR FAMILIES!"

"Okay. Settle down. Sounds like we all agree. Now let's go over the plan that Chris and I devised earlier."

The men all drew back, still with adrenaline pumping through their lithe bodies, and squatted on the ground surrounding Maunea.

"Basically we'll divide up into three groups. I will lead the group that will enter the village from the uninhabited side. Chris will lead the group attacking the flank in the harbor area and Leani will head the group that will be the long range snipers hidden in the thick brush adjacent to the dock area."

"Before we leave here I'll tell each of you the group that you will be in. The ones assigned to be the long range snipers, make sure you get the best rifles, preferably with scopes if possible. I know we were able to confiscate some when we were skirmishing with the Japs. If anyone has a scope at your cave bring it back tonight. The rest of us will get what's left of rifles and side arms along with the grenades."

"Okay men, go back and spend some time with your families. Try to rest. It's going to be a long night. If anyone is apprehensive on going along tell me now. It's okay. I want everyone to know the dangers of this skirmish. Even though we have surprise and probably numbers on our side, they still are trained soldiers and it will be dangerous. It will not be held against anyone who feels he is not capable of doing this. In fact it would be better not to go and be a detriment to the rest of the group."

He stood and looked at each man. He studied the reactions and could only see resolve in every face. He smiled broadly and said "I'm proud of my brothers. Our forefathers are looking down upon us, holding their heads high with the dignity, in the self respect this band of Polynesian warriors has brought upon themselves. We will go into battle tonight to bring honor back to our people. No longer to be under the boot heel of the monsters that drove us out of our village."

A resounding cheer rose from the entire group. They were ready.

"Go home brothers and come back one hour before sunset, ready to avenge our families and friends."

The group dispersed and Maunea sat and composed himself. He bowed his head and murmured "Please dear God help us to overcome this adversity."

He rose to his feet and strolled to his cave to rest for tonight's showdown. He felt like the weight of the world was on his shoulders.

Once in his cave he tried to rest but was wide awake while lying on his mat. He tossed and turned and finally fell into a restless sleep. His dreams turned into nightmares and he awoke drenched in sweat. He lay there trying to bring himself back to reality. Going into battle is traumatic for every man, no matter how brave he may be. Maunea knew this to be true but it was still hard to accept.

As he sat up, Chris appeared at the cave entrance. He smiled at his good friend and said "Hello fellow warrior."

Maunea smiled back and answered "You've heard?"

"Yes, the camp is stirring with excitement. Maunea you've instilled in these men the pride that has made Polynesians a great people. I'm as proud of you as you are of your men. It will be an honor to do battle along side of you."

"Thank you Chris, but you are a very large part of what has happened here and as I told you, we feel that you are a brother. I too feel it is an honor and privilege to have you on our side."

"Okay my friend" said Chris, with a twinkle in his eye, "then I guess we'd better gather up our warriors and prepare to do battle."

Maunea chuckled as Chris hugged him and both men felt the tension leave their bodies.

When they reached the big cave, at least half of the men had already gathered and a steady stream followed them.

"It looks like most of the weapons are here. Chris, help me issue them. Okay, snipers first. Step up and claim your rifle and scope."

It worked out that each of the six snipers had a good long range rifle equipped with a scope. "Now remember on Leani's signal, you men will start popping off any one you see on the docks or in area surrounding the headquarters office. No one has seen the camp commander yet so we don't know if he has already left or is still in the building. Knocking him off will be a big advantage."

Maunea continued "Chris' group will work their way on the other side of the dock and will attack when the soldiers gather to defend against the sniper attack using grenades and arms fire. When the soldiers turn and advance to defend against the attack from their flank, my group will have made our way through the deserted village and will form a pincer attack from their rear also with grenades and more arms fire."

"I want everyone to know that this plan was taught to Chris when he attended R.O.T.C. at the University of Purdue in the good old U.S.A. and he has graciously passed it on to us."

Rounds of congratulations and thanks were directed at Chris by the entire group which brought a wide grin from Chris.

"Well men I guess that's it, unless anyone has a question."

Maunea hesitated and scanned his men. When no response came he said "Okay then get in your group and take further orders from your leader. Good luck men. We'll gather at the dock after the battle."

CHAPTER THIRTY THREE

This may be the final entry in this diary. Later today I will join my Polynesian brothers and rid our island of the Japanese scourge. Eva is being cared for by Kellea and she has promised to keep her safe until Rosie or I can come for her. My future is questionable. I have a feeling of doom but I have kept my positive attitude before my fellow warriors. If this diary is ever found please pass it on to those who may have an interest on what happened on this island during the war years.

The hike down to the encampment started at the fall of darkness. Each group traveled separately but stayed within hailing distance. Finally when they reached a predetermined spot they broke off from each other and proceeded to their entry point of the attack.

Maunea's group had the farthest point of entry at the far end of the deserted west end of the village. Chris' group had to skirt the dock area and stand ready to attack the flank. The snipers would reach their spots first but must wait until the signal from Leani to begin shooting. Leani would wait for Chris' signal and Chris must wait for Maunea's signal which were calls of a night bird.

The snipers were in place hidden deeply in the brush. Some had palm fronds tied on their bodies to further hide them from the campsite. The wait was excruciating. It was a warm humid night and all were perspiring heavily. The smell of fear was in the air and the men grew restless.

"Shh" whispered Leani "it will be soon."

There was some activity on the docks but not like the previous night. There were six or eight men moving cargo about and two armed guards watching. They were smoking and had their rifles leaning on the building beside them.

"Easy targets" thought Leani. He whispered to the man on his left "I'll take the one standing and you take the one squatting. Pass the word to the others to pick off a dock worker when we get the signal. When the soldiers come running out of the barracks, pick them off."

Chris' men had made their way to the far side of the docks and were concealed but the brush was not as thick here. They would need to work fast after start of the sniper attack. But they must wait until the soldiers left the barracks or be in danger of getting attacked from the rear. They waited.

Maunea and his men entered the village and worked their way east. Yes, they verified that this part of the village was deserted, but they still must use caution and not cause a premature start to the battle. They passed the prison compounds and saw the freshly turned earth. It burned each man deeply when they thought of the innocent families and friends covered in that mass grave. They were now in sight of the barracks and the headquarters office. The docks were still beyond their line of sight.

Maunea whispered "find a spot to conceal your selves until the battle starts. We cannot make our move until after Chris and his men draw the soldiers back to them." They settled in and waited.

When his men were properly concealed, Maunea made the sound of a night bird calling loudly to his mate.

Chris and his men were waiting in the sparse brush hopeful that the signal would come soon since they were not concealed as well as they had hoped to be. Then the signal of a night bird calling to his mate was distinct. After a few quick seconds Chris answered the call of the night birds mate.

Leani heard both calls. Everyone was in place. Now it was up to him to make the next move.

He loudly exclaimed "Pick your targets and fire."

Six shots fired rapidly. The two soldiers fell over mortally wounded. One did not stir after he was hit. The other crawled on his hands and knees but soon collapsed and lay still.

Three of the dock workers fell over, dead before they hit the ground. One was wounded and went screaming towards the barracks. It was just seconds later when the barracks doors flew open and Japanese soldiers in various stages of undress came running out but even though some were only half dressed they all were armed. The wounded man pointed to the thick underbrush and spewed a torrent of Japanese.

"They're coming after us" yelled Liani "try to hold them back until Chris can attack.

The snipers fired again but not as successfully as before. Only one soldier hit the turf and he was only wounded. But the volley slowed the soldiers down and they just fired randomly at shadows. None of the snipers were hit.

Chris' men were anxious to join the battle but Chris said "Hold it. Hold it. Let all the soldiers come out where we can see them."

He waited a few long minutes in anguish before he said "Okay let's roll."

They charged at the soldiers who were firing blindly into the brush, firing the rifles and side arms as they ran. Two or three grenades were lobbed at the half dressed group. But more fully dressed and armed men were emerging from the barracks. Two grenades were lobbed into the nearest barracks and screams permeated the night air.

The soldiers now turned to battle Chris and his men. They had something to shoot at and they fired rifles and a crew had set up an automatic weapon. They fired a burst and wounded one of Chris' men but his mate quickly threw a grenade and it hit home. The machine gun nest was wiped out.

The snipers also had new targets with the soldier's backs to them. But the superior force was pushing Chris and his men back to the brush.

Suddenly a new force was heard from. Maunea and his men charged in from the village side. The Japs were now caught between three forces and were taking a beating. More and more fell dead with the villagers casualties limited to wounds though some were bad wounds and would require treatment soon.

The leader of the Japanese force was the brutal sergeant. He was fiercely standing in defense of the dock area. He was firing a fully automatic weapon and it was exacting a toll on the attackers. Several in Maunea's force fell from his assault. He turned to face the attack from his flank and he spied Chris who stood out from the Polynesian warriors and was a head taller than most.

"There is the Yankee dog whose wife caused me so much trouble. Now I will get my revenge. You will die slowly you pig as he fired a burst towards Chris' legs and two bullets hit home. Chris fell to the ground writhing in pain.

"Ha! You Yankee dog. Suffer a while until I put you out of your misery."

He ran to the fallen body and jammed the muzzle of the weapon at the forehead of the still conscious American.

"Now die! I will go to my ancestors knowing that I have killed my enemy" he said with that evil face grinning and emitting a final laugh before a swinging machete took his head off cleanly and it fell to the ground. The headless body stood for a split second before it crumpled down and lay across Chris' inert body.

Maunea stood with the bloody machete in his hand and stared at what he had done. He retched and dropped the ancient weapon before he pulled the headless body from on top of Chris.

"Chris. Chris" he called "are you hurt bad?"

But there was no response. Chris had blacked out as the muzzle was slammed against his head. His leg wounds were bleeding profusely.

The shooting had all but stopped with only an occasional burst and an accompanying scream from a Japanese defender.

Suddenly a fusillade of gun fire sprayed the Polynesians. Two of the Japanese soldiers had set up a machine gun nest on the edge of the dock among a pile of supplies and machinery that was stacked to be shipped. Maunea ducked down and pulled Chris to safety behind a hut.

He yelled "Get down! Get down!"

After a quick visual check he determined that he was the closest to the enemy soldiers who had already killed or wounded several of his men. Fortunately they were concentrating their fire on the village side and his men were well under cover by now. However the machine gun fire continued when ever they detected movement.

He carefully scooted on his belly around the hut. He crawled towards the back side of the pile of supplies and machinery that was protecting the rear of the nest. When he reached the pile he slowly raised his head. He could see the backs of the two men who were concentrating on firing at the Polynesians who were hunkered down.

Slowly he pulled the pin on a grenade. Released the handle for a short count and then tossed it with a hook shot that landed directly in the nest. The gunner saw it and made a grab to toss it out but it exploded as he put his hand on it. Both men were thrown backwards as the blast hit them, both bleeding from shrapnel wounds. The gunner was killed instantly and the other man was badly wounded but alive and moaning.

Maunea leaped over the barrier into the nest and put the wounded man out of his misery with a killing shot to the head.

He then scanned the dock to make sure all was secure and it appeared to be so. He sat down on the dock and the flow of adrenalin still pumping through his body made him dizzy. He sat until his head cleared and then stood when he was sure the shooting had stopped.

The snipers came out of the brush and Maunea yelled "Leani, check everything out. Make sure we got all of them. Some may have tried to escape to the rain forest. I will do what I can for Chris but it looks bad. Assign some men to attend to our other wounded."

Maunea took off his shirt and tore some strips to make tourniquets for Chris' leg wounds to try to stem the flow of blood. It seemed to work but he knew it was only temporary. There was no one with the knowledge to treat this kind of wound or for that matter other wounds that he saw among the rest of his attack force. What should he do?

And then, a miracle appeared before his eyes. As he looked out at the entrance to the harbor, a submarine with Old Glory flying from the mast was steaming its way in.

And then four motorized rubber rafts hit the water off the main deck and four armed men, in each raft, raced into the dock area. As the first one emptied Maunea recognized Donovan, Jones and Kowalski.

"Over here Lieutenant" yelled Maunea.

Donovan answered "I'm on my way" and as he got there he said "Looks like you guys have done our work for us. Did you leave any for us to clean up?"

"I think we got them all but Chris is hurt badly and I don't know what to do."

"We've got a medic with us. Let me get him over here" and he yelled "MEDIC".

A Navy enlisted man with a Red Cross arm band appeared and said "What have we got Lieutenant?"

"Looks like some bad leg wounds and an awful lot of blood loss."

"Oh boy looks like the femoral artery is severed. He needs blood but I don't know his type. No dog tags."

"He's a civilian. Can we get the doc off the sub to set up a triage area and then a field hospital of sorts? There are quite a few wounded Polynesians too. These guys did our work and we owe them something."

"Sure thing sir. The sub is tying up now. I'll report to the doc and I'm sure he'll set it up." And he skedaddled off to the sub.

It wasn't long before a work party headed up by the sub's doctor was headed their way. This was a new class submarine, much larger than the

Cod and carried a full fledged doctor instead of a Chief Pharmacists Mate in charge of sick bay.

Once the triage was set up, the wounded were carried or walked to see the doc. When Chris was brought in, the doctor said "We've got to type this man quickly or he's going to shut down from blood loss."

The medics set about doing this immediately and while they awaited the results the rest of the wounded were attended to.

Maunea and Donovan were comparing notes. Maunea asked "How did you guys happen to steam in here just when we needed you?"

"To tell you the truth, we didn't even know you were here until we got close enough to hear all the shooting. But let me start from the beginning. When my crew and I got back to the sub the other night and I made my report to the skipper, he decided that we should steam over to the other side and shadow the supply ship that was leaving. We did and when we saw that he was headed north and we saw a Jap freighter headed into the island we decided to lay a few torpedo's into both of them."

"I've got to tell you Maunea I've never seen anything like these new warheads. Three direct hits on the supply ship and two direct hits on the smaller freighter completely destroyed them. The supply ship must have been carrying some ammo because the explosion shook the sub. The sonar man's ears won't quit ringing for a month."

"The freighter was so old and decrepit that it just disintegrated right before our eyes. We surfaced to see if there were survivors but all we saw were dead bodies and a lot of sharks."

"Then the skipper said 'Well there can't be much left on the island. Let's be pretentious and sail right into the harbor in a display of power and wipe out the rest' and here we are."

"Well I was never in my life happier than when I saw that sub with the U.S. flag proudly flying from the conning tower mast" Maunea said.

I'm glad we made it. Now I hope the doc can do something for Chris. Let's check with him."

They walked over to the quickly set up field hospital and saw the doc working on Chris. They waited until he was done and then asked "What do you think doc? Is he going to make it?"

"We got some plasma in him. The next 24 hours are going to be critical."

Maunea asked "Do you have a feel for the rest of my wounded men yet?"

"Not all of them but it looks like you have four that are dead and two more very critical that might not make it. Six more wounded, that look like survivors. The Japs are all dead. There was one wounded but he died on the way to the triage before your men got him here."

"Oh how I hate to lose such fine warriors" said Maunea "well I guess I'll collect the rest of my men together and see about getting some chow. They deserve a little break."

"Hold on" said Donovan "I'll get the sub's galley to fix your guys up. They deserve the best, not just a break. Let's see if I can get them aboard."

CHAPTER THIRTY FOUR

AT HONOLULU

It took four different flights and five days before Rosie made it to Honolulu. It was there that she was finally able to arrange an overseas telephone call to Mr. and Mrs. Conner, Chris' mom and dad.

When she finally got through to them at their Kansas farm, the first few minutes were filled with a tearful conversation.

Finally when the three of them composed themselves, Mr. Conner said "The government was kind enough to inform us that you had been rescued but no detail was given about Chris or as to where and when you would be in touch with us."

"I've got so much to tell you" Rosie stammered "Chris is still on the island of Tongolo and living in the mountains with Polynesian Islanders. The last I heard was that he is safe. I also want to tell you that you are grandparents. Our daughter, Eva, was born on Tongolo on October 12, 1942. She's a beautiful baby and I miss her terribly. When I see you I can explain how and why I feel that they are safe."

"When can you get back here on the mainland Rosie? We want to see you as soon as we can."

"I can catch a hop tomorrow and be back at the Navy Base in Alameda late tomorrow night. They'll put me up for the night in the Waves barracks but the next morning I'm on my own."

She hesitated. "Mom and Dad, I have no money, just the clothes on my back and nothing else. Will you help me? I've been told that I can fly with a woman's group that tests and delivers planes for the Navy and the Army Air Corps. That will give me some earnings."

"Oh Rosie, you're family. Of course we'll be there to help you. We'll leave as soon as we can and drive to Alameda. We'll get a room or an apartment right away and leave word at the base office where to reach us so we can pick you up" said Mrs. Conner.

"I knew I could count on you" Rosie said "I'll be so happy to see you. I'll go over this whole ordeal with you"

"By the way honey, don't worry about money" interjected Mr. Conner "since we were the only heirs, when you and Chris were reported lost at sea, all the airplane insurance and the rest of your estate that was in the bank went to us. We just could not believe you and Chris were dead so all the money went into a special account in memory of you both, with the stipulation that it was yours and Chris' if and when you returned. We did not accept the Life Insurance so the companies held it in escrow. Even so you've got quite a nest egg."

"I didn't even think about any of that. I guess I should contact the same attorney that handled the estate and make sure every thing is done legally" Rosie answered.

"Good idea" said Mr. Conner "we'll see you soon. Mom and I can hardly wait."

They signed off and Rosie checked in at the airfield. While she was walking back to the barracks she heard a call.

"Excuse me Miss. Aren't you Rosie Conner?"

"Yes I am. Can I help you?"

"I thought it was you. I'm Chad Ericsson. I'm with Lockheed on assignment here in Honolulu. I worked with your husband Chris in California. That was back before the war."

"Oh yes, now I recognize you. You were in engineering with Chris."

"That's right. I.....I hesitate to ask...I heard about the crash back in 1940. Is Chris....?"

"It's okay. Yes we both survived the crash. And it's been a long story since then but Chris is still alive and hopefully doing well on an island called Tongolo. The last I heard Tongolo was still under Japanese control but he was safe and hopefully our military plans are to take it back from the Japs in the near future."

"Thank God you both survived the crash. I'll bet you could write a book about it."

Rosie laughed "Well I'm sure there will be many stories coming out of this war. Ours is only one of many."

"What are your plans? Have you had a chance to make any?"

"I'm heading back stateside tomorrow. Chris' folks are meeting me in Alameda. I've got some legal things to get squared away since everyone thought we were dead. Then I'll volunteer with the group of women that help the war effort by testing and delivering aircraft. I'm hoping to hear from Chris soon and then find out how we can get back together. We also have a daughter and I'm so anxious to see her again."

"I'll bet you are. Say I know that my wife would love to see you. We have a temporary bungalow here at the field. How about dinner at our place tonight?"

"I'd love to. I think I remember your wife. Is it Anne?"

"That's her. She did some flying too. By the way I'm going to check with Lockheed to find out Chris' status. If I'm not mistaken he was still employed when you guys went down in the Pacific."

"Yes, he had taken an extended leave of absence but he loved his job and only did it for me and my obsession to complete the Earhart flight."

"I'll check it out and see you tonight. Here I've written the address" said Ericsson.

Rosie's mind was in a whirl. She needed to lie down and clear her head before she could function. So much had happened.

She returned to the barracks, found her bunk and took a long nap.

That night was pleasant, just dining and visiting with friends. She enjoyed reminiscing with Anne about the old days before the war.

Finally Ericsson was able to chime in "I checked with corporate and yes Chris was still an employee at the time of the crash. When he returns and I'm sure he will, Lockheed would like to discuss a position for him. They are also checking into any benefits he and you, as his dependant, might have coming. They want him back. He was a valuable and capable aeronautical engineer."

Rosie's eyes filled with tears and she said "Oh thank you so much. You've both been so kind and helpful. I won't forget you and what you've done to help restore my confidence. There were times when I thought I'd never be with civilized people again."

"We know that you've been through a lot Rosie and we're proud to be able to give you some support."

After a pleasant evening of visiting, Rosie realized she should get some rest before her flight the next day. She bid them goodnight and promised to keep in touch and update them on Chris.

The flight to Alameda was uncomfortable but uneventful. Flying in a huge cargo plane was not a luxury but it was also free. She arrived late at night and bedded down at the Waves barracks.

The next morning she checked in at the base office and they told her there was a party parked at the Main Gate waiting for her. She caught the base bus outside of the office and was on her way to the gate.

The reunion was as joyful as any could be. When everyone settled down Mr. Conner said "We were able to rent a small apartment on the edge of town. It's not much. There's a real shortage of housing here as well as everywhere since the war started. We'll stay until you get settled in and we can get all the legal entanglements out of the way. You can come back to Kansas with us if you want. You know you are welcome."

"Thanks dad but I want to be here and work towards getting back to Chris and Eva. I'll stay in touch with some contacts in the military and while I'm waiting I'll do some flying with the Women's Airforce Service Pilots. Maybe I can be of service and return some of the help that has been given to me by our military."

The next days were filled with reestablishing herself with civilization. But soon she was settled in. Her funds were in an account that she could access and the Service Pilots Group were anxious to have her flying experience.

Mr. and Mrs. Conner felt that they should return home after they got a promise from Rosie to keep in constant touch and come to Kansas as soon as she could.

Rosie found her niche with the Service Pilots Group and was asked if she could do some long distance flying to Honolulu and back to Oakland. She agreed, if the group would agree to base her out of Honolulu. She felt it would offer a better chance to reunite with Chris.

Later, while she was in Honolulu and checking with Navy Intelligence, she was told of the raid on Tongolo. But they would give her no details other than plans were to establish a P.T. Boat Base.

This was top secret, and other than the island was thought to be no longer occupied by the enemy, they could not tell her more. She explained that her husband and child were on the island and she just wanted to get back to them.

"Can I get to the island in some way....some how?"

The Commandant said "I sympathize with you but that is out of the question. But I will promise to try and get some information on the status of the island residents. Check back with me in a few days."

You must understand, Mrs. Conner, that there are hundreds of thousands of displaced people in today's world. We'll do what we can but also understand that as important as Tongolo is to you there are many more important targets out there that the military are fighting for. And I might add doing a tremendous job of driving the enemy back. We just got word that our Navy scored a decisive victory in the Battle of Leyte Gulf. The Japanese fleet there was annihilated. Every cruiser and most of the other Japanese ships were sunk with very few survivors."

"Thank you Commander. I understand that little Tongolo is pretty insignificant in the whole scheme of things. I have some aircraft deliveries to make, and then I'll check back with you when I return."

After she left she couldn't help but think of Lieutenant Nakamoto. He was transferred to a cruiser based in the Leyte Gulf. She was sure he died doing his patriotic duty as much as he would have hated doing it.

Weeks went by. Rosie continued flying aircraft for the Service Pilots Group. The only word she got was that a P.T. Boat Base had been quickly constructed in the protected harbor of Tongolo by Polynesians from another island since the native Polynesians chose to return to the mountains.

She also learned that some wounded civilians had been evacuated but no names or detail was given.

The only notoriety in that area was about a Lieutenant from a wealthy family whose P.T. 109 was sunk. He was rescued and had saved one of his crew members by swimming with him in tow to a spot where they were picked up.

She reported for her next assignment and was asked to wait in the outer office. When they called her in, she saw two other women standing at the Commanders desk.

"Rosie, I had you wait so I could ask if you'd like a special assignment. And it's strictly voluntary."

"What is it sir?" asked Rosie.

"The Air Corps guys need planes in New Guinea. I understand that you have had experience in that neck of the woods."

Rosie laughed and said "That's putting it mildly sir."

"Well anyway, we've got to get a squadron of planes there. It's a long haul and means a couple of stops. We have some experienced Army Air

Corps men available but not enough to transport the whole squadron. Would you go along with these two ladies and a few others to deliver the planes?"

"I'm ready, willing and able sir" answered Rosie "when do we leave?"

"Excellent! I knew we could count on you. It'll be a few days yet but get your affairs in order. It may be a while before you get back."

Rosie left the office with a giddy feeling. Soon she would be in the part of the world where she could be united with her husband and child. Maybe this was her break.

"Please God take me to my loved ones" she prayed.

CHAPTER THIRTY FIVE

BACK ON TONGOLO

"How's he doing, doc?" Maunea said.

"If your talking about Conner, I've done all I could for him. We can thank God for these new drugs, Sulfa and this newest one, Penicillin. If it wasn't for those two antibiotics I would have had to take both legs. One thing that this war has done is rush the creation of some miracle drugs. I've been able to keep the infection to a minimum but we still have a chance that gangrene may set in. He needs surgery, beyond our abilities here, and needs it soon."

"Is there anything we can do doc? It would be terrible if he lost his legs."

"That's the least of it. He could die from gangrene too."

"Can you take him somewhere on your sub? You've got to do something doc!" he asserted.

"Now take is easy fella. It's not up to me where this sub goes and I guarantee you its main job is not hauling wounded civilians to a hospital."

"Okay, okay I know, I guess I'm just frustrated."

"And I'm sorry I leaped on you. There is one possibility but it's a long shot. The Sea Bees are due to arrive soon. Maybe even tonight or tomorrow. They're being transported by a newly commissioned troop transport called the U.S.S. General J.C. Breckinridge. I'm not sure what medical facilities she has but they've got to be 100% better than this field hospital. Being part of the U.S.N.S. Command they also transport civilian dependants so I think we can get him aboard. The best thing we can hope for is that they can keep him alive until they reach a hospital ship where surgery can be preformed. Maybe they can even save one or even both legs with a little luck."

"That would be great. Do you know if any hospital ships are in the area?"

"We heard that the U.S.S. Constellation is anchored at Tarawa. That would only be about a two day run for the Breckinridge but that's not saying that they will do it. They have their orders too, ya know."

"Thanks doc. You and your men have been great. We all really appreciate what you've done."

"Well…you guys did a pretty good job here too."

"Can I see Chris now?" Maunea said.

"Sure you can but don't make any rash promises to him until we know something definite" said the doctor.

"Don't worry doc. I won't say anything" said Maunea on his way to the field hospital.

When he got there, along with Chris were three of his Polynesian warriors. They were all in pretty good shape and Maunea talked to each and told them how proud he was to have them along side him in battle.

"Rest up for a few days and then you can go back to your families" he told them.

Then he looked in on Chris who was gaunt and only semi conscious. Doc had mentioned that he was keeping him on morphine for the pain in his badly mangled legs.

"How ya doin' buddy" he said.

Chris turned his head to look Maunea's way. "I feel like I'm about half way between" he said with a slur in his weak voice.

Maunea chuckled "between what?"

"I don't know….I just….don't know. Where am I?"

"Just rest Chris. The docs have you on some pain medicine. Just sleep and let me take care of things."

"Okay….okay…I will" as he drifted off.

Maunea left feeling very low. Chris really needed help. He went back to the temporary camp with his men.

The next morning Maunea walked back towards the field hospital. He looked out over the docks into the harbor and saw a huge gray U.S. Navy ship anchored right in the mouth of the harbor.

"Wow" he said to a hospital corpsman also looking out at the ship "I guess that's as close as that baby could get in this harbor."

"Yea. I guess the Sea Bees will need barges to get their equipment into shore, but I'm sure they've done it before" he answered.

"Looks like they're starting already. Here comes two boat loads of men now" Maunea said.

"Those guys don't waste any time. They'll be working at it by this afternoon."

As they were standing on the dock, the first boat tied up and discharged a tough looking crew of Sea Bees. The submarine doctor also jumped out of the boat.

"Hey Maunea, I've got good news. We can transfer Conner to the sick bay on the Breckinridge. They won't be leaving for about three days but they are picking up some army and marine guys in Tarawa for transport back to the states. They can then transfer Conner to the Constellation there. The Constellation has the surgeons and operating facilities that he needs. The sick bay on the Breckinridge is state of the art and although they don't have the surgeon aboard to do all the work, the head medical man seems to think he might help him until he can get the expert help he needs. He claims to have had success with similar wounds on some evacuees."

"That's great doc. When can we move him?"

"The sooner the better. Let me line up a boat. Can you and one of your men give us a hand?"

"I'll meet you at Chris' bedside with my strongest guy in five minutes" Maunea said in happy anticipation.

The transfer went without incident. After Chris was settled in on the Breckinridge he looked up at Maunea and said "My friend I must ask you to do one more favor for me."

"Of course. What is it?"

"Go to Kellea and ask her to keep Eva until I return. After I'm back in shape I will find Rosie....I must find Rosie.....And then we will come for Eva. If there is any way that I can send for Eva before I find her I will arrange it. Please keep her safe"

"You need not worry about Eva, Chris. Kellea loves that child and I will personally see to it that no harm comes to either one of them. Kellea is special to me."

"Thank you my good friend" whispered an emotional Chris.

"Good bye Chris" and as he turned away, choking back a sob, he was not able to say any more.

CHAPTER THIRTY SIX

It was now the spring of 1945 and the Allied forces were smelling victory in Europe. The Pacific war was also progressing but the Japanese still vowed to fight to the last man. Many lives were lost on both sides.

Rosie managed to stay on assignment at New Guinea, but try as she might she could not find a way to get to the island of Tongolo. She was able to get the information that the U.S. Navy, with the help of the locals, had rid the island of Japanese and established a P.T. Boat base. But as with many things it was top secret or at least she was told that it was.

But she was pretty sure that her little family was safe. She made one of many trips to headquarters on the base and was told quite plainly that she was becoming a pain in the ass. As she was leaving the headquarters office, her commanding officer called to her.

"Hey Rosie I need you to make a quick run. Could you grab one of your pilots and deliver a DC-3 to New Britain and bring one back for periodic maintenance? It's just a short hop. You'll be back for dinner."

"Okay, I'll grab Stephanie. I need to work off some frustration anyway" Rosie answered.

Less than an hour later, the two pilots were winging their way across the Huon Gulf.

They landed at New Britain and taxied to the maintenance hanger where they shut down and hopped out of the plane. They were met by some G.I.'s who gave them the razzle dazzle about staying over and going out for drinks later.

The girls laughed and said "No thanks guys. Do you have a plane that needs to go back to New Guinea?"

The soldiers also laughed and said "Yeah we've got one plus a few passengers."

"Well that's a new one. They didn't tell us it would involve passengers. Okay.....what have you got and where are they?"

"Yeah this one's a little different. It's a Polynesian couple and a little girl. The guy is huge and his wife is a cute gal but the really strange thing is that the little girl is white. Definitely not theirs. And that's not all. They got here by P.T. Boat."

"Locals? Flying on a military plane and on a P.T. Boat? They must have some clout to get that."

"Apparently they do. A pretty high up Navy officer authorized the paperwork. A Commander Donovan. He's a submarine skipper."

Rosie was aghast. "Wait a minute...where are these people?"

"Here they come now" said the soldier.

Rosie turned and couldn't believe what she saw. "It has to be an apparition" she whispered, her eyes clouding up with tears. She rubbed them as if trying to wipe out what she saw and she was rooted to the spot. She stretched out her arms and sobbed. "Oh....Oh!"

Kellea and Maunea with Eva in his gigantic arms stopped short.

Kellea screamed "ROSIE....ROSIE...IT'S REALLY YOU!!"

They ran to each other and embraced both sobbing and blubbering. Kellea finally drew back and said "Look who we brought with us."

Maunea walked up and put the beautiful two and a half year old girl in Rosie's trembling arms.

The little girl drew back. She really wasn't sure who this lady was.

"It's mommy, my darling Eva. Its mommy" cooed Rosie.

"Mommy?" questioned Eva as she looked back at Kellea.

"Yes honey, its mommy. Remember how I told you about mommy?" Kellea said.

"Daddy too?" Eva asked.

"Yes darling. You will see daddy too" Kellea answered.

Rosie gave Kellea a questioning look and Kellea in turn looked at Maunea.

He said "Rosie, we received word that Chris is in a rehab hospital in Port Moresby, New Guinea. He will be discharged soon and sent word by Donovan to bring Eva to him. He also said that he was sure he could find you because you were somewhere in New Guinea."

"Oh my God. Is he alright? What kind of rehab? Was he hurt?"

"He's okay now. I'll give you the whole story but shouldn't we get moving?"

"Yes, yes of course. Oh my God he's just on the other end of the island. This is too much, first Eva and now Chris. Stephanie can you fly this monster? I'm not sure I'm capable."

"Don't you worry, honey. Just hang on to that baby. I'll get us home."

By the time they landed in Papua, Maunea briefed Rosie on the last year or so on Tongolo including the battle with the Japanese.

"All these months that I've been here, trying to get back to Tongolo to my darling husband and he has only been a couple hundred miles away. Can the two of you go with me to the rehab hospital?" asked Rosie.

"Sure we can. Our paperwork says that we are to deliver Eva to her father. And Donovan said there is a bus that goes to Port Moresby from Papua. Let's get moving I can't wait to see Chris' face when we all waltz in on him."

The bus ride was hot, crowded, bumpy and just uncomfortable, but no one complained. By the time they reached Port Moresby Rosie and Eva had bonded as if they had never been separated.

Eva was laughing and playing peek-a-boo with her mommy until she drifted off to sleep. Rosie cuddled her into her bosom and was the picture of peace and tranquility holding her closely and staring into her beautiful little face.

Maunea nudged Kellea with his elbow and said "That picture is worth a thousand words."

He continued "Ya know little lady, we might want to start thinking about the pitter patter of little feet."

Kellea turned and gave him a long reflective look "The thinking stage is over my observant husband. I thought you might notice but anyway... You're going to be a daddy too."

Maunea was speechless. He just gawked at Kellea with a dumb looking smile on his face and then he grabbed her and kissed her all the while saying "Oh Kellea... Kellea...I'm so happy."

Rosie turned to look at them, smiling that kind of smile that meant she knew what was going on. In fact it wasn't long before the whole bus knew because Maunea couldn't contain himself and loudly announced it.

The bus erupted with several languages and in several dialects but a round of applause was the universal sign of approval. Eva slept right through it all.

They were able to catch a cab to the rehab hospital when they reached Port Moresby and after a short ride they found themselves at a pleasant, well landscaped building.

They entered through the main entrance in the front and stopping at the reception desk asked for patient Chris Conner. The lady looked through her file and advised them that after the rehab session the patients usually gathered in the rear garden area for some rest and relaxation before dinner. That's probably where they will find Mr. Conner.

The garden area was a tranquil spot and many of the military men who were rehab patients were quietly sitting and talking among themselves in groups, while others were reading.

They spotted Chris who was talking to a young man in a wheelchair. His back was to them and when the young man glanced their way, as they walked down the pathway, Chris turned his head and stopped in mid sentence.

He awkwardly stood on his damaged legs and tried to step forward but instead he extended his arms. By that time Rosie had raced to his outstretched arms. The embrace was tender and the kisses were wet with tears.

The words were those of love and devotion but intelligible only to those uttering them..

Cheers and encouragement rang out from the previously tranquil setting. The other patients knew that this was a special reunion and they responded in a manner befitting the occasion. Most had known the story of why this civilian was in a military rehab center.

"Sit back down my darling" Rosie said as she lowered him back to his chair.

"I'm okay honey" he sobbed "the legs are getting stronger. I just need to learn how to walk again. Now with you by my side I can do anything."

"Daddy, daddy" called Eva as she toddled towards him in short, uneven steps. He reached down and swept her up in his arms and said. "I've been expecting you little sweetheart but I didn't know you were bringing mommy with you."

Eva pointed to Rosie and said "Mommy came too."

Chris grabbed Maunea's hand with both of his and then kissed Kellea. He said "How can I ever thank you for bringing my family back to me?"

"You will always be my warrior brother, Chris. There is a bond that will always be there and that I am thankful for."

It was a momentous occasion and the other patients respected their privacy and drew off to the side.

Months later Chris was discharged from the rehab center able to walk again. Maunea and Kellea had returned to Tongolo.

He had made contact with Lockheed and was offered an engineering position in Honolulu and Rosie contacted a Pilot Training School and was accepted as a teacher.

These were the waning months of the war and travel to Hawaii was by ship. The day they landed in Honolulu was August 14, 1945. The streets were filled with revelers. It was VE day, the day that Japan had signed an unconditional surrender.

All was well.

CHAPTER THIRTY SEVEN

TONGOLO 2006

Teddi had just completed reading the entire diary when Kent walked into their hut.

"Oh honey this has answered so many questions for me but there are so many blank spots. Ben said that the old woman living on the edge of the village is named Kellea. I must go see her and find out if she is the one in the diary" said Teddi.

"Go do it now, honey. From what I've heard, she is very old and very frail. You don't want to miss this opportunity" Kent answered.

"Do you want to go with me?" she asked.

"This is your heritage and I think a one on one is in order. If you need me, I'll come."

"Thank you darling. I'll send for you if I feel you can help."

She picked up the old diary and walked to the edge of the village. It was in the oldest part, some of which she was sure was here during the war.

As she approached the old woman's hut she saw a small wizened figure sitting in a large bamboo chair in front of the hut. The old woman was dozing and as Teddi approached, the lady awoke with a start.

"Oh I'm so sorry" said Teddi softly "I didn't mean to startle you."

"Oh that's alright" she answered in a quavering voice "it seems like that's all I do is nap all day and sleep all night. Are you looking for someone?"

"Yes I am. My name is Teddi Allison."

"Ah yes I heard there were some folks that came here to live on our island. My name is Kellea."

"Can I ask you some questions Kellea?"

"Yes, but I'm afraid I can't give directions anymore. I can't see very well."

"No Kellea I don't need directions. Let me explain why I'm here."

"Go ahead my dear, but go slowly, I'm not as sharp as I once thought myself to be."

"A few days ago, Ben Fletcher Adams, my husband, and I went exploring in the caves on the mountains."

"Ah yes, the caves. Yes, I once lived there. Is that your question?"

"Well yes that is part of it, but let me explain. In one of the caves, in a hidden spot, we found an old diary. The diary was written by Rosemarie Conner but was abruptly cut off and finished by her husband Chris Conner. Kellea did you know these people?"

Kellea sat silently and stared off in the distance with her failing vision. She wasn't seeing but rather was trying to bring back distant memories.

Teddi waited, knowing that she had stirred something in this old lady's memory that was long ago. Finally Kellea turned and looked at Teddi with a sparkle in her eyes.

She said "Oh yes, my dear, I knew them very well. Rosie was my best and dearest friend and when the Japanese took her from us I cried every night. Chris Conner? Yes, I loved Chris but only as a sister could love a brother. I cared for him when he was next to death. And little Eva? She was like my own for almost two years. I knew that Rosie was keeping a diary but I never knew what happened to it."

"Kellea, I have something important to tell you."

"Alright......Alright, my dear" Kellea said haltingly.

"Rosemarie Conner was my grandmother and Eva was my mother. I was born in Hawaii in 1976. Unfortunately my mother, Eva, died giving birth. My father grieved himself to death and died when I was two, but I remember none of it. My earliest memories were when I was being raised by my grandmother, Rosemarie Conner. I barely remember my grandfather Chris Conner. He died before his time due to complications from his wartime wounds. He was considered to be a hero and was well spoken of. It was also unfortunate that my grandmother contracted Alzheimer's and died when she was 76. Before her death, during her more lucid moments, she was able to tell me some of what happen to her and grandpa during the war. But it was sketchy and she died when I was young."

Teddi took Kellea's hands and gently held them in her own. "Are you okay?" she asked the old woman.

"Yes. Yes. I'm alright" she said with glistening eyes "My husband Maunea died last year. I'm the only one left now. It went so fast….so fast."

"Can you tell me what you remember about my grandparents? I don't want to tire you though and I can come back tomorrow."

"I'll tell you as much as I can remember today. My daughter will be here soon to help me and she stays until I go to sleep. You can come back tomorrow. She may remind me of some things I passed on to her that I have forgotten. You have stirred up many memories young lady, many things that I would not have remembered. And I am thankful that you have done that."

"Just take your time and reminisce. I'll listen to anything you want to tell me. When you feel you want to rest or are too tired to go on please tell me. I can come back tomorrow or any time you feel you can talk to me. I want to be your friend."

"Thank you dear. I know I'm going to like you" she said with a little more strength in her voice. She then went on, telling of all the happy times with Rosie and Chris. She told of the battles and the abduction. She told of the time with Eva and the reunion of the family in New Guinea and all she could remember in between.

But soon she was tiring. Her daughter came to feed her and get her ready for retiring for the night.

Teddi met the daughter, turned to Kellea and said "You can't realize how much you have helped me to understand my heritage. I'll be forever grateful."

She gently hugged the frail body and said "I'll stop by tomorrow and if you want to talk some more, we can. But if you are too tired I can come another day."

"Please stop by, my dear. Even just to say hello" said the old lady who was showing signs of tiredness.

The daughter helped her to her feet and Teddi turned to leave feeling very gratified.

When she got back home, Kent and the children were already there. She hugged all of them and told of her very pleasant day.

"I must write this down. She told me so much. Can I tell you while I'm writing? I don't want to forget a single thing" she said so excitingly that she almost tripped over her own words.

Kent laughed and said "Go ahead honey. I'll get the kids something to eat while you're writing. I know it's very important to you."

"Thank you honey" as she concentrated on her day with Kellea.

That night she was still so excited that it was hard for her to sleep. She couldn't wait until the next day to visit Kellea again. Finally it was morning. The kids went off to school and Kent went off to work on his boat. She was free to gather more information.

She walked to Kellea's hut and as she approached she saw a gathering of people outside. One was the daughter that she had met yesterday.

The daughter separated herself from the crowd and approached Teddi. She said "I have bad news. My mother passed away early this morning."

"Oh no" Teddi said "that sweet old lady. Oh…..I hope I didn't tire her too much yesterday. I feel so badly."

"Please don't feel that way. We've been expecting this for some time now. My mother was very ill and didn't want to be a burden on anyone. I was with her as she passed and her last words were 'Soon I'll be with my husband and my two dearest friends'. She was smiling as she closed her eyes and breathed her last."

"I'm just so sorry that I hadn't met your mother before. She was such a sweet, dear person" said Teddi.

She met the rest of the family, spent some time with them and then left in respect of their privacy.

She was alone in her hut and reflected on the past few days. It was the end of an era.

She felt that she covered her heritage back to her great grandparents and learned much about her grandmother's life, piecing together her early life as a young racing pilot, her marriage to the love of her life, the crash in the Pacific, the encounter with the Japanese during the war and her life in Hawaii.

She was a great lady and lived a complete and eventful life.